About the Author

Colin Denby was born in Yorkshire on the 29th November 1938 at the start of the Second World War. Always a sickly child, he had 11 different homes in the first 14 years of his life, most were of poor construction, many with water running down the walls in winter, and when it rained. Doctors told his mother that in their opinion her son would not reach his teens.

As a child he was frail and weak with the most horrendous stammer. An elderly spinster teacher of English used to take great pleasure in exploiting this defect by selecting him to read to the class every day. When the words failed to come forth from his trembling body, she would drag him by the ear to the front of the class and scold him for being stupid. She would then place a dunce hat on his head and have him stand in the corner of the classroom. Because of his stammer he had to endure bullying every day. He hated school and failed the 11+ examination.

Throughout his formative years his mother was his rock and saviour, as he lay in his sick bed sometime barely able to breathe. She would sit by his side and sing to him pieces of music from the great operas. She would tell him time and time again; "Heal yourself ... Fight ... there is no CAN'T."

In June 1960 he was conscripted into the armed forces, one of the last to be called upon to perform National Service. He was sent to the Royal Military Police training depot at Woking, in Surrey. Sixteen weeks later having passed all the tests, he was sent to Supreme Headquarters Allied Powers Europe, France (S.H.A.P.E.). The most prestigious posting in the British Army. He was by now an athlete of some note, this opened doors which were closed to others. Whilst there he guarded most of the heads of states of Europe, as well as America. He was involved in the showdown between JFK and Nikita Khrushchev. For twenty-five years he was subject to the Official Secrets Act, so his military experiences have remained secret.

In 1963 he married his childhood sweetheart Brenda. They celebrated 50 years of marriage in 2013. They had two sons, Paul and Craig. Paul was killed at the age of 15 having been hit by a car. They were devastated beyond belief. However, they donated his eyes and kidneys in the hope that others might benefit. A young boy from Luton received Paul's kidneys and managed to track them down (never been done before), resulting in all three of them appearing on the Anne Diamond and Nick Owen Television programme; Breakfast TV, (November 84).

In the 2010 Parliamentary Elections Colin was the UKIP candidate for Rochdale.

Now aged seventy-six, Colin spends his time writing about his life's experiences.

Dedication

This book is dedicated to all the National Service men who served their country for so many years, and were paid a pittance for doing so.

This story is based largely on fact, names and localities have been changed at the writer's discretion.

Colin Denby.

Colin Denby

THE PRICE OF FREEDOM

AUSTIN MACAULEY
PUBLISHERS LTD.

A CIP catalogue record for this title is available from the British Library.

ISBN 978 1 78455 326 5 (Paperback)
ISBN 978 1 78455 331 9 (Hardback)

www.austinmacauley.com

First Published (2015)
Austin Macauley Publishers Ltd.
25 Canada Square
Canary Wharf
London
E14 5LB

Printed and bound in Great Britain

Acknowledgments

My books would not be possible without the help of the following people;

My wife Brenda for her patience with me.

My friend, agent and IT wizard Martin Jones.

My friend Dr. David Holding. BA (Hon). MA. Ph.D. LL. MSc., for his military research.

My friend and solicitor Simon Robinson.

My friends Liz and Mick Finan for their support and enthusiasm.

My friend David Hamer for his historical input.

And last but not least, Brian Kenny ex. Green Jackets, the latest avid supporter of my work.

"2379. Corporal Davenport, Sir!"

Chapter One

The brown envelope addressed to Mr. Conrad Davenport, with the stamp HMS, fell onto the hall carpet of the Davenport's modest house, in the small Yorkshire town of Bridlington. It lay there for several hours, its contents known to but a few faceless civil servants. When Mrs Moira Davenport arrived home from her mundane job in the local confectioners' shop where she worked to supplement the households' meagre income, her hand went to her mouth instinctively and she cried out 'Oh please God, not Conrad, you've already taken one of my two sons from me, isn't that enough for you?' She stumbled into the kitchen and sat down and cried. As all mothers have done since time began, when their sons or daughters are about to be taken from them, for the 'safety and glory' of the country or whatever excuse is put out by the powers that be.

When her sobbing had ceased, she heaved herself to her feet drying her eyes as she did so before starting to prepare the evening meal knowing that Conrad would soon be home from work and would gobble down his tea prior to rushing off to night school. She paused for a moment and let her mind wander back to the time she lay on a hospital bed in Bradford, as she gave birth to her second and final child, another boy, at the start of the Second World War. Conrad came into the world, not with a fanfare of trumpets, but with coughs and splutters and gasping for breath. He remained a sickly child for most of his formative years; every ailment that could afflict a child, Conrad contracted it. Mumps, Measles, Scarlet Fever, Chicken Pox and of course, Bronchitis. All these ailments took their toll on his already feeble body. Bronchitis seemed to affect him more badly than any other illness. The rationing during the war years did nothing to help nurture him or thousands more like him. For with everything in such short supply, all children were deprived of the essential vitamins necessary to build healthy bodies.

Looking back however, she recalled with pride the numerous times the various doctors had told her with all the sincerity and compassion that they commanded in those days, that in their opinion, it was extremely doubtful that Conrad would reach his teens.

As the tears rolled down her cheeks again, she recalled the hours she had sat by his bedside telling him to 'Heal yourself, there is no can't, fight, fight, get well.'

The front door opened to a jangle of Chinese door alarms, the kind you buy from any cheap general home accessory shop in any town in the land.

'Hello Mum, where are you?' Conrad was home.

'I'm in the kitchen love,' she replied.

The kitchen door opened and in walked Conrad, six feet two and a half, a fine example of a young, healthy male and the apple of his mother's eye, singing to himself "Gounod's Ave Maria", one of his favourite pieces of music, it was also one of Moira's favourites.

Over the years, Conrad had inherited his mother's love of classical music, probably from the hours she had spent singing to him as he lay gasping for breath, as bronchitis once again racked his feeble body.

'What's for tea Mum, I'm starving,' her heart almost burst with pride as she turned to face him, he looked so handsome and innocent, tall, broad shouldered, dark curly hair with green piercing eyes and pink cheeks. For a moment she could not speak, she turned away from him, in order to regain control of her emotions.

'Shepherd's pie,' she replied, with a husky voice.

'Wonderful,' he replied, 'my favourite.' Whatever his mother made him, it was Conrad's favourite. 'Are you OK Mum?' he asked.

'Yes, of course,' she replied. 'The onions have made my eyes water that's all.'

Humming Ave Maria, he went to the bathroom, washed his hands and face, and then changed into some casual clothes, before returning to the kitchen. 'Any post Mum?' he asked.

Moira's stomach churned over and with a less than casual voice said, 'Behind the clock in the front room.'

Conrad, still humming Ave Maria, went to collect his mail. He found the brown envelope behind the old brass, ornamental clock on the mantelpiece above the unlit coal-burning fire, one of two that were the only source of heat in the house. However, due to the usual warm summer weather, there was no need for a fire, although his mother had placed the small paper rolls surrounded by pieces of wood and coal in a neat pyramid in the grate, ready to ignite it should it suddenly turn cold. He noted the HMS stamp on the front of the envelope and for a moment, his hand poised above the letter, then he picked it up and with a feeling of trepidation, ripped open the envelope with his thumb.

The letter inside was short and to the point. "Dear Mr. Davenport, having recently been examined by one of Her Majesty's approved team of doctors; I am pleased to inform you that you have been passed as A1 Medically Fit to serve in her Gracious Majesty's Armed Forces. Upon receipt of this letter you should now make arrangements to terminate your employment forthwith and report to the Royal Artillery Depot, Oswestry, Shropshire, using the enclosed travel warrant." Conrad read the letter three times before the enormity of the instructions registered. Where the hell was Oswestry? What about my job? What about my future?

What about Mum? WHAT ABOUT ME?

He went into the kitchen and sat down at the small dining table, the letter in his hand. Moira turned from the oven, the plate containing his meal of mashed potatoes, meat, onions, beans and a crusty cheese topping with gravy, clutched tightly in her hand for fear of dropping it.

'Well Mum,' he said 'what do you think of this?' he said placing the letter on the table in front of her. Moira's hand trembled as she picked up the sheet of paper. Her worst fears were now confirmed, 'A1 medically fit for service.' The child she had nurtured, scrimped for, slaved for, and defied all the medical advice that was available to her, was now about to become a target for all the riff raff that the world outside England could muster.

'So Mum; Conrad's A1 how about that, eh, top of the pile?' Looking at his mother full in the face, he said 'How many doctors told you that I would not reach my teens?'

Moira broke down again. Her baby was about to be removed from her once more, as he was when the doctor drew him from her womb, twenty-one years ago, with the words "Mrs. Davenport, you have a son." Now, some faceless thing was about to perform a similar operation, but far more clinically than a doctor could ever do, and without any trace of blood on its hands. 'It's wonderful' she said, as tears rolled down her cheeks.

After a pause which seemed to be an eternity, for both, Conrad, with mist in his own eyes said 'Don't cry Mum, you know the buggers won't beat me, no matter what they may do to me, remember, there is NO CAN'T.'

Slowly, he eased his hand into his pocket and withdrew his wage packet, from which he withdrew his housekeeping money and passed it to Moira, 'Here's my housekeeping money for the week Mum,' he said, in a voice not as confident as normal, and placed three pounds ten shillings on the table, leaving himself with the same amount.

For a few precious moments, mother and son clung to each other, both lost in their own private thoughts of the past. Finally, Conrad eased his mother away from him and said, 'Mum, I'm going to run down to Heather's, and tell her the news, I shall not go to night school tonight, for there is no point now.'

Heather was Conrad's childhood sweetheart and he adored her. Heather was petite, gentle, and stunningly good looking, with a small rounded face, pink cheeks, blue eyes, a small nose and full sensuous red lips, plus a curvaceous body. All this natural beauty was crowned by a head of close cropped dark hair. She was the archetypal English rose. It often surprised him to think that he would think nothing of tackling two, three, or more 'hard cases', causing a disturbance and yet, in tender moments together with Heather, he had never been able to find the courage to tell her that he loved her. On the other hand, he did not think it was necessary to do so, for he just assumed that they were meant for each other.

The seven miles round trip to Heathers' was nothing for Conrad, for ever since he had seen a feature profile of Emil Zatopek, the great Czech runner, on the family's tiny black and white TV screen, with the clip-on magnifier, he decided that he would try to follow in Zatopek's footsteps, and run and run, in order to shed his illnesses, and get well. It paid off!

As he ran to Heather's house, he wondered what her reaction would be when he told her the news. In the company of male companions, the stories of "whilst the cat's away, the mice will play," were rife. Conrad ignored such rhetoric. It began to rain! A soft, warm, English May rain, that freshened and revived all that it touched. Conrad loved to run in the rain. But for propriety, and the fear of being locked up, he would have run naked, as if reborn, having being cleansed of the confines of the womb by the nurse's soft hands and warm water, as she carefully and loving as though it were her own child, prepared to present the new arrival into the arms of its mother.

Conrad sucked in the warm rain running down his face and into his mouth. His eyes closed to the sheer ecstasy of man against the elements and again, his mother's sobs of "There is no can't" came into his mind.

Where would men be, he thought, without the love and determination of their ladies?

Turning the corner into Heathers' road, he suddenly realised that he was wet through, his long curly locks now hanging limp against his face. What a sight I must look, he thought, still, Heather would not mind, she liked him no matter how he looked.

When he knocked on the door of Heather's house, he was soaked to the skin and panting, for he had spurted the last two hundred yards, he was greeted by Heather's mother. After a brief greeting, he asked if Heather was at home. She informed him that Heather was having to work extra duties at the hospital and would not be home until the weekend. She did not comment on his appearance. Conrad and Heather's mother did not have a loving relationship! Having made his apologies for disturbing her, he turned and began the run home. If only we had a telephone, he thought.

When he arrived home his mother was still in the kitchen, 'I didn't expect you back so soon,' she called out.

'Heather wasn't at home,' he replied, 'she's having to work late. I'm going for a bath, Mum, I'm wet through.'

'All right love,' she replied 'there's plenty of hot water, I put the immersion on for you.'

'Why did you do that?' said Conrad. 'It costs money to use that thing; I could have had a cold bath.'

'What, and catch pneumonia!' she replied. Conrad shook his head and smiled to himself, his mother still thought he was a small delicate child, even though he competed in cross country races during the winter, and braved all that the elements could hurl against him plus the efforts of all the other athletes taking part.

He lay in the warm, soapy water, and wondered what lay in store for him, what adventures if any, might he encounter, would he be involved in any armed conflicts during the next two years. It was perhaps as well that he did not know what the future held for him, for had he done so, he would have rushed from his bath screaming.

Conrad could not reach Heather until Sunday lunch time. When he told her that he had something important to tell her she replied, 'Is it exciting?' They agreed to meet at the Red Lion that evening at about seven.

Conrad was ten minutes early, Heather was five minutes late. After they had settled down in a quiet corner, Heather said 'So, what's the important news you have to tell me?' Conrad passed her the brown envelope. She read the letter and then returned it to the envelope. 'So that's your news, I thought it might have been something else,' she said looking at him. 'So we only have three weeks left before you leave.' There was a pause as both searched for the right things to say.

Finally, Conrad said 'I hope you will write to me once in a while.' And with a little embarrassment he added, 'I would expect you to enjoy yourself in my absence, for you do have a large circle of friends.'

Heather sat for a moment and thought, how typical of him, always thinking of others, never himself. 'Of course I will write to you, just let me know where you are,' she replied. They left the pub in a sombre mood and, after a clinging embrace near to Heather's home, they parted.

The next few days were hectic for Conrad; Heather was working night shifts at the hospital and taking exams, so apart from a few calls via the public telephone, that was their only contact. With two days to go before he left, they met for a farewell meal at a small restaurant. It was a subdued evening, both making small talk whilst picking at their food.

Afterwards as they sat stirring their coffee, Conrad whispered, placing his hand over hers as he did so, 'I've always loved you and always will, so please take care of yourself.'

A lump came into Heather's throat, she coughed to clear it and said 'I know you do and I will take care of myself, you do the same.' She squeezed his hand as if to endorse what she had just said.

For a while they looked at each other, locked in a precious pocket of time. 'Is everything all right for you sir?'

It was the waiter with the bill, who unknowingly, had just shattered their private moments.

Suddenly, dragged back to reality, Conrad looked up at him and replied 'Yes thank you, it was fine.' He paid the bill and then they left. That was the last time they saw each other, for over two years.

The parting from his mother was one of the worst experiences Conrad could remember. Nothing he said or did could stop the river of tears that gushed from his mother's eyes. In the end he had to be firm and say, 'Mum, I have to go, please stop crying, I cannot bear to see you like this.' She lifted her tear-swollen face and looked at him. 'I'm sorry love, take care of yourself, I'll think of you every day.'

With just one backward glance at his mother, Conrad began the walk to the railway station, tears now rolling down his cheeks, his chest heaving with emotion. He wondered what the future had to offer.

When he arrived at the station, he walked onto the platform and noticed several other young men standing around with suitcases and holdalls of various shapes and sizes and he realised, that he was not the only one about to start his National Service. It was June 1960 and after the July intake, National Service was being abolished. Just my luck to be caught, he thought.

The train pulled into the station and he and the rest climbed on board. Conrad settled down at a window seat and lay back.

'Are you going to Oswestry?'

Conrad looked up at a young man of about his age, with long fair hair. 'Yes I am,' Conrad said.

'Me too, Alan's my name, Alan Faby, mind if I join you.'

'No, not at all, my names Conrad Davenport, pleased to meet you.' They shook hands and settled down, each with their own thoughts.

After several stops en route, the train finally ground to a halt at Oswestry and about a hundred young men alighted, Conrad was surprised by the number. They were met by four army wagons and two men in uniform, clutching clipboards. One said 'Gentlemen, when I call your name, answer "here Corporal".'

Alan whispered in Conrad's ear, 'Well he seems all right, perhaps the stories one hears about the army are untrue.'

The trucks travelled a few miles then came to a halt in a cloud of dust and exhaust fumes in front of some derelict looking sheds. The tailboards of the trucks dropped down and several men in uniform suddenly appeared.

'All right you fucking miserable looking people, get down, line up in a straight line and be quick about it, you're in the Army now.' It was the soldier who had met them at the railway station! Several more expletives poured from the rest of the mouths of the soldiers, none very complimentary.

So this is the Army, Conrad thought. As he did so, the Corporal who met them all from the train, appeared in front of Conrad holding a clipboard. Conrad took an instant dislike to him. The first thing Conrad noticed about him was the number of spots on his face, the second was his dirty fingernails, and the third thing was his bad breath.

'Name!' he barked.

'Conrad Davenport,' he replied.

'Corporal,' the soldier screamed.

'Conrad Davenport; Corporal,' Conrad replied, looking him straight in the face. The Corporal it seemed did not have a name, looked at Conrad, and saw the steely glint in his narrowed eyes and something deep inside him sent a shiver up his spine. Then he looked down at his clipboard, made some note on it with the stub of a pencil and went to the next in line.

The Corporal went down the line of men and then stopped in front of one, 'Name?' he asked. The unfortunate person replied, 'Peter Bentley Corporal.'

'And what are you doing here?'

'Reporting for National Service Corporal,'

'But you're deformed,' the Corporal said, with a tinge of sympathy Conrad thought.

'The Medical Board passed me A1 even though I have had Poliomyelitis Corporal,' Peter said, beginning to shake with emotion.

The Corporal looked at him for a few moments more then said 'Fucking doctors, right, all but Bentley pick up your gear and take two steps forward.' They had all by now been stood out in the open for a couple of hours and sweat was soaking their clothes. The tarmac they were standing on which was very hot began to permeate the soles of their town shoes causing some to lift their feet in order to ease the discomfort they were feeling. This was pounced on by the soldiers and another tirade of abuse ensued.

Having checked all the names on his list, the Corporal shouted at the top of his voice, whilst standing in front of Conrad, 'Right you fucking lot of misfits, I'm going to give you all some fucking good advice, forget your fucking mothers, your homes and especially your fucking tarts at home, who I have no doubt will be getting shagged tonight. You now belong to the Army for the next two years.' Conrad decided at that moment that the first chance he got, he would have to hurt this foul mouthed person who had just abused Heather. The Corporal did not miss the look of defiance in Conrad's face. This was of course they realised later, the start of the de-humanizing period of the conscripts, prior to rebuilding them and turning them into soldiers. When they were all in line, the Corporal announced that they were now going to be 'processed', and then fed and watered. He led the way, leaving Peter Bentley behind with another NCO (Non Commissioned Officer).

The 'processing' was degrading to say the least. In a long building called a Nissen hut, a relic of the Second World War, 'civvies' (civilian clothes) were handed over to various people and stored on rows of shelves, then in return each new recruit was given army clothing. The men passing out their new 'wardrobes' would shout out, 'Size?'

'Nine,' was the reply, 'These should fit', and a couple of pairs of boots were thrown at you. Some did fit, some did not. The same demand for your size applied to everything. You began with boots and socks, then shirts, trousers, etc., until you came to the end of the line. Eventually, you had a pile of all kinds of strange clothing which looked as though it had been made a hundred years ago, which you then crushed into a kit bag (a large rough canvass bag) and you staggered outside with your new wardrobe and waited for further instructions. In a daze, the recruits were then escorted to what would be their home for the next few weeks.

The Nissen huts are long, low tunnels of corrugated iron with cement floors. These relics of the Second World War stank of coal smoke, which came from and old cast iron pot belly stove sited in the middle of the hut, plus sweat and cigarette smoke. Beds were placed every six feet or so down each side of the tube, with a small metal locker by each bed.

In a bemused state not knowing what to do, the Corporal suddenly appeared and told them where to 'kip', 'kip' being the army term for sleep. He then said, picking up a collection of aluminium tins, which fitted one inside the other, 'These are your billycans, they are for holding your food; we don't have plates in the army, and these are your eating irons.' He held aloft a stainless steel knife, fork and spoon, which were held together by a clip. 'These must be kept spotlessly clean at all times.' he said. And then with a smirk on his face, he said 'Recruits,' he emphasised the word, 'We are now going to have tea.'

They were led to yet another Nissen hut but this one somewhat larger than their sleeping quarters. Odours totally foreign to what Conrad had ever experienced in his mother's kitchen, assailed his nostrils. As if watching something out of an old World War II film, they had to stand in line with their billycans in front of them, whilst various people in white aprons and trousers, poured ladles of slop into the cans.

No-one attempted to eat more than a couple of spoonful's of the slop, so far as Conrad could see, which included himself; however, Corporal 'Spotty', as Conrad had christened him, overlooked the scene with a smile on his face.

Once again, Conrad decided that he would have to teach Corporal 'Spotty' a lesson, and very soon.

That evening after they were left to their own devices, prior to going to bed (lights out at 22.00 hrs. army terminology for 10.00pm), there was a ringing of bells outside the huts. Someone nearest to the door looked out and said, 'Fucking hell men, there's a chap in a van outside selling food and drink.' As one, the hut emptied and everyone rushed outside clutching some of the precious few pounds they had brought with them from home, and bought a bag of food together with a varied selection of drinks, but no alcohol.

When the lights were extinguished at exactly 22.00 hrs, a strange calm settled over the hut. Conrad lay in his crude army bed and thought of home. In the distance he heard the sound of a train. He wondered where it might be going, what stations it might pass en route to its own journey's end. Might its destination be Bridlington, Yorkshire, home? As melancholy began to engulf him, he realised that he was thinking a fool's thoughts.

At around midnight he was awakened from his slumbers by a strange noise. For a moment or two he could not make out what it was, then the truth dawned on him, it was Fraser, a young lad of twenty, from Sunderland, his first time away from home and in the next bed to himself, crying!

He got out of bed and shook Fraser's arm. 'Stop crying', Conrad whispered, so that no one else would hear, 'don't let the bastards grind you down, just remember this, there is no can't.'

Fraser turned his tear-streaked face and looked at Conrad, 'I cannot take this treatment Conrad.'

'What do you mean?' Conrad asked.

There was a pause, and then, 'The Corporal BUGGERED me tonight in the showers.'

Conrad sucked in his breath, 'Do you mean Corporal Spotty?'

'Yes,' Fraser replied.

Conrad said nothing for a while. When he spoke again there was a sinister edge to his voice, 'Fraser,' he said, 'I promise you this... No-one will ever violate you again whilst I am around, least of all that piece of garbage, Corporal Spotty.'

Fraser looked at Conrad, and after a few moments said, 'There is something about you Conrad that frightens me, I almost feel sorry for Corporal Spotty.'

'Don't be,' Conrad hissed.

At six o'clock the following morning, the first recruits into the showers found Fraser, hanging by his neck, DEAD! An army belt was tied around his neck and fastened to one of the roof supports. When Conrad heard the news of Fraser's death, he was mortified. When the news of the death of Fraser became common knowledge, all activities were cancelled, and all the recruits were confined to their quarters prior to an investigation by the S.I.B. (Special Investigation Branch) of the Royal Military Police.

After all the interviews and written statements had been completed and recorded by the S.I.B., it took a mere two days for the S.I.B., staff to complete their investigations. The official army statement was that "Recruit Fraser, Arnold, Army No. 238---23 took his own life, whilst being of unsound mind, and in the service of his country, may God rest his soul." So, Conrad thought after reading the newsletter given to all the new recruits, a young innocent man's life is cut off in his prime, by a piece of perverted trash by the name of Corporal Nicholson.

After a few days, almost everyone had exhausted their supply of money, no letters had been allowed to be sent home, therefore no parcels or money orders could be received from the outside world. The only solution to hunger was to eat what you were given! This one did, despite the fact that on many occasions, deposits from animal life flying from end to end of the building due to all the windows and doors being open to allow ventilation because of the hot weather, had a tendency to fall into your food. With every meal, there was a pot of tea, no other beverage was offered. The tea was laced with Bromide, which, if left to stand for a while, formed a sickly looking skin which you could remove with a spoon. However, the effects of Bromide on the system when digested would be the same, which was to curb the natural thoughts of intercourse between healthy young men with those of the opposite sex.

Three days after the death of Fraser, the camp was getting back to normal, the S.I.B., had left, so it was back to basic drilling (marching techniques) which became the order of the day. As if to mock them, the June sun of 1960 blazed down on them from dawn until dusk, from a cloudless sky.

Under the direction of Drill Sergeant Morgan, with Corporal 'Spotty' acting as his assistant, the new recruits were drilled hour after hour on the 'Square' as it was called, including Peter Bentley with the deformed foot, until one day, Bentley collapsed. Sergeant Morgan, a family man, finally brought some sense to bear and Bentley's anguish to an end, by refusing to take any further drill classes which included Bentley.

The story going around the camp was that a private doctor had been called in to assess the physical condition of Bentley, and his verdict was that he should never have been passed fit for army service when first examined by the Medical Board. Conrad watched the sickening scene as Bentley was carried from the Square, and noted the sneer on Corporal Spotty's face as the unfortunate Bentley was removed. Conrad decided that now was the time for something serious to happen to Corporal 'Spotty'.

Three days later, Conrad had the opportunity he had been waiting for. During some self defence training, Corporal 'Spotty' announced to the group of recruits that he was going to show them how to defend themselves if attacked by someone with either a knife or bottle in their hand. He called for a volunteer to demonstrate to the rest how to disable a would-be assailant. No one stepped forward at first, for all had been warned back home, never to volunteer.

Corporal 'Spotty' looked at all those before him, 'What no offers,' he said with a sneer on his face. Then Conrad stepped forward, 'I'll help you Corporal,' he said.

Corporal 'Spotty' could not believe his luck; he had never liked Davenport from the first day he had met him at the railway station. There was something about Davenport that he could not fathom, and anything he could not understand, bothered him. Davenport's offer to assist him sent a glow through him; he decided he would play with him like a cat plays with a mouse. Now he would be able to vent his pent up feelings for Davenport in front of all the recruits, and when he had finished with him, all the recruits would realise that he was a hard case, and not a man to be crossed. This he was going to enjoy. This he would savour for a long, long time. Unfortunately for Corporal 'Spotty', he did not know what he was facing!

Before Conrad was called up, he had spent six months training with Bill Long, an ex-SAS Sergeant PTI. (Physical Training Instructor) retired, and friend of the Davenport family for many years, a truly 'hard case'. Bill had no family and loved Conrad like a son. When Bill heard of Conrad's 'call-up', he took him in hand. He taught Conrad many, many, things in those six months, and brought him to a level of fitness which would be far superior to anything he would encounter in normal army life.

Corporal 'Spotty' barked out, 'Now watch what I'm about to show you, you pathetic lot, it may save your life for you, if you ever make it to a war front.' He then went through a series of moves and counter moves in slow motion, showing how to use the body as a lever, and counter lever when faced by someone who was bigger and stronger than you. Having performed this scene many times in the past, he now had the attention of all the recruits, building the tension almost word by word, which everyone now was beginning to feel. It was obvious to all, that Corporal 'Spotty' was going to hurt Davenport.

'Have you got all I've been telling you?' the Corporal shouted, there was a chorus of 'Yes Corporal.'

'Right' he said, 'Davenport, have YOU got the moves in your mind?'

'Yes Corporal,' Conrad replied. There was a pause, then 'Spotty' said, 'Is that you humming Davenport?'

'Yes,' Conrad replied.

'What the fuck are you humming?'

'Ave Maria Corporal, one of mine, and my mother's favourite songs.'

Corporal 'Spotty' looked at Davenport and thought to himself, what a fucking odd ball, he must be as thick as shit, I'm going to put him in hospital, and he's humming some fucking song. 'Right, let's do it then in real time, I've got a knife, and I'm coming at you Davenport, defend yourself.'

Corporal 'Spotty' rushed at Davenport, knife in hand. Those watching simply saw a whirl of bodies, then Corporal 'Spotty' fly over Conrad's head, heard a loud crack, followed by screams of pain, and Corporal 'Spotty' on his back, his arm broken, and the knife he had been carrying, stuck up to the hilt in his leg, his Achilles tendon severed. 'That's for Fraser,' Conrad whispered, bending over 'Spotty'.

News of the accident to Corporal Nicholson spread like wildfire around the camp, and as in most cases when a story is passed from one person to the next, it became embellished, and the truth was lost along the way. However, the officer commanding the unit was far from satisfied as to what really happened that day, even after interviewing all the recruits who had witnessed the unfortunate incident. In the end, he had to report in his daily log that a new recruit, soldier Davenport, Army No.2379... had accidentally been responsible for causing severe physical injuries to one, Corporal Nicholson, Army No.1764... whilst engaged in unarmed combat training. Due to the severity of those injuries, it was the opinion of the camp Medical Officer that Corporal Nicholson would no longer be able to continue to carry out his normal duties in the armed forces, and should be discharged, once he had recovered from those injuries. A small Army pension was recommended.

Sometime later in a building many miles away from Oswestry, in a branch of the army known to a few as 'Special Services' based in Kensington, a clerk going through his daily duty of recording 'elements of interest', came across the report. After a while, he went to a large ledger, one of many on a shelf with the title, 'Recent Field Abnormalities', and began to read.

A week after the 'accident', Conrad was 'posted' to the Royal Military Police Depot, Woking, Surrey, and a new chapter of army life was about to evolve, one that would change his life forever.

Chapter Two

When Conrad and a few other recruits from Oswestry arrived at their new home … Inkerman Barracks, Woking, they were shocked to learn that it had once been a prison. The building was old, austere, and built of stone with a huge Square in front of it. In some places there appeared to be areas marked out in white and yellow paint, which they later found out were used for drill instruction.

After they had all alighted from the two trucks which had transported them from the railway station, they found that there were twenty-eight of them. Two Corporals came out of the guard house by the main gates, each carrying a clipboard, one began to call out names, and those called were told to fall in behind him, the rest behind the other Corporal. Conrad noted how immaculate they looked, from the top of their red pleated hats, to their gleaming boots. Their shirts were pressed with almost razor sharp creases, and everything was in line. The creases down the front of their trousers looked as though you could cut your hand on them. They were a far cry from those they had just left behind.

Once the two columns were sorted and each recruit reunited with his kit bag, they were marched around the Square (no one crossed the Square) towards the huge drab building. Once inside, Conrad and a few others were told that they were in Squad 792 and that Sergeant Crouse was in charge. They were then marched away to their new quarters, which turned out to be on the second floor of the building. As they climbed the stone steps, their boots sending out waves of noise, the walls seemed to close in on them, and Conrad wondered what stories these walls could tell. They entered the barrack room and Conrad noted that the wooden floor was spotlessly clean, and shone like the proverbial new pin. There were several other people in the room, who apparently had arrived earlier in the day, the squad of twenty-eight (two weeks later, two were returned to their previous unit, as they could not meet the physical demands required of them) was now complete.

Each of the new recruits was given a bed with a pile of sheets and blankets, and a large metal locker. The Corporal told them to make their beds, and then lay out all their gear on the bed, ready for inspection by their Sergeant, when he arrived. The Corporal then left them to their own devices. After they had all introduced themselves, they began to sort out all their equipment, and lay it out on the bed as instructed. After about an hour, the barrack room door opened and in walked a Sergeant. 'I'm Sergeant Crouse' he announced. Everyone jumped to attention, not knowing what was expected of them. He was perhaps in his thirties Conrad thought, a little over medium height, with a powerful upper body, and immaculately dressed, his boots gleamed beneath his white webbing gaiters, his right hand which was raised up, gripped the end of a swagger stick, which was held in place under his right armpit. He looked very impressive, and intimidating. Everyone's eyes were fixed on him.

He slowly looked around the sea of faces surrounding him, and then in a voice with a slight Welsh accent to it said 'Well I've seen worse Squads, but not many,' he said with a degree of humour in his voice. 'Right, stand easy, you can smoke if you want.' There was a pause then he continued; 'Now I know all of you don't want to be here, because National Service will be abolished in a couple of weeks. But here you are, and you are here for at least sixteen weeks of your two years, so my advice to you all is to make the best of it. For those who may be thinking, I'm going to be as difficult as I can, for the next two years, forget it, for the Army will break you.' He looked around slowly as if to emphasize what he had been saying. One could have heard a pin drop.

'Right,' he said breaking his spell, 'let's have a look at your kit.' He then began to rummage through all the kit as it was laid out. When he had finished, he proceeded to show one and all how kit should be displayed in the Royal Military Police, especially bedding. The Sergeant demonstrated how each sheet had to be folded so that each formed a square, then he did the same with the blankets which then surrounded the sheets, almost like a sandwich, next came the actual blanket on the bed, this had to have square corners, and finally how to place the bundle of sheets and blankets at the foot of the bed, in the middle. He then picked up someone's boots, 'Do these fit you?' he asked.

'No Sergeant,' the recruit replied.

'What's your name?' asked Sergeant Crouse.

'Hallam, Sergeant.'

'No it's not,' said the Sergeant 'from now on your name is Probationer Hallam, Sergeant, that goes for all of you; you are all Probationer's in the Royal Military Police.' Returning to the subject of the boots, Sergeant Crouse said 'What's wrong with them?'

'They are too tight Sergeant.'

The Sergeant looking around at everyone said 'Well the best way to soften boots is to piss in them, and then walk around for a few hours, and if that doesn't work stuff them with wet paper.' After a few laughs, the Sergeant then showed everyone how to prepare one set of boots for dress purposes. This as every soldier will know to a greater or lesser extent, involved the 'magic circles' routine.

The back of a spoon handle is heated over a candle and when hot, it is rubbed over the surface of the leather which, apart from the toe cap and heels, has a rough pimple effect. The hot spoon eventually wears the pimples down leaving a smooth surface. Then the 'magic circles' take over. Hour after hour after hour of monotonously applying black boot polish in a circular motion, via the use of the index finger covered in a duster, numbs the mind. At regular intervals, one has to spit on the leather then add yet more polish (which the individual has to buy). This process eventually brings forth a high shine. It would be impossible to calculate the man hours this process takes.

Having completed his instructions, Sergeant Crouse said, 'It's now late Friday afternoon, you have the weekend to practice all the things I have just shown you, if any of you are not sure of something, ask someone, work as a unit, for on Monday morning we start to make soldiers out of you.' He looked around at the sea of faces surrounding him and continued, 'For the past two years, I have produced the best Squad at the pass out parade, so as you are going to be my last Squad, I intend to make it three in a row, do as I tell you, work hard and I will make you proud of yourselves.' Finally, he said before leaving, 'This as you may have noticed is an old building, if you want hot water to shave with in the mornings, be in the ablutions before six o'clock. And when on parade, there is no excuse for not being properly shaved.' He looked around and noted the expressions on some of the faces. 'For those who want to eat, there is a list of the times the mess is open behind each door of your lockers.'

With that he strode to the barrack room door, opened it, then turned around and said 'I will see you all on Monday morning at nine o'clock, beds made, floor polished, boots cleaned, no litter anywhere, all shaved, shirts pressed, all brass work cleaned, windows cleaned, you will find a cupboard with all cleaning gear in it that you will need. Work in teams and you will get the work done quickly.' Then he left. Conrad was impressed by Sergeant Crouse.

'Fucking Hell,' someone said, 'we'll never be able to do all that work before Monday, fuck this for a game of soldiers, I'm going home.' Suddenly the tension disappeared, and everyone burst out laughing. Everyone talked to each other, and discussed how best to tackle the workload, in the end all the various jobs were written down on separate pieces of paper, then put into a box, shaken, and then each in turn took out a paper. Conrad drew window cleaning along with a big, gangling, slow speaking bloke called Barry Rolf from

Keighley, Yorkshire, who by sheer chance had the bed next to him. They became buddies immediately, although as different as chalk and cheese.

After some priceless moments of social verbal intercourse, everyone collected their belongings and arranged them in their lockers. Having done so, they then made their way to the Mess, each carrying their 'irons'. As they entered the Mess hall, Conrad said to Barry 'I wonder what slop the Royal Military Police will serve up.'

'God only knows,' replied Barry. When Conrad and Barry arrived at the serving counter of the Mess having queued for several minutes, they were pleasantly surprised to find a variety of dishes available to them namely: Baked fish with roast or mashed potatoes and a choice of vegetables. Cold beef salad. Fried eggs, sausage, tomatoes, and chips, or a combination of all, with a choice of two puddings plus of course, the usual pot of tea. For the first time in his brief military career, Conrad actually enjoyed an army meal as did Barry.

Back in the barrack room, Conrad and Barry flopped onto their beds and looked at the ceiling above them, each thinking their own thoughts. Conrad was thinking about Heather and what she might be doing, for no letters had been allowed to be sent to those at home, and he wondered how his mother was coping. Barry said 'What are you thinking about Conrad?'

Conrad turned his head and looking at Barry and said 'Home, Barry.'

'Me too,' Barry replied. They both returned to their own private thoughts. After a while Barry turned to Conrad and said in a low whisper 'Conrad, will you help me to get through the training programme?'

Conrad turned to face him and said 'What do you mean?'

Barry replied 'Just help me get through the physical training; I'm not sure I can make it on my own, and I don't want to fail.'

'Of course I will, if I can,' Conrad replied.

The weekend was spent cleaning all their equipment, boots, clothes, webbing, and of course their individual barrack room tasks. In between all this feverish activity, they discovered that the army food in the MPs, a phrase they all began to use more and more frequently, was far superior to any which they had experienced in the past. But of course nothing like home cooking, which was still fresh in each and everyone's mind.

By Sunday evening, each and everyone felt that come Monday morning, Sergeant Crouse would have nothing but praise for all their efforts over the weekend, and each felt that his kit would pass any muster. A feeling of togetherness was beginning to bind them all.

Later that evening prior to lights out, some in the Squad who had previously not done a great deal during the course of the day, for the collective benefit of the Squad, were now dusting the areas around their beds, giving an extra polish to their boots, and to anything else that they thought would benefit from their extra attention. No doubt they thought that their inactivity had gone unnoticed by the rest of the Squad, which of course it hadn't. No-one realised at the time that this was the start of the formation of team spirit, which is of course the keystone of all military thinking and training.

As the lights went out at 11.00pm precisely (an extra hour at weekends), each member of the Squad climbed into his bed, and thought his own private thoughts. In the darkness, there appeared tiny pin points of light, almost like stars appearing in the night sky, as some lit a cigarette and tried to draw down some form of comfort from the smoke they inhaled, in order to ease their personal predicament. Whispered conversations were exchanged from bed to bed. Occasionally an expletive such as, 'Watch your fucking ash on my floor,' could be heard, 'Sorry mate', came a reply from the offending party. Slowly but inevitably, fatigue overcame them all, and eventually each member of the Squad, succumbed to the seductive temptations of sleep, whilst wondering what was in store for them tomorrow morning.

The alarms went off at 5.00am the next morning. Sheets were thrown back from the bodies of the sleepers as if by magic, and a stream of young men in various stages of undress, some still naked, each clutching the various accoutrements of hygiene, a toothbrush, toothpaste, razor, shaving soap, after shave and towels, rushed to the ablutions in order to be the first to avail themselves of the limited supply of hot water, with which to cleanse themselves. A more incongruous sight would be hard to imagine.

Ablutions finished, it was back to the barrack room, then grabbing their eating irons, a fast march to the Mess hall, before the rest of the 'inmates', as all probationers were called, arrived on the scene. By being first in the queue, you had the benefit of the hottest and freshest food, (there is nothing worse than hard baked eggs and bacon dripping in lukewarm fat to put you off food) with the possibility of a little extra, for no-one knew just how many would attend breakfast, and the cooks did not like to waste the food they had prepared, because they had to justify the purchase of all provisions.

There are many stories told about the ACC., the Army Catering Corps, or as many 'old swet's' (old soldiers) will refer to them as being, 'Andy Clyde's Commandoes'. They are: Butchers of food, egg, bacon and chip specialists, lumpy-mashed potato experts and islands in porridge artists. And so on, the list is endless. In actual fact the ACC., produced a diet that would sustain a fighting man in the field of conflict, and at the same time could create a meal fit for a King. They are perhaps the most maligned of all the branches of the Army.

After a breakfast of mixed cereals, bacon egg and sausage, with of course the usual pot of bromide tea, it was back to the barracks, to tidy up, and prepare for the arrival of Sergeant Crouse, at nine o'clock. As soon as Conrad and Barry had washed their eating irons, and cleaned out the rings of bromide in their pots, they set about preparing their beds as previously instructed, and laid out their best pair of boots. Barry's boots looked positively dull compared to Conrad's. Barry, for whatever reason, just could not raise a high shine.

With half an hour left before the Sergeants' arrival, the barrack room was a hive of activity. Dusters, floor buffers, brooms, dust pans, chamois leathers, all were being deployed in every corner of the room with feverish haste.

At one minute past nine o'clock, the door opened and in walked Sergeant Crouse, swagger stick under his arm, as before. He surveyed the lines of men standing to attention at the sides of their beds, sweat already showing on some of the faces, and under the arms of those he was about to inspect. He had of course in his long army career seen similar sights many times before. 'Stand at ease,' he barked. His voice cut through the silence like a knife through butter. All stood at ease as one. Slowly Sergeant Crouse walked up and down both sides of the room, his eyes darting from one man to the next missed nothing. Having completed his tour, he stopped at the middle point of the room and addressed them all.

'When I left you on Friday I told you I wanted this place clean when I came back this morning, obviously some of you did not hear me.' With that he strode to the bed of probationer Hallam and picked up his fork, 'What the hell is this?' He asked Hallam holding up the fork.

'Egg Sergeant.'

'What is egg doing between the prongs of your fork?'

'I don't know Sergeant,' replied Hallam, trying to keep a steady voice.

'You don't know?' roared the Sergeant, 'is this or is this not your fork?'

'Yes Sergeant,' replied Hallam.

'Then I will tell you why it's got egg between the prongs, it's because you're bloody idle, and have not bothered to clean it.' There was a deathly pause before the Sergeant spoke again. 'Am I right Hallam?'

Hallam swallowed, and then he replied 'Yes Sergeant.' Sweat now running down his face.

Sergeant Crouse went to each and every man and found fault with either him or his equipment. When he got to Rolf's bed, he had a field day! His blankets were not evenly folded and there was a stain on his pot which he had missed when drying it and the inside of his locker was a mess. Then he looked at his boots. Looking up at Rolf, for Rolf was a good six or seven inches taller than the Sergeant, he picked up his boots, 'What are these supposed to be Rolf?'

And Barry in his slow speaking way replied after giving the question serious thought 'Boots Sergeant.'

Sergeant Crouse almost burst a blood vessel, 'I know they are boots you idiot, what I want to know is why you haven't bothered to clean the bloody things as I instructed.'

'Excuse me Sergeant,' Rolf said, 'but there's no need to use bad language, my mother always told me that bad language is a sure sign of a poor education.'. Rolf was of course serious, (such was his strict Methodist upbringing, which came to light later) for no one ever heard him swear.

Sergeant Crouse stood there unable to comprehend what he had just heard. Around the room, some of those that had heard the exchange were trying to stifle laughs, shoulders heaving with the effort, however some sound did escape their lips, which only added to the theatrical element of the situation. After what seemed an eternity, Sergeant Crouse regained control of himself, and with a flick of his swagger stick, sent Rolf's boots flying through the air before they made contact with the far wall, and fell to the floor. Everyone suddenly went tense and wondered what would happen next. They did not have long to wait to find out. Immediately Rolf had retrieved his battered boots when told to do so, Sergeant Crouse said 'I want this shambles of a barrack room tidy when I return in half an hour, and then we shall do some drill in the nice warm sunshine, in fact we shall probably do drill all day.' He lingered on almost every word, for he was well aware of the fact that every new soldier since time began, hated drill.

As he was about to leave, the Sergeant turned to Conrad and said 'what's your name?' looking at Conrad with more interest than normal.

'Probationer Davenport, Sergeant,' replied Conrad, looking him straight in the face.

Sergeant Crouse returned the look, then after a few moments said 'Right, get to work all of you; I shall be back in half an hour.' He turned, and left the room.

The unknown clerk in Kensington had not wasted any time informing his Superior, and he in turn informed the CO., (Commanding Officer) Major Harris, of the incident in Oswestry. After some deliberation, he reopened two files on his desk and proceeded to read them again. Having done so he put his chair into recline mode, took out his pipe, lit it, and after the sparks had settled down and he was sure the pipe was drawing to his satisfaction, he closed his eyes and thought.

Later in the day on a secure line, he telephoned the CO., at Woking, Major Darnie, and had a lengthy discussion regarding some 'sensitive' programmes he was currently dealing with, which came under the banner of 'TOP SECRET'. At one point, Major Darnie expressed his utter disgust at what his opposite number was proposing, and wished to have his views recorded. However, whilst both men held the same rank, Major Harris had almost unlimited 'clout' in high places. He had turned down numerous offers of promotion over the years, for he was a 'man's man', and wished to stay in a position where he could control men and not paper. He was in fact on the same salary as a General, although very few people knew this, therefore he usually got his way in matters of importance. Eventually, Major Darnie capitulated, and with a heavy heart he agreed to set in motion an agenda that could not be terminated. The two officers then entered into a dialogue on the future of the armed forces for the foreseeable future, and then Major Harris ended the conversation.

When he replaced the telephone Major Darnie sat for a while and mused over what had transpired this day. With great foreboding, he slowly opened his bottom drawer and retrieved a bottle of fifteen year old Scottish malt whisky. Slowly he poured himself a large glass of the amber fluid, he watched as if in a trance as the daylight sparkled on the facets of the glass, and its contents. Slowly he raised the glass to his lips and took a long draught of the fiery liquid. As he replaced the glass on his desk, he said to the emptiness of the room 'May your God go with you, and may my God forgive me.' With that, he drained the rest of the whisky in the glass, shuddered slightly, and then arose from his chair. He picked up his hat and cane, checked his dress in the long mirror which adorned part of the wall by the door. He looked at himself for a few moments, adjusted his hat slightly then opened the door of his office, he paused on the threshold a few moments as the warm summer sun surrounded him, he watched a Sergeant drilling his men at the far side of the Square and smiled to himself, then he slowly closed the door behind him, locking it as he did so, then walked down the side of the Square to the main gates and out of the barracks, acknowledging the salutes of the sentries on duty as he did so.

Chapter Three

Sergeant Crouse returned to his Squad exactly thirty minutes later, he slowly paced around the room and noted that everything was back in place. Without any reference to the previous inspection or any individual, he simply said 'Right, we are now going to learn how to drill (march in Army terms). Drill is probably the most important element of Army training for, when done properly, it creates pride in oneself, comradeship and respect for others. Some of you will find it difficult, but at the end of sixteen weeks, all of you, will be as good as the next man, this I promise you. That means that you will be the best there is in the whole of the British Army.' He paused for a moment to allow the enormity of what he had said to register. He continued 'The Royal Military Police only take the best, therefore as you are my last Squad, I intend to make you the best there has been, it will be difficult but not impossible, providing you work hard.' After a long silence, the Squad left the barrack room and made its way down the stairs to the Square behind Sergeant Crouse who, as always, was immaculately dressed.

The day had begun badly for Rolf, however, it was about to become infinitely worse! Once out on the Square in the bright, hot, summer sunshine, they formed three lines, standing at ease. They listened intently as the Sergeant described the various manoeuvres he wanted them to perform. Having described them, he then demonstrated exactly what he expected of them. Conrad thought he was very, very good. Having brought the Squad to attention, Sergeant Crouse then proceeded to march them up the Square, left, right, left, right, left, right, however after covering only a few yards there was chaos as some of the front rank stumbled, unkind words were leaked from the clenched teeth of those concerned, until Sergeant Crouse brought them to a halt. After some well-chosen words, he realigned them and started again. Once more after a few strides, there was chaos. After the third attempt to march a few yards, Sergeant Crouse discovered the cause of the problem, Probationer Barry Rolf.

'Rolf, you bloody clown, can't you march?' roared the Sergeant. He stopped the Squad and brought poor Rolf to the front. After informing Rolf which was his left arm, left leg, right arm, right leg, he proceeded to attempt to march alongside him. It was pitiful to watch, big, innocent, gangling Rolf, arms and legs still dysfunctional, trying to march with one of the Army's elite. Some in the squad could not contain themselves, and ripples of laughter could be clearly heard. This of course only aggravated an already tense situation. No matter how the Sergeant tried to help Rolf, he only made matters worse, for Rolf was by now a nervous wreck. Sergeant Crouse nursed him, cajoled him, and finally cursed him, but to no avail, Rolf just could not swing his arms in unison with his legs. Eventually Rolf was put back into line and the Squad awaited further instructions from the Sergeant. By now, all were sweating profusely, including the Sergeant, for the sun beat down on them from a powder blue sky.

Once again, Sergeant Crouse brought them all to attention, and then commenced to march them up the Square…again, chaos, caused by Rolf! By now the shouts of Sergeant Crouse had attracted the attention of other instructors on the Square. Now, all eyes were on Sergeant Crouse's squad. If there is one thing that a senior instructor cannot stand, it is the thought that a junior instructor thinks that he, is better than his senior, and that he has the best Squad. Expletives poured from the mouth of Sergeant Crouse all directed at poor Rolf.

After several hours of misery on the baking hot Square, Sergeant Crouse dismissed them and sent them to their barrack room. When they were out of earshot of anyone in authority, most of the Squad turned on Rolf with a vengeance. 'You stupid Yorkshire sod, look at my fucking boots.'

'You bloody Yorkshire pudding what's wrong with you?'

This tirade went on for some time until Conrad stood up and said 'Why don't you leave him alone, he hasn't set out to be difficult, he just cannot march properly.' Turning away from them, he began to hum Ave Maria to himself as he divested himself of the course, soaking wet khaki shirt, stained with the white salt rings of sweat from his body. Then he examined the red raw abrasions under his armpits that the rough crude material had created. He winced as he tenderly explored them with his fingers.

'And who the fuck do you think you are,' came a voice two beds away from Conrad.

Conrad turned slowly, still humming and faced the speaker, his eyes never wavering from the speaker's face 'I know who I am, what's your problem?'

The speaker was Bernie Allen from Birmingham. He was a strong, burly chap who rarely spoke to anyone. 'My problem matey is the Yorkshire dumpling next to you, he's so fucking stupid he's going to make us a laughing stock on the Square, and something has to be done about him.'

Conrad laughed. 'And just what do you think we can do about someone that cannot march properly that will transform him overnight into a drill expert?'

'We can knock some sense into the Yorkshire idiot and make him march properly,' Allen replied. At this, Rolf came forward and tried to pass Conrad, who put out his arm and stopped him. Whilst the vocal exchanges had been taking place, no one seemed to notice that the barrack room door had opened quietly and Sergeant Crouse had entered the room. He now witnessed the confrontation between Davenport and Allen.

'Just try and lay a hand on Rolf, and I'll break your fingers,' Conrad said casually, and half turned away. The barracks fell silent as the expectation of a fight gripped them. No one moved, and all eyes were focused on Conrad, Rolf and Allen. You could have heard a pin drop. Ignoring the warning, Allen lunged at the two of them. He was within two feet of them when Conrad went into action. He swayed to his left and then pivoted, bending his knees slightly, then driving upward with his right hand extended like a knife blade. He hit Allen in the throat, the blow only travelling eighteen inches. Bright lights flashed before Allen's eyes, and for a few moments, he thought that he was going to choke. Conrad stood back and watched as Allen slowly sank to his knees, clutching his damaged throat, a strange animal like noise coming from his mouth. Conrad moved in and was just about to administer the coup-de-grace on his fingers when Sergeant Crouse shouted out 'Davenport stand still.' Conrad stepped back from Allen and came to attention immediately, as Sergeant Crouse approached him.

SAS Sergeant Bill Long would have been proud of his pupil!

Sergeant Crouse however, having witnessed Conrad's talents first hand, now realised that he had in his Squad a seemingly passive person, who, according to his Army file, had a love of opera and all things British but could, under certain conditions, suddenly turn into a very, very dangerous individual. Sergeant Crouse now realised why he had received the sealed envelope containing the orders to 'stretch' Davenport almost to breaking point.

Some seven years previously, Sergeant Crouse had been faced with a similar situation and having pushed the unfortunate individual to the limits, had watched with both horror and dismay, as the young healthy Probationer, wilted and waned under the constant pressures imposed upon him. He eventually ended up in the psychiatric ward of one of the Army hospitals on the south coast of England, where he stayed for several years. He was never the same person again. Sergeant Crouse was now afraid that history was about to repeat itself, for he now began to harbour the same uneasy thoughts he had had seven years ago, when he received his orders. He hoped with all his being that Davenport would not suffer the same fate as his previous charge had done. Sergeant Crouse could not face that prospect again.

'What the hell is going on here?' bellowed Sergeant Crouse.

No one answered at first and then Rolf said 'We were just practising unarmed combat moves sergeant, and Allen slipped.' Big gangling Rolf just stood there and looked at the Sergeant, as innocent as could be. Allen was now beginning to get to his feet, still clutching his throat, his face scarlet with pain.

'Are you all right Allen?' the sergeant asked, Allen could only nod, looking at Conrad as he did so, hate burning in his eyes.

Sergeant Crouse turned to Conrad who was still stood at attention, minus his shirt. As someone who knew how to condition men, the Sergeant realised that Davenport was in the best of condition, well-muscled, good shoulders, slim waist, athletic and carrying no surplus flesh. 'Stand easy Davenport, so you were practising unarmed combat moves were you? Well don't practice them again in the barracks, do it in the gym or outside with the PTIs., (Physical training instructors) do I make myself clear?' There was a mumbled 'Yes sergeant' from all the Squad, except Allen of course, who still could not speak. Conrad just looked at the Sergeant.

As Sergeant Crouse half turned to leave, he paused, turned back and said to Conrad 'If you have time to spare, do something useful, and get Rolf to march properly,... in fact, that's an extra duty for you, train Rolf to march'. With that, he strode from the room.

After the door closed, some of those closest to Rolf and Conrad gathered round them and talked about how Conrad had dealt with Allen, they wanted to know how Conrad had learnt how to fight the way he had, they were all impressed. Conrad just said 'I've read a few books on the subject.'

When all the admirers had gone back to their beds, Rolf, quietly so he would not be heard by anyone else, thanked Conrad for what he had done. 'Forget it.' Conrad said, 'what we now have to do is to get you to swing your arms correctly when you march, it's not difficult if you think about it.'

Conrad tried all he knew, which was not a great deal, trying to get Rolf to swing his arms in unison with his legs. He tied one of Rolf's arms to his and then marched with him, then repeated the process with the other arm. Had anyone seen them they would have thought that they were mad. However, after three hours of practice, even though lights out had been called some time ago, they continued to practice in the dark. Then at some time just past midnight, Rolf finally got the message, and marched up and down the landing outside the barrack room, arms swinging in unison with his legs, but still very ungainly. Rolf could not, even with the most generous of imaginations, be described as being elegant to look at when marching, however, he could now march properly, and consequently he would not be an embarrassment on the Square. The Sergeant in his wisdom, put Rolf next to Conrad when marching, and from that moment on, a strong bond was forged between them, and suddenly there was a different atmosphere on the Square.

'Get out of those bloody pits (beds) you idle buggers, we are all going for a nice early morning run!' someone screamed.

When the Squad had awakened from their slumbers and realised that they were not dreaming, they all exited their beds in quick time in many cases, their maleness evident to a greater or lesser degree. It was 05:00hrs, June 1960 and the barrack room lights blazed down on them.

'Right you miserable lot, you there, whatever your name is, pointing at Hallam, put your dick back in your pants, I've never seen anything like it before in my life.' He shouted 'Get dressed in fatigues, now, all of you, and be quick about it, then line up outside.' By now, everyone was wide awake and back in the real world. They grabbed their working clothes and hastily dressed, then ran downstairs onto the square. The Corporal who had disturbed their slumbers was a new PTI endeavouring to stamp his authority on the squad. He was well muscled, with a shaven head, dressed in a white tee shirt and black skin tight trousers.

'Right you pathetic bunch of people, let me introduce myself, my name is Corporal Marsh, some call me Corporal Harsh, because I don't like amateurs, like you lot. I'm a professional soldier with fifteen years of service.' He drew in his breath and expanded his chest, as if to impress the Squad. Everyone stood impassively, looking to his front. 'For our first run I'm going to be easy with you, just a few miles, I hope all your boots are broken in, if not you'll have some blistered feet.'

He led the way down the side of the Square heading towards the main gates. 'Which one of you is Davenport?' he asked, running on the spot as they filed past him.

'I am, Corporal,' Conrad replied. Marsh came alongside him, fell into step with him, appraising Conrad as he did so. Conrad looked to his front impassively. After a few moments, Corporal Marsh increased his pace and went to the front of the file and took up his position in the lead.

Corporal Marsh led the procession at a slow jog, in single file, as they approached the sentries at the main gate. Once outside, they ran on the road which skirted the barracks, then after a mile or so, they left the road and began to feel soft earth beneath their boots. The sweet scent of pine trees floated over them like an invisible mist, and the full orchestra of bird songs began to fill the air, reaching to a crescendo, as they welcomed the warmth of the rising sun. A barn owl en route to its nest no doubt, and with its breakfast firmly held in one of its talons, alighted on the branch of a tree, and looked down at the file of perspiring men as they passed beneath it in the early morning mist. It gazed at them for a few moments as only owls can, then blinked an eye, and launched itself into the sky with that slow, almost lazy action, that is so special to the owl. Conrad loved running in the countryside and especially through woods, he was in his element!

Corporal Marsh began to increase the pace, and soon, in order not to stumble over the man in front, Conrad had to keep dodging around people as they failed to keep pace with Corporal Marsh. Very quickly, Conrad found himself close behind the Corporal, with an ever widening gap between himself and the next man. Marsh looked behind him and saw that only Conrad could keep pace with him. Once again he raised the tempo and still Conrad was behind him. At this point, Conrad noticed that Corporal Marsh was wearing light running shoes, whilst he was wearing boots! A smile broke out on Conrad's face as he realized that he had the measure of Corporal Marsh / Harsh.

They reached the halfway point of the run and Corporal Marsh called a halt whilst the rest of the Squad caught up. He was very red in the face and blowing hard. Conrad on the other hand was simply jogging on the spot, arms loose by his side, inhaling the sweet fragrant air that surrounded them. He loved this environment! When all the Squad had reached the halfway point, some were in various states of distress due to their footwear. However this did not seem to concern the Corporal in the slightest. He had by now regained both his breath and his composure and was ready for the return run back to barracks.

Leading from the front, Corporal Marsh set off to a chorus of 'My boots are killing me Corporal.' He in turn replied, 'Remember this; there is no gain without pain.' He looked at Conrad, who was at his shoulder, and he realised that he could not out run him.

As they approached the barracks, Conrad stayed two feet behind Marsh, with the rest of the Squad spread out behind them. They passed through the main gates and made their way around the Square to the point from whence they had started.

As they came to a halt, Corporal Marsh turned to Conrad and gasped 'Why didn't you come past me, for I know you could?'

Conrad looked at him with a degree of respect that one athlete has for another and replied 'I could have passed you as you say, but that would have undermined your authority with the Squad.' Then he turned away as the stragglers came into the Square and was delighted to see big 'carthorse' Rolf, as ungainly as could be, pounding his way through the gates, trying to overtake the man in front of him, which he failed to do. There was something simple, innocent and endearing about Rolf that Conrad liked.

When all the Squad were assembled, the Corporal simply said 'Right, off you all go and get a shower then some breakfast, then stand by your beds and await an inspection by Sergeant Crouse.' With that, he cast a sideways glance at Conrad, paused for a moment, and then jogged away to his quarters.

After they had all showered and eaten, they returned to their quarters and changed into their second set of fatigues then made their beds. By now this was almost second nature. Once again the barrack room talk was all about Conrad, and how he had matched, or even bettered the Corporal on the cross country run. Having done so, they then cleaned their boots as best they could bearing in mind that they had just run more than seven miles in them. Some of the Squad could barely walk due to the blisters on their feet from the ill-fitting boots, some were actually bleeding.

Sergeant Crouse arrived at 09.00hrs., having examined the layout of the all kit, he could only find fault with Conrad's, which he pulled to pieces and left strewn on both the floor and his bed. Conrad was told to report to Corporal Marsh at 18:00hrs for extra duties. Those with the bleeding feet he sent to the MOs, (Medical Officer) for treatment. The Squad, apart from Allen, whose throat was now slowly recovering from the blow inflicted upon it by Conrad's hand, gathered around him and questioned why his kit had been picked on, for his was the best laid out in the barracks, thanks to the training of SAS Bill Long. After some lengthy discussion, no one could figure out why the Sergeant had picked on Conrad and one by one they returned to their beds and started to clean their boots, followed by washing their stained clothes in the wash hand basins before another day began. Later, most of them went to bed earlier than normal, except for Conrad. He reported to Corporal Marsh.

Two hours later having cleaned five WCs, the Corporal's boots, and run up and down the stairs twenty times, Conrad was allowed to return to the barracks. He opened the door quietly and crept inside thinking that everyone would be asleep. He was wrong; almost all were wide awake waiting for him to return. When asked what he had had to do, Conrad simply told them the truth. There were cries of 'The bastards'… 'The shit bags' … plus many other descriptive phrases. After a while, everyone returned to their beds and settled down. By this time Conrad was exhausted, and no sooner had his head touched his pillow, he was asleep.

For the next six weeks this routine continued, always it was Conrad who was picked out for extra duties, and no matter what he had to do, he did so without a word passing his lips in protest.

The eighth week of training marked the halfway point in the RMP training programme and included a fifteen mile speed time trial with full pack. At various points along the course, 'Brass' (high ranking officers) watched the event unfold from Land Rovers, binoculars pressed to their eyes. By the halfway point, Conrad, having started from the back was in the lead and much to the surprise of all concerned, in second place, was Rolf! Big, gangling, flat footed, awkward Rolf pounding along like a big carthorse. He did not try to jump over hedges, he went through them. Brambles stuck to his trousers which were stained with blood, his boots were now void of any polish, and would thus require many hours of spit and polish to bring a shine back to them. But Rolf was happy, he had reached the halfway stage in the training programme, only two had failed to reach this point, and he was not one of them, thanks to the help of his friend Conrad, who was way out in front of him. Rolf felt good, and for some strange reason the words of Sergeant Crouse came back to him "Do as I tell you, and I will make you feel proud of yourself." Rolf was proud of himself!

At the end of the fifteen mile exercise, seated on a temporary grandstand overlooking the finishing line, were several high ranking Officers. Also in the group was the RMP (Royal Military Police) RSM., (Regimental Sergeant Major) and Sergeant Crouse. The attendance of Sergeant Crouse caused a few heads to be turned in his direction, especially when it was noted that he sat next to Major Harris! As Conrad crossed the finishing line, three hundred yards ahead of the next man, Wilson, a young man from Cheltenham managed to overtake Rolf ten yards from the line thus depriving him of second place, behind his friend and hero. The officers and guests applauded the victor, and the rest, with a vigorous clapping of hands led by Major Harris.

After watching some of the stragglers come home, Major Harris turned to Sergeant Crouse and said 'Sergeant Crouse, it would appear that you have done a good job so far, our man looks in perfect shape, so tell me, what exactly do we have in Davenport?'

Without rising to his feet or offering a salute, as previously instructed, Sergeant Crouse paused for a moment, then opened a folder he carried with him, with 'TOP SECRET' stamped across the front of it in large red letters. He began to read: "Conrad Davenport, born Bradford, Yorkshire 1938 always a sickly child. Numerous homes prior to parents settling in Bridlington, East Yorkshire 1950. Has a deep rooted love of opera, probably due to his mother, who had an outstanding operatic voice. From information to hand, it would seem that his mother is his 'pillar of strength'. Believes that British is best.

Education not very good, failed the 11+ (probably due to disrupted war years) but then blossomed when he went to Technical College, at age seventeen. Joined a local harriers club (track and cross country) at the same age. Good at all sports apparently, again not mentioned previously, and prior to call-up for National Service, spent some time being trained by ex SAS PTI Sergeant Bill Long, (one of the best apparently) which would seem to account for his outstanding physical fitness, and the fact that he seems to be afraid of no-one. From information supplied by Special Branch, he has a command of the Arts of Self Defense, second to none! He should be approached with extreme caution! Has a girlfriend, Heather Newton, a nurse, whom he has known from childhood. From information to hand, it would seem that there has been no other woman in Davenport's life. End of report."

Sergeant Crouse closed the folder and looked at Major Harris. He did not reply immediately but when he did, he had a smile on his face. 'Well Sergeant, it would seem that I was right in picking young Davenport, what a sly young fox he has turned out to be, all these skills and he never mentioned them.' He chuckled and said 'We have got ourselves a dark horse. What a good day this has turned out to be.'

'Yes sir,' replied Crouse, also smiling.

Again another pause, 'Very well Sergeant keep up the good work, and I will see you towards the end of his training, if anything important happens before then, you know where to contact me.' With that he got up and slowly walked away, his shoulders rising and falling as though laughing to himself. Sergeant Crouse watched him disappear then he too wandered away, deep in thought.

As he passed a bunch of Officers he saluted them and they returned his salute. He was about to pass by when one of them, 2nd. Lieutenant Mitchell, one of the Medical Officers, waved him over, 'Yes sir.' Crouse said, 'Damn fine show today Sergeant, first class in fact, tell us who was the chappie of yours who was way out in front.'

'Probationer Davenport sir.'

'Davenport eh, I don't think I've seen him on sick parade Sergeant.'

'No sir,' Crouse replied, 'he's a very healthy young man.' This brought a loud guffaw from the group and a 'Quite, quite' from Mitchell then 'anyway Sergeant, a damn fine show.' They exchanged a few more words then Crouse excused himself by saying that he had to go and see to his men. Out of earshot, he said, imitating Mitchell's very refined voice, "Damn good show Sergeant, damn good show."

Chapter Four

The daily routine for the Squad intensified with more and more drill, sessions in the gym, forced marches, weapon training, and using those weapons on the firing range. On one of those range days, the Squad had been issued with SMGs, (sub machine guns) with live ammunition. Before using them, the weapons' instructors gave a demonstration of how to approach the targets, then on command drop to one knee, then fire at the targets. He also informed the Squad what to do in case the weapon jammed, which was to stay in the firing position, lower the weapon, and raise the left arm in the air. The targets were wooden frames with a type of cardboard covering, with the picture of a soldier painted on them in black paint.

All went well until the last three men came to the firing line. One of the three was Rolf. The instructor gave the order 'Advance in line and fire in groups of five rounds, then advance five paces and stand still, advance'. They went forward and began to fire, when Rolf suddenly stood up and turned round with the weapon still in both hands and said 'The gun's jammed.' Never have so many men moved so quickly. One of the instructors from the safety of a wall of sand bags bellowed out 'Rolf stand still you bloody idiot, everyone get down and stay down.' Conrad peered over the sand bag wall and saw big gangling Rolf, still stood there with the SMG. in his hand, half turning to his left then right, wondering no doubt where everyone had gone, he prayed that the weapon would not suddenly burst into life, for the two who had been with Rolf were still flat on the floor, one on each side of him.

Again the instructor addressed Rolf only this time in a softer voice 'Rolf, very slowly, put the weapon on the floor and then stand back, do it now.' There was a great sigh of relief by all concerned as Rolf lowered the weapon to the ground, and then stood up with a dazed expression on his face. The instructors ran over to Rolf, one stood by him while the other bent down and gingerly picked up the offending weapon. He was facing the targets as he inspected it. Suddenly, and for no apparent reason, the weapon burst into life and one of the targets disintegrated as a number of rounds leapt from the muzzle of the offending weapon and found their mark.

When calm was restored, Rolf was visibly shaking, he looked a pathetic sight as the two instructors hurled a tirade of abuse at him, pointing out that he could have killed one or more of his comrades because of his stupidity. Needless to say, he was put on a charge and then all were marched back to the barracks in quick time. Once inside, the usual boisterous atmosphere was replaced by a more sombre mood. Hardly anyone spoke, when they did, it was in hushed tones that were barely audible. Almost everyone stayed by their beds polishing their boots and equipment, almost like robots, thankful that they had not been injured or worse.

When they returned from the Mess hall after their evening meal, one of Sergeant Crouse's assistants brought them some mail, he called out the names of those fortunate to have a letter or parcel, whilst making lewd comments about some of the letters that had a trace of perfume on the envelope. This was a soul destroying time for those that did not receive mail. It was also a bad time for those that received the dreaded, 'Dear John'. This was a letter from a girlfriend saying that she had found someone else, due to his absence. Some even returned engagement rings with their letters.

This particular day most of the squad received mail including Bernie Allen. Conrad received two, one from his mother and one from Heather with a picture of her with her scooter. Everyone went to their beds and lay down to read their mail, some took out cigarettes and smoked them, blowing lazy clouds of blue smoke up to the ceiling, as they savoured every line they read, whilst all the time wishing that they were back home with their girlfriends and families. Always there were many damp eyes when everyone had finished reading their letters, and usually no one spoke for some time afterwards, in case their voices betrayed their emotions.

Bernie Allen was the first to move from his bed, he went directly to the ablutions tossing his letter into the waste bin by the door as he did so. No sooner had the door closed than one of the squad retrieved the letter and quickly read it before tossing it back into the bin. 'Fucking hell, Bernie's girl has sent him a 'Dear John',' he called out. 'We all better watch out from now on, for he's going to be a bastard to live with.' There was a mixed reaction of feelings around the barrack room at the news. Some genuinely felt sorry for him, whilst others said it was what the sod deserved, for very few in the squad had any time for him, he was arrogant, crude, and a bully.

When Allen returned, he went straight to his bed, undressed, pulled the sheets back, climbed into bed, then drew the sheets over his head and went to sleep, much to the surprise of the squad. However, there is little or no privacy in a barrack room, therefore in bed, covered by a few flimsy pieces of cloth, is as near to privacy as one can get.

Those who had work to do set about doing it, Rolf went to clean the ablutions after all had finished using them. This was day one of his fourteen day fatigues punishment for the firing range incident, and Conrad went to help him, unofficially. Whilst they were cleaning and polishing, Rolf said to Conrad, 'You want to watch out for Allen, because since you almost choked him he has been working in the gym lifting weights, and he has let it be known that he is going to get even with you.' Conrad looked at Rolf and said 'Thanks for the warning Barry, I've been expecting something for some time from him, but don't worry, I can look after Allen.' With that, he went back to polishing the taps on the wash hand basin, and very soon afterwards he was humming Ave Maria. 'What is that tune you are always humming Conrad?' Rolf asked. Conrad explained at some length, but Rolf could not appreciate what Conrad was saying, having virtually no understanding of classical music.

As they were about to leave the ablutions, Rolf grabbed Conrad's arm and said 'Conrad have you ever wondered why you are always being given extra duties, even though your kit is always immaculate, and why are the PTIs always trying to race you, even though you beat them?'

Conrad paused before answering, when he did so he simply said in a matter of fact voice, 'Perhaps they don't like me, anyway Barry, no matter what they may do to me, they will not break me.' He looked at Barry for a few moments and then walked the last few yards to the door. With his hand on the door handle he paused, then turned about and faced Barry. 'Barry I'm going to say something to you now that may be of help to you in the future when times are bad, and you think there is no hope; it's simply this "There is no Can't," … think about it Barry.' Then he turned, opened the door and left the room, closely followed by a very puzzled looking Barry Rolf.

Once inside the barrack room, they took off their boots and flopped onto their beds. They lay there for several minutes, eyes closed, as their exhausted bodies relaxed and began to recharge. Exquisite sensations washed over them as their nervous system settled down and began to relax. Pins and needles attacked their feet almost as a 'thank you' for freeing them from the heavy cumbersome and restrictive boots that had for many hours restricted them. Finally they arose, undressed then climbed into their beds; both were asleep within a few moments of their heads touching the pillows.

At five o'clock the next morning without the aid of an alarm clock, everyone was awake and with razors and other toilet requirements in their hands they made their way to the ablutions and the small amount of hot water that would be available for the early risers. Having washed and shaved it was back to barracks, bed making, boot cleaning, floor polishing, and anything else that had to be done prior to the usual morning inspection, then breakfast.

Having returned from the Mess hall, all the squad went to the ablutions, cleaned their teeth and eating irons, then returned to the barrack room and began putting away their utensils ready for the inspection.

Conrad was humming Ave Maria when he opened his locker door which had the picture of Heather stuck to it and began to arrange his knife, fork, spoon and mug. Then a voice loud enough for most in the room to hear said, 'I bet she got shagged last night.'

Silence suddenly fell on the barrack room. Conrad slowly turned to face the owner of the voice. He looked at the leering face of Bernie Allen but said nothing. Allen began to repeat himself when Conrad said 'If you are talking to me and referring to my girlfriend you had better say no more, otherwise this time I will break your fingers.'

Rolf had moved up behind Conrad whilst he was addressing Allen but Conrad pushed him back. Allen laughed out loud and replied 'I bet she got s...' That was as far as he got, Conrad covered the eight feet or so between them in a flash, the edge of his right hand smashed into Allen's nose, breaking it and causing it to bleed profusely. Allen staggered back under the ferocity of Conrad's attack and he hit the floor head first with a sickening thud. Conrad had his hands around Allen's neck and was squeezing the life out of him when the word 'Davenport,' thundered out. Conrad held onto Allen's throat, several hands dragged him off.

When he stood up, he was looking into the faces of Sergeant Crouse and Corporal Marsh, Rolf, and some of the others in the squad. 'What the bloody hell's going on here?' demanded Sergeant Crouse. Before anyone could say a word, Rolf stepped forward and told the Sergeant exactly what had happened, and that Allen was the cause of the trouble, others in the Squad now found their voices and endorsed what Rolf had said.

Crouse went over to Allen who was by now getting to his feet, aided by a couple of the Squad, the front of his shirt was covered in blood, his nose was swollen and the marks of Conrad's fingers were clearly visible about his neck. Having assured himself that Allen was all right he sent him to the medical centre with one of the Squad to have his nose checked.

After they had left, he turned to look at Conrad and said 'Corporal Marsh take Probationer Davenport to the guardhouse and wait for me there, but for the time being do not make out a charge sheet, do you understand?'

'Yes Sergeant,' Marsh shouted. Then he barked out 'Probationer Davenport, to the guardhouse in quick time, quick march, left, right, left, right, left, right.' They both marched to the door of the barrack, and then paused whilst Marsh opened it and then they disappeared.

There were murmurs of dissent from the rest of the squad at this treatment of Conrad, who was liked by all. 'Quiet,' shouted the Sergeant, 'and get this mess cleaned up before I return.'

He turned to leave and was confronted by Rolf. 'This isn't right Sergeant, Conrad did no wrong, Allen started it.'

'Move aside Rolf otherwise you'll be in the guardhouse as well.' Reluctantly Rolf stood aside, and Sergeant Crouse left the room.

On the way to the guardhouse Sergeant Crouse called in at the Sergeants' mess and went to a telephone with a secure line, he dialled a number and after a few moments a voice said 'Harris.'

'Major Harris, Crouse here with a report sir.'

'Carry on Sergeant,' then listened whilst Crouse told him what had happened. When he had finished his report, Harris said 'So, our man almost killed him eh,' with a slight chuckle in his voice.

'Yes sir,' replied Crouse. 'How's his training going?'

'First class sir, excels in virtually everything, especially self defence and physical training, the PTIs cannot keep up with him.'

'Good.' There was a pause then Harris asked 'How much longer to pass out?'

'Just over two weeks sir.'

'Right Sergeant, that sounds fine, I have already sanctioned Davenport's posting to S.H.A.P.E. (Supreme Headquarters Allied Powers Europe., Paris) with a Top Secret clearance.' Again there was a pause then Harris said 'keep our man in the guardhouse for a couple of days, but don't charge him, I will be with you sometime tomorrow and talk to him. Before I do so I shall require all Davenport's incoming and outgoing mail which we have withheld.' Again another pause then 'Incidentally Sergeant, when one of 'my people' visited the Davenport's house for assessment, he was shown Davenports' bedroom by his mother and judging from the books on display, I am delighted to say that it appears that Sir Winston Churchill was a boyhood hero of Davenport's.'

'Oh, right sir,' replied Crouse unable to understand the significance of the statement.

'Anything more I need to know Sergeant?'

'No sir, except that I have not charged him, I thought it best to speak to you first, in view of the current situation.' replied Crouse.

'In that case I will say goodbye for now, and I will see you shortly, you have done well Sergeant, I am impressed by the way you have handled this matter.' The line went dead and Sergeant Crouse was left with only his conscience for a companion, unfortunately his conscience afforded him little or no peace of mind.

Chapter Five

Sergeant Crouse left the mess and walked slowly to the guard house and checked that no charge had been entered against probationer Davenport. Having satisfied himself that all was in order, he and Corporal Marsh returned to the Sergeants mess for several drinks.

Upon the instructions of Sergeant Crouse, Probationer Allen was kept in the medical wing for a few days, under light sedation, as suggested by Major Harris.

The Major arrived at 14.00hrs, the next day and summoned Sergeant Crouse to the Officers mess. Major Harris waited at the entrance for Crouse and then signed him in. Harris went straight up to the bar, 'Care for a drink Crouse?'

'Thank you sir.'

The major scowled. 'Sorry,' Crouse said, 'Force of habit.'

The major smiled 'I understand, drink?'

'A pint of bitter please.'

The Major turned to the barman. 'A large Black Label, a pint of bitter and have one yourself.'

'Thank you sir,' he replied. This time there was no questioning the 'sir'.

'We will be sitting over there.' He pointed to the far corner of the room.

'Very good sir, I'll be with you in a moment.' The Major nodded his head then led the way to the window table and sat down. No one spoke.

The barman arrived a few moments later, immaculate in his white shirt, black bow tie, red cummerbund, black trousers and shoes. He carried a silver tray at shoulder height in one hand, and weaved his way through the many tables and chairs that were placed at random around the floor. He laid a crisp white napkin on the table in front of the major, and then put a chunky cut glass tumbler containing the large Black Label on top of it. He then placed a small jug of water to the right of the Majors' drink, again on a crisp white napkin. He then repeated the process with the Sergeants' beer.

'Is there anything else you require sir?' enquired the barman.

'No that's fine thank you,' Harris replied. With that the barman retired. 'Cheers,' said Harris raising his glass,

'Cheers,' repeated Crouse raising his glass, then he took a sip from the white foamed top and settled back in his chair. For a few moments, both men just sat and enjoyed their drink.

'Have you brought the material?' the Major asked quietly.

Without saying a word, Sergeant Crouse put his hand inside his jacket and withdrew a large brown envelope, which he slid across the table, then took another drink of his beer.

The Major picked up the envelope and weighed it in his hand 'Quite heavy, how many letters?'

'Forty-seven,' replied Crouse.

'Anything special in them, that I should know about?'

'Apart from the letter and picture of Davenport's girlfriend you allowed to be passed, albeit three weeks late, not a great deal. Although I am sure that by now Davenport's girlfriend probably thinks that as he has not written to her for several weeks, he has either found someone else, or finished with her. As for his mother, she must be in a state of torment.' He looked at Harris but only 'dead eyes' returned his gaze.

'You don't like this business do you?'

'No I don't,' replied Crouse.

'Nor do I,' replied Harris, 'but it has to be done, I'll arrange for someone to call and see Mrs. Davenport and put her mind at rest, duty to the country and all that. Whilst on the subject of the Davenports, I have to say that you getting Corporal Marsh to provoke Allen into a confrontation with Davenport over his girlfriend was a touch of genius, especially after him receiving a 'Dear John'?'

Crouse put down his beer he was about to drink, and looked at Harris 'How do you know about the 'Dear John' Allen received?'

Harris looked back at him. 'One of my specialist handwriting people sent it,' he said slowly.

For a moment, Sergeant Crouse was speechless, then gathering himself he said 'You sent the 'Dear John'?'

Harris nodded. 'Jesus,' said Crouse, 'just what the fucking hell are we into here.'

There was a long silence then Major Harris said 'Crouse, I want you to know that I have covered you as far as your Army record goes. No one will be able to point a finger at you and say that you had any part in what is about to happen. Your reputation is intact, your promotion opportunities are unblemished and your pension is intact.'

There followed another long pause whilst Sergeant Crouse looked at the last of his drink which he slowly swirled around in the bottom of his glass. Gradually, he raised his head and with tears starting to form in the corners of his eyes he looked at Harris who simply stared back at him. 'And is my fucking conscience intact, Sir.'

Harris looked at Crouse and for a moment his mask fell, he placed his hand on Crouse's arm just for a moment then said 'My friend (he had never used the word before) try to forget what has happened these past few months and the hurt which has been caused and may continue to be caused. If you need to find a reason for what has happened (and I cannot tell you), simply think of the safety of the country and under those circumstances, everyone is expendable, you have my word that I will do all I can to protect young Davenport.' The Major allowed Crouse to gather himself before saying 'Come, it is time to leave, I have to go and see Davenport and be back in London by 19.00hrs for a meeting.'

As they walked to the guardhouse, Harris stopped and faced his Sergeant. 'Crouse, this sadly is the end of the road for us, make sure that no ill befalls Davenport from here on in, unfortunately I shall not be here to see Davenport's Pass Out Parade as I shall be abroad on other business.' With that he threw protocol to the wind and saluted Crouse, Crouse instinctively returned the salute so fast that anyone watching would not have known whom had saluted first.

Upon entering the guardhouse, Major Harris produced his credentials and was immediately escorted to the rear of the detention block to the cell which housed Conrad.

Looking through the bars of the cell, he was shocked at what he saw. 'Who ordered this?' he demanded, rounding on the orderly Sergeant.

'Standard procedure Sir,' he replied.

As Major Harris waited for the doors to Conrad's cell to be unlocked, he looked at the figure he was about to interview. Conrad had been divested of anything which might have assisted him in the taking of his own life, belt, braces and shoe laces, and so he stood in the middle of the room his left hand holding up his fatigue trousers, whilst his right hand instinctively rose to his forehead in salute to an officer. Major Harris returned the acknowledgement then turned to the guard and demanded Conrad's clothes.

A few moments later, Conrad now properly dressed, sat behind a table facing Major Harris, sipping a cup of tea. The guards had been sent outside by the Major so that the pair of them could talk in absolute privacy. For the next hour, Major Harris explained to Conrad the reasons for all the extra duties he had had to perform, the barrack room confrontations and the fact that the best of the PTIs. could not match his level of physical fitness; he had without knowing, surpassed all expectations, and was therefore ideally suited for a special mission known to only a select few, a mission with

International ramifications. For several moments, Conrad just sat there unable to fully understand all that the Major had said. The hairs on the back of his neck seemed to suddenly stand out, and a shiver ran down his spine, his hands felt cold and damp, even though the room temperature was in the high seventies.

Major Harris sensing that Conrad's mind was in turmoil said 'If there was some other way, or some other person that could successfully achieve that which I am asking you to undertake, I would not be here, alas, there is no one else.' He paused whilst Conrad tried to absorb all that he had said.

Finally, Conrad said, 'Well sir, it would seem that I do not have a choice, but supposing that I fail, and the worst should happen, will you look after my mother?' Major Harris nodded his head in acknowledgement, 'and will you explain to my girlfriend what has happened? Although as I have not heard from her for some time now, it may be that she has found someone else whilst I have been away.' At this he lowered his head in order to hide the tears that began to form. When the moment had passed and he had regained his composure, he looked at the Major expectantly, and once again Major Harris nodded his head in agreement.

They talked for a while longer then Major Harris stood up and said that he had to leave. He went to the front of the guardhouse and summoned one of the guards and demanded to inspect the daily log book. Having done so and noted that there was no charge entered in the name of Davenport, he left the building with Conrad. When they reached the gates, Major Harris turned to Conrad and bade him farewell, Conrad saluted and the Major returned the salute, then left. He forgot to mention the letters he carried belonging to Conrad.

Chapter Six

After Major Harris had left, Conrad returned to the barrack room and was greeted by one and all; Rolf was particularly pleased to see him. They sat on the edge of Conrad's bed and discussed what had happened during the course of the past seventy-two hours, although Conrad did not mention any details of his conversation with Major Harris, for he was now under oath, and bound by the 'Official Secrets Act'.

When at last they each climbed into their beds and the lights went out, both lay for some time, eyes open looking at the ceiling, and wondering what the next few days would bring. As weariness finally began to overpower them, Conrad turned his head and whispered 'Goodnight Barry.'

'Goodnight Conrad,' Barry replied. Within two minutes both were sound asleep.

The next few days were filled with nonstop activity as they prepared for the 'Passing Out' ceremony. Sessions of drill followed sessions of drill, then more drill, the polishing of boots and brasses reached a fever pitch with each and every one trying to 'out do' the next man. By this time, Allen was back in the squad, having been discharged by the MO. although he still had two black eyes. It was noticeable however that he stayed well away from Conrad, and hardly spoke to anyone.

The big day finally arrived with blue skies, sunshine and with no trace of any rain, much to the relief of all concerned. Families of all the Squads on parade had been invited to attend this special day, after weeks of postal 'black out'. Temporary seating had been erected around the Square, and by midday most of those seats had been occupied by fathers, mothers, brothers, sisters, girlfriends, uncles and aunts and in some cases, grandfathers and grandmothers. The ladies resplendent in all the finery that only women seem to be able to muster regardless of budget, created a Technicolor background for the main event.

To a fanfare of trumpets and drums, the Parade got under way. Each member of the various Squads now sporting the rank of Lance Corporal on their shoulders, (no longer Probationers) headed by their Sergeants, marched into the Square resplendent in their uniforms (as opposed to drab fatigues) and took up their positions. The company Officers and invited high ranking personnel, all in their dress uniforms, with sunshine flashing off their highly polished boots, swords, spurs, chain mail, and other dress items, completed a spectacle that only the British can produce.

The ceremony went like clockwork, every manoeuvre was performed without fault (it is truly amazing what repetition can achieve) and for those watching the silent marching section, it must have been difficult for them to understand how it was possible. No commands are given, every sequence performed by numbers, counted in each individual's head, in unison with everyone in the Squad!

At the end of the spectacle, the Squad's all stood facing the gallery of Officers; the senior Officer Major General Adams addressed the assembly, slowly and with dignity, in a rich 'plummy' voice. 'Ladies and gentlemen, today you have been privileged to witness the 'Passing out' ceremony of this, the last group but one of National Servicemen to serve their country. You have all just witnessed how the British Army with training and discipline can mould a collection of men from all walks of life into one working unit. I have to say that I have never seen a better parade in my entire career. I commend all those who have today, made this a day to remember. Our country can rejoice in the knowledge that its young men, when put to the test, will not be found wanting.'

As the General spoke sweat ran down the faces of all the Squads, but no one moved or flinched, but stood ramrod straight and proud of themselves for what they had achieved this day.

The General continued. 'These young men have today completed one of the most intensive and arduous training programmes in the British Army, some that began the course fell by the wayside, as they were unable to attain the highest standards, as required by the Royal Military Police.' He paused in order that his words were understood by all. He continued 'It is now my duty to announce the winner of the best Squad on parade, this has been no easy task I can assure you, for as I have already stated, I have not seen a better body of men in my entire career. However, I am charged so to do, therefore after much deliberation, I have awarded the Best Squad Title to Sergeant Crouse and his 792 Squad.' Cheers resounded around the Square as the families of all those watching realised that their son was in the best Squad.

Again no one moved, the sweat from their bodies now soaking their shirts, but every member of the 792 Squad was elated by the news.

The General called for order then said 'I now call upon Sergeant Crouse to come forward and lead his Squad from the Square.'

Sergeant Crouse strode to the front, immaculately turned out, pride written all over his face, his stick under his arm, cradled by his right hand. When he reached the front, he paused, then at the command of 'Parade Attention,' everyone came to attention with a crash of leather on tarmac then the order 'Quick March' was given and Squad 792 marched from the Square, followed by the rest. As they strode around the Square, Conrad noticed that there was hardly a dry eye amongst the visitors, some ladies / mothers were weeping uncontrollably, no doubt from sheer personnel pride in their offspring. His own eyes could not hide his true feelings no matter how he tried. He glanced to his right and left and noted the same condition.

When they were back in the barrack room, their individual pent up emotions burst forth in a torrent of phrases 'Best fucking squad', 'Fucking Crouse does it again'... 'Jesus Christ I can't believe it', 'I need a fucking cig.' And so it went on. Some collapsed on their beds, others could not keep still, and walked up and down shaking hands, talking in loud animated voices, when the door burst open and there framed in the doorway was Sergeant Crouse.

He was now red-faced and sweating; he paused for a moment then asked 'Is there any man here who is not proud of himself this day?' No one gave him an argument. He came into the room and faced them all. He looked around the faces (his faces) and said, 'This is one of the proudest moments in my life. When I first saw you all four months ago, I never thought I would get you through training, especially with Rolf in the Squad, where is Rolf?'

'Here Sergeant.' Crouse turned to face Rolf. 'You did well today Rolf, are you proud of yourself?'

'I am indeed Sergeant,' he replied.

'Corporal Marsh,' Crouse shouted, 'bring in the beer.' All heads turned and in came Marsh carrying a crate of beer; he put it down on a table, went outside and returned with another. 'Help yourselves,' Crouse said 'you've earned it.' Happy banter followed for some time then Crouse said 'For those of you who are going home on leave today, I shall probably not see you again as you will then be reporting to your postings so I will wish you good luck. For the few of you who are reporting back here after your leave, I will see you when you get back. I now have to go to the Sergeants' Mess where I have no doubt I shall get pissed.' With that he strode from the room, before his eyes betrayed him, followed by Marsh. With his hand on the door knob, a voice shouted 'Sergeant Crouse does it again.'

After Sergeant Crouse and Corporal Marsh departed, the room came alive again and everyone had something to say about Crouse, like, 'Who would have thought Crouse was human?'

'I can't believe what Crouse has done!'

'Did you notice that Crouse was on the verge of tears?'

'Pass me another bottle before the bastard comes back and takes them away,' this last remark caused a huge laugh to echo around the room. Eventually they all left the barracks to make their way home on a seventy-two hours pass. Most went by train courtesy of an Army travel warrant, those fortunate to have parents with motorcars and therefore with no strict time tables to adhere to, departed with less haste, having being invited to sample the delights of the Sergeants' mess.

Conrad along with several others making their way to the North of England, climbed into the back of an old Army truck which had been commissioned to take them to the local railway station. There was much banter about what they would be doing whilst on leave, however deep down there was also a sense of loss, for after months of living together in the confines of the same room, sharing all the highs and lows that their new harsh environment had imposed upon them, they had in effect become a family. Sadly, that family was now about to be fragmented, possibly never to meet again.

At the appointed time, the train destined to take Conrad and his fellow passengers to the North of England pulled into the station, belching out great clouds of steam as it did so. After everyone had boarded this iron colossus and settled in their seats, the Station Master blew on his whistle, waved a green flag to signal that all was clear and once more this great iron automaton belched out clouds of steam from its belly, as its iron forged wheels sought to find purchase on the metal rails that supported it. Having done so, it began its slow, remorseless progress forward, gathering speed with every revolution of its wheels, until finally it reached its optimum speed.

After a while with the 'clickety-clack' noise of the wheels over the rails, Conrad began to doze, before sleep overcame him. When he awoke, he was looking at a pair of long shapely legs, crossed provocatively and a white blouse partly undone, which barely contained that which it was supposed to do. For a few moments, Conrad looked at the owner of the legs with that vacant expression that travellers have, she in turn looked at Conrad, with the same none seeing look. Then for the first time in months, Conrad felt a stirring deep inside him and he couldn't help but smile to himself as he realised that he was back in the land of the living, and the dreaded 'Bromide' was apparently no longer a part of his staple diet. Conrad picked up the paper he had been reading and opened it fully in order to obscure his embarrassment from the lady, as the stirring gathered pace.

Eventually the train came to a stop at the Bridlington railway station and disgorged all its passengers who were destined for the East Coast resort. Conrad stepped down from the train onto the platform and looked around for any familiar faces, having recognised no one he began the long walk home. As he did so he tried to contemplate the kind of a reception he would receive from his mother when he opened the door. He increased his walking pace and as the ground was eaten up by his stride, he wondered which of his favourite meals his mother had prepared for him.

Whilst walking he wondered why he had not heard from Heather during the past couple of months. Had she found someone else? Had she moved from the area in order to follow her nursing career? In the end, he gave up trying to think of what might have happened but decided to go and see her tomorrow. He began to smile to himself as he thought of that meeting, would she approve of the physical change in him since their last meeting (he was now twenty pounds heavier and all muscle)? Would she recognise him? Would she approve of the new Conrad? After a while, he put aside all these negative thoughts, increased his walking speed, as he headed for home, the forty pound bag he was carrying made not the slightest difference to his progress. As the sweat began to run down his face, he reveled in the fact that he was supremely fit and that nothing was impossible.

Chapter Seven

The back door was open as Conrad knew it would be. Only the rich locked their doors.

Quietly he put down his bag, his white shirt now soaked with the sweat from his exertions. As he straightened his six foot two inches frame, his nostrils absorbed all the scents and odours of home, which he had almost forgotten. He crept into the kitchen and inhaled deeply, the glorious aromas of Shepherd's Pie, rich gravy, apple crumble and custard assailed his taste buds, causing his mouth to water copiously. He stood there for a few moments, swallowing several times in order to clear his throat. Home, he thought, is Heaven on earth.

As quiet as a cat he made his way down the hall to the front room where he knew he would find his mother. He tried to peer through the opaque glass of the door in order to discern who was in the room with her. Eventually he gave up and, taking a deep breath, he opened the door and went inside. Moira sat in one of the two easy chairs placed either side of the central coal fire, ten feet away sat ex-SAS sergeant Bill Long, already on his feet at the slightest noise from the door as Conrad made his entrance. Conrad immediately went into a defence mode as he faced Bill, then after a brief pause both burst out laughing, their macho moment lasted only a fraction of a second and then Conrad was smothered by the embrace of his mother. Tears rolled down Moira's face, closely followed by those of Conrad. Mother and son clung to each other for several minutes, glorifying in the special relationship that only a mother and a cherished son can understand.

For a fleeting moment, Bill Long watched the intimacy between Moira and Conrad, then in order to afford them the privacy they warranted, he turned away to gaze unseeing through the front room window, as moisture began to swamp his world weary eyes, for Conrad was the son he never had, and he adored him.

'Bill,' Conrad said at last, easing himself from the embrace of his mother, 'I can never thank you enough for all the hours you spent coaching me, especially the unarmed combat training.'

Bill spun round in true army fashion and with an obvious trace of moisture still in his eyes he replied with difficulty, 'The pleasure was all mine Conrad.'

There followed an embarrassing silence as the two men looked at each other, which was eventually broken by Moira saying 'I've made Shepherd's pie and apple crumble for tea, so who wants to eat?' They all laughed as one, as if to break the tension then clutching Conrad, Moira led the way into the dining room. She placed Conrad and Bill at opposite ends of the table facing each other, whilst she sat in the middle in order to serve the food she had prepared.

During the meal, Moira kept up an incessant demand for information on everything that he had done so far in training. And so Conrad told her all about the good times he had had so far, but he omitted to relate any of the problems that he had encountered in order not to distress her. Bill sensing that Conrad was not telling the whole story, made no comment.

Eventually they retired to the front room and each flopped down into a chair. 'Mum,' Conrad said, 'that was a magnificent meal.'

Moira smiling replied 'I thought you liked it for there was not a crumb left on your plate.'

'The Army teaches you not to waste food, any food,' Conrad replied and Bill nodded his head in approval. There followed some small talk about local things then Conrad said

'I think I will run down to Heather's house tomorrow and see how she is for I have not heard from her for some time.'

Moira looked at Bill and then turned to Conrad. 'Are you sure that's a good idea love in view of the fact that you have not written to her for a long time.'

Conrad looked at his mother 'What do you mean I have not written to her for a long while? I have written to you both every week since I've been away! Have you seen Heather?'

'I saw Heather's mother in town a while ago and she told me that there had been no post from you for several weeks.'

Moira then turned and looked at Bill who spoke for the first time. 'In view of what you have just said, I think your letters have been subjected to censorship and withheld, for whatever reason.'

Both Conrad and Moira looked at each other. Conrad spoke first. 'Why would the Army withhold my mail?'

Bill shrugged his shoulders and raised his eyebrows 'I don't know, unless it's because you are being posted to S.H.A.P.E., which as you well know, has the highest security rating in the British Army and therefore no stones are left unturned and vetting has to be thorough.'

After a few moments Moira said, 'After listening to you both, I think I can throw some light on the matter. During the past two months, I have had two visits from people from the MOD (Ministry of Defence). They produced identification and asked me questions about Conrad. I was told not to mention their visit to anybody, because it came under the Official Secrets Act, and if I did so, I could face a heavy fine, jail, or both. So obviously I haven't done so until now.'

At this point Bill said, 'Well I think we now have the answer to the missing mail, someone has read Conrad's letters and decided not to pass them on for whatever reason whilst hiding behind the cloak of the Official Secrets Act, which of course they can do, without any fear of reprisal or prosecution.'

All three discussed the matter for some time until Conrad said that he was going to go to bed for it had been a long day.

As he arose he turned to Bill and asked, 'Do you fancy a ten mile run in the morning Bill?'

Bill looked up at Conrad and laughing replied 'I'm not in your league now Conrad, so I would only hold you back.'

Conrad smiled and responded with, 'Well I will make allowances for an old man and friend and not run too fast.'

Friendly banter was exchanged between the two men before Conrad gave his mother a hug, said goodnight to Bill and went upstairs to his bed.

Having washed and put his clothes away, Conrad climbed into bed and was asleep within two minutes. He awoke at five the next morning and was about to jump out of bed and run to the ablutions when he realised where he was. Smiling to himself, he laid back and thought about his missing mail and the various points they had discussed the previous evening. Suddenly, he realised just who was behind it, Major Harris. As for why, Conrad was lost for an answer. In the end he gave up and dismissed the matter for the time being.

Half an hour later he got out of bed and went to the bathroom where he washed and shaved, returning to his room he made his bed as he was conditioned to do then went downstairs. Hearing a noise in the kitchen, he opened the door and found his mother preparing breakfast. 'Why are you up so early Mum?' he enquired.

'Couldn't sleep a wink all night,' was her reply. 'All that missing mail and things, I've been thinking about it ever since Bill mentioned it.'

Conrad sat down and enjoyed a meal of orange juice, bacon, beans, egg, toast and honey washed down with two cups of tea. They chatted for some time then Conrad said that he was going to run the few miles to Heather's house and then call in at Bill's.

Moira looked concerned and said 'Heather's house is in the opposite direction to Bill's, so if you plan to run ten miles with Bill, by the time you get home you will have run something like twenty miles!'

Conrad laughed. 'So... I run twenty miles with forty pounds on my back in training, it's no problem.' Moira looked at him and marvelled at what he had become.

Conrad went upstairs, cleaned his teeth again, put on one of his old track suits and a pair of his favourite Adidas road running shoes and set off for Heather's.

The morning air was fresh and cool with the first hint of autumn. After a while he began to stretch his legs. The few miles to Heather's house were quickly eaten up and he found himself outside her front door, barely out of breath. He rang the front door bell and waited, he rang again, but no one answered. He was about to ring for a third time when the next door neighbour opened her front door and came out. 'If you want the Newton's they have gone away on holiday and won't be back for a week.'

Conrad looked at her and asked 'Do you know if Heather has gone with them?'

'I believe she has,' she replied.

Unfortunately, the lady had given Conrad the wrong information, Heather was in fact at the hospital working night shifts and staying in the Nurse's home.

Conrad stood there for a moment, his expectations of seeing Heather dashed. 'Thank you for your help, if you see Heather or her parents would you please tell them that Conrad Davenport called.' Then he turned away and set off jogging in the direction of Bill's house.

When he arrived at Bill's, he was waiting for him dressed in a maroon track suit with his SAS badge prominently displayed on the left hand side of the track suit top. After a few miles, Bill said 'Conrad I've been giving a lot of thought to what was said last night and some things don't add up.' Before Conrad could answer, Bill continued 'I think that you have been selected for a special mission which you cannot talk about, hence all the MOD activity, am I right?'

Conrad stopped and turned to face Bill. 'You're right Bill, I cannot talk about it, all I can say is that if anything happens to me, will you promise to look after Mum and tell

Heather that I have always loved her and that there is no one else?'

Bill looked at Conrad, pursed his lips and said 'Christ Conrad I did not realise it was as serious as that.'

Conrad looked at Bill, but said nothing. Finally Bill replied, 'You can count on me, you know that.' Then for the first time since Conrad had known Bill, tears began to form in his eyes as he said 'Take care of yourself Conrad, for you are like a son to me and I don't want to lose you.' With that he turned away and began to run, his shoulders going up and down with emotion. Conrad watched him for a while and then followed at a distance. When he judged that Bill was composed, he came alongside him effortlessly and they ran side by side in silence, each too occupied with their own private thoughts to speak.

The next day, Conrad and Bill met on the beach and did some strenuous training, culminating in a five mile speed run back to Moira's house. After they had bathed and freshened up they had one of Moira's special meals, meat and potato pie with oxtail gravy and Heinz beans. When they had finished, they all retired to the front room where a glowing coal fire greeted them.

Whilst Conrad and Bill settled themselves in a chair, Moira switched on the old gramophone and put a new needle in the pickup arm then placed a long playing record of Giacomo Puccini's magnificent opera Madame Butterfly on the turntable and set the machine in motion. All sat back and enjoyed the wonderful, emotional experience of the master composer's music. Gradually, a feeling of wellbeing and contentment enveloped them all like a cloak, until both Moira and Bill dozed off leaving only Conrad awake.

As he fondly looked at their slumbering forms, he smiled to himself and thought of everything they had done for him over the years, especially his mother. As he gazed at her, tears began to flood his eyes and there and then he decided that whatever sacrifice was required of him in the future, he would not be found wanting, for this family scenario was more than likely being repeated in every decent home in the land, rich and poor alike and must be cherished and protected in the name of both democracy, decency and freedom.

All too soon, the seventy-two hour leave pass came to an end. The day Conrad prepared to return to Woking, his mother was beside herself with grief, for while she had said nothing further about the missing mail, she had a premonition that something dreadful was going to happen to her beloved Conrad. Eventually Conrad convinced his mother that she should not accompany him to the railway station in order to save her further distress, adding that Bill would go with him, this she finally agreed to.

As the train pulled into the station and rolled to a stop, Bill turned to Conrad and with his arm outstretched grasped Conrad's hand. In a husky voice he said, 'Conrad, I've taught you all I know, physically you are in top class condition and more than a match for anyone, look after yourself and make sure you come back safe and sound to your mother and me.' Conrad looked at Bill for a few moments and squeezed his hand then he turned abruptly and mounted the train, almost on the point of tears.

After placing his bags on the luggage rack in the carriage, he lowered the window as the train belched out a cloud of steam and prepared to move off.

He looked at Bill and called out 'Remember Bill, look after Mum for me.' As the train began to move, Bill did something quite extraordinary, he snapped to attention and saluted. Conrad withdrew from the window, as tears began to roll down his cheeks.

Chapter Eight

Conrad arrived back at the Woking barracks late in the evening. He reported to the guard room and signed in. He then went straight to his old barrack room where he found two others from his old Squad putting their things away. After some small talk was exchanged, he put his civvies away, had a wash, and then went to bed. As he lay there he pondered his future, slowly he began to doze then eventually fell into a deep sleep.

They all awoke at 05.00hrs the next morning and rushed to the ablutions in order to avail themselves of what little hot water there was, just as they had done for the past sixteen weeks. They need not have bothered for today there was only a handful of them, the rest of the squad having already been 'posted' therefore the precious hot liquid was in abundance. After ablutions, they changed into fatigues then went to the Mess for breakfast, having dined they went back to the barrack room to clean their eating utensils, tidy the room, as per normal and to await instructions as to what was required of them. No more the frantic energy of recent weeks.

At 09.15hrs, the door to the barracks opened and in walked a Corporal with a list in his hand. 'Morning all,' he said, 'here's a list of duties for you, report to the various places at the appointed time.' With that he placed the list on the table and left the room.

Conrad was to report to the Sergeant's Mess at 10.00 hours for mess fatigues, which meant washing dishes, pots, floors, walls, in fact anything that was not clean, plus, peeling dozens of potatoes and vegetables. The benefit was the fact that the Sergeants ate and drank well and therefore so would anyone working there.

Conrad reported at the Mess with five minutes to spare. The Sergeant on duty let him in and gave him his first job, cleaning a small cupboard in the corner of the room. Conrad opened the cupboard door and then stared in amazement at the contents. Facing him were fourteen dirty pint glasses, some with small amounts of beer left at the bottom of the glass, some even had dead cockroaches in them! The sergeant liked his beer Conrad thought. Later it came to light that fourteen pints a day was the Sergeant's daily intake! Taking the glasses to a huge metal sink half full of hot soapy water, he began to wash them.

An hour later the Sergeant placed a pint pot of hot tea on the table together with a thick bacon and egg sandwich and called Conrad over. 'I have to go out for a while,' he said 'so I'll see you later.' With that he turned and walked to the door, with his hand on the door handle he turned around and with a smile on his face he said 'By the way, there's no Bromide in the tea.' Laughing, he opened the door and was gone.

Conrad dried his hands and sat at the table and tucked into the sandwich, if this is working in the Sergeant's Mess I can handle this, he thought. He had almost finished the sandwich when a side door opened and in walked a blond haired man in a black tracksuit carrying a file. 'Are you Davenport?' he asked.

Conrad stood up and replied 'Yes.'

The man waved him down 'Carry on with your refreshment.' He pulled up a chair and sat facing Conrad, opening the file as he did so. Conrad finished the sandwich and took a drink of the tea then sat still looking at the man in front of him.

After perusing the file for a few moments the man said, 'My title is Captain Marcus Johns,' at this Conrad straightened in his chair. Johns smiled at this respect of rank then said 'Forget that, we haven't the time for formality.

Major Harris has assigned me to instruct you in the dubious arts of counter espionage during the next three weeks which, I have to say, I believe to be an impossible task. However, those are my orders, so I shall endeavour to fulfil them.' They exchanged eye contact for a few moments then Johns spoke again, 'What happens from now on is Top Secret; you must not speak to anyone about what we do, or where we go. As of now, if not before, you are bound body and soul by the Official Secrets Act.'

Captain Johns went on, 'As we speak all your equipment and personal possessions are being removed from your barrack room and taken to a secure unit not far from here. As of now, you are a part of the Army Special Intelligence Unit.' He continued 'there is no rank in this unit, there is no saluting, there is no 'Sir' we use only initials for addressing each other; for example, you are CD I am MJ.' There was a knock on the door then it opened and in walked another person also dressed in a black tracksuit. 'And this is my colleague Lt. Robin Jackman, RJ.' Conrad looked at RJ and a pair of green eyes looked back at him impassively. He put out his hand and Conrad took it noting the firm grip. They shook hands for a few moments then RJ in a cultured voice said 'Glad to meet you CD you have an impressive file.' A faint smile briefly softened his young fresh face.

For a brief moment no one spoke then MJ said 'Right let's get started,' and turning to the door from which he and RJ had entered the room, proceeded to open it, when Conrad said 'But what about the Sergeant, when he returns and finds me gone what will happen?'

'That's already been attended to, when the good Sergeant returns someone else will be here in your place, and by the time the Sergeant is into his tenth pint of the day, he will not even remember you.' They all laughed as MJ led the way through the door. Outside was a black nondescript looking car into which they all climbed. RJ took the wheel with MJ. alongside him, Conrad in the back. The car had one-way windows, those inside could see out, but those outside could not see in. The reason for this became apparent at the main gates when the car came to a halt. RJ lowered his window slightly and showed some kind of pass to the Guards, who immediately waved them through. However the Guards had no idea of the features of the occupants in the car.

As they passed through the main gates, MJ turned to Conrad and said 'Just in front of you in the rear of RJs seat is a black band, put it over your eyes for the duration of this ride, sorry about the cloak and dagger stuff, but it's for your safety, whilst at the same time keeping our destination secret.' Conrad looked at MJ and raised his eyebrows in surprise, MJ smiled back and nodded his head. Conrad slowly stretched out his hand for the band, at the same time noting the time of day on his wristwatch. He put the mask over his eyes and was immediately rendered as blind as the proverbial bat. He lay back against the car's black leather seat and thought to himself, what the hell is going on? This is the kind of stuff you read about in boy's adventure books. This cannot be happening to me, I'm just a nobody from Yorkshire! But it was. And it was just the beginning.

For some of the journey, the car seemed to be running on well-made roads, for there was little or no bumping, but after a while the car began to lurch a little from side to side and go up and down, as if negotiating potholes and uneven ground. Eventually it stopped and the engine was turned off. Then MJ. Spoke 'OK CD you can take off the blindfold now, we have arrived at our HQ' (Headquarters). Conrad took off the blindfold and blinked for a while whilst his eyes refocused. Then he slowly leaned forward in order to return the band to its original pouch behind the driver's seat, as he did so he casually noted the time. They had been driving for approximately forty minutes, the last two or three miles over bumpy terrain. Therefore Conrad reasoned that if they had been doing thirty miles an hour on the roads, their destination should be somewhere in the region of fifteen to eighteen miles radius of the barracks. As he alighted from the car, the familiar scent of pine trees assailed his nostrils and, smiling to himself, he decided that he had a good idea of just where he was.

As he looked around, he noticed a large prefabricated hut tucked away in the trees almost invisible to the untrained eye. As he looked at it MJ said 'Our home for the next three weeks, it has been specially built for this project, when we have finished with it, it will be dismantled and removed, trees will be planted in its place and the ground returned to its original condition.' As Conrad was about to move to inspect the hut MJ said, 'By the way CD I noticed your little exercise in the car with your watch, so what do you think is the distance from the barracks to our base here?'

Conrad looked at MJ. 'Between fifteen and eighteen miles,' he replied.

MJ looked at him 'Very good CD,' he said 'it shows you are thinking, I like that, now let's get inside and see what goodies we have been left.'

The hut was bigger than Conrad had thought, it went back into the tree's quite a way, for there was a large room with a table and six chairs placed around it, three bedrooms, a bathroom, kitchen and a store room. In a corner of the large room, stood a projector, a folding screen and a pile of reels of film. The hut also had electricity, for very faintly in the background could be heard the rhythmic hum of a generator.

Once all their belongings had been brought in from the car, MJ turned to RJ and said 'Will you prepare something to eat whilst CD and I stack all this gear.'

'OK,' RJ replied and went to the kitchen. Once inside he opened the door of a large freezer and surveyed the contents; numerous packs of meat, chicken, vegetables and bread greeted him. He then went to a fridge which was as big as the freezer and found that was packed with eggs, milk, bacon, potatoes, carrots, tomatoes, apples, bananas, tins of beer, corned beef, tuna, beans, condensed milk, butter and various odds and sods. On the bottom shelf, he was surprised to find several bottles of wine. He withdrew one and looked at the label, 'Chardonnay 1958,' he said out loud. Impressed, he returned the bottle to the fridge and then checked the rest of the kitchen. Having satisfied himself that they had everything they needed for the next three weeks, he began to prepare a meal.

A short while later, he entered the main room and began to prepare the table, 'The Army Catering Corps have done us proud,' he announced, 'we have all the provisions we need, food in about fifteen minutes.'

The meal began with a piping hot bowl of thick soup, followed by a huge sandwich of tuna fish and mayonnaise, topped with tomatoes and cucumber; and to wash it down, a bottle of Chardonnay. Conrad opted for a glass of iced water instead of the wine.

As they began to clear the table, Conrad, throwing caution to the wind said 'I did not realise until now, that those who join the forces voluntarily, should reap benefits, so far removed from those that are conscripted. Such benefits I find perverse, to say the least.'

The two Officers stopped dead in their tracks; slowly they turned and looked at Conrad. MJ spoke first, 'CD whatever you may think of the present circumstances, we (he indicated to RJ and himself) are here to give you the benefit of our collective skills, as instructed to do so by the highest authority in the land and at great expense to the tax payer.' He paused then added 'this,' raising his arms and looking about him 'is all for your benefit, such is the importance of our mission.'

'Bollocks,' Conrad replied 'what you actually mean is that amongst the tens of thousands of you so called Officers and gentlemen, there is not one of you capable of carrying out this operation and so you want me, no doubt in your books, an 'expendable item' to do your dirty work for you.'

As soon as Conrad had finished speaking, RJ indignant at Conrad's remarks, rushed at him, issuing various expletives as he did so. He managed to get to within two feet of Conrad, then with a quick turn of his hips and a lowering of his body height, Conrad's left arm whipped out and stuck RJ in the throat, felling him to the ground like a chopped tree.

'Bravo, well done CD,' MJ said and clapped his hands. 'In all the time I have known RJ, I have never seen anyone do that to him, normally it's the reverse.' He went to RJ's side and helped him to his feet, 'Are you ok?'

RJ nodded, whilst holding his neck with his left hand, his face now red from coughing. He approached Conrad and held out his right hand. Croaking, he said, 'No hard feelings CD.'

Conrad took his hand and shook it. 'No hard feelings RJ.'

'Excellent, well done both of you, we have no time for bearing grudges,' exclaimed MJ, 'So gentlemen, let us get down to work, for time is of the essence.'

They cleared away the table, washed and dried the crockery and cutlery, then put everything away in its rightful place, before returning to the main room for their first briefing. Sitting around the table each with a pen and note book to hand, they patiently waited for MJ to sort out his piles of files and papers before chairing the meeting.

For the next two hours, MJ outlined the daily programme that he had prepared. The first week would mostly be spent looking at films of various people and their organisations, with questions and answers as required, plus some basic French lessons for CD.

The second week would deal with methods of gaining and passing information, with again questions and answers, then more films from the first week, plus codes and contacts followed by another revision period on the first week's work.

The third week would deal with anything that CD had a problem with, a revision of the first and second week's work, finishing with the final element. 'What's the final element?' Conrad asked.

There was a pause before MJ replied 'I'll tell you that in week three.' That was all he would say. 'Anyone care for a drink?' MJ asked. RJ nodded his head, saving his throat, Conrad opted for a beer. MJ went to the kitchen and returned with two glasses of wine, and a beer for Conrad.

They all sat quietly with their drinks in their hands. Suddenly Conrad said 'Do we have any writing paper? I need to write home.'

MJ looked at CD and said quietly 'We've already taken care of that for you.'

'What do you mean?' asked Conrad.

MJ looked at him for a moment or two, then replied 'One of our hand writing experts posing as you, has written to your mother and girlfriend informing them that you are going away on a course for three weeks and that you will be unable to correspond, due to a lack of postal services.' MJ then lifted his glass and took a sip of the wine.

Conrad put his drink on the table and looked at MJ. 'Did you sanction that action?'

MJ lowered his glass and said 'Yes I did, why?'

'Because it was necessary,' he replied.

'But you've interfered with my private affairs.'

MJ raised his glass to his lips again and sipped the liquid, then returned it to the table and faced Conrad. Slowly and deliberately he said, 'CD you no longer have any private affairs, this is the Army and we have a mission to complete, this is not 'civvy street' where you can please yourself what you do, the Army owns you, as it does myself and RJ and as the one in charge of this mission I have the authority to do whatever I think appropriate, to achieve a successful conclusion.' There followed an embarrassing silence broken by 'I hope I have made the situation crystal clear CD.'

Conrad looked at MJ for a few moments before replying, 'Crystal clear MJ,' then lifting his beer to his lips, he swallowed the remains of the tin, crushed it in his hand then placed it on the table. There followed another embarrassing silence whilst MJ and Conrad looked at each other.

In order to break the tension RJ croaked, 'I think I will go and prepare some food, it's getting late.'

MJ looked up 'A good idea RJ. It's been a long day. I think some hot food would do us all a power of good.' The meal was eaten in almost complete silence after which, they cleared the table and put everything away. MJ informed them that they would commence work the next day at 06.00hrs with a five mile run followed by breakfast, before commencing the first week's programme. Having done so, he walked to his bedroom bidding them both goodnight as he did so.

As Conrad rose to go to his bedroom, RJ caught his arm, 'A moment CD please,' he said. 'MJ's a good chap, but has a bastard of a job to do, he did not want this mission, but he's got it, just remember that.'

Conrad looked at him for a moment, then smiled and said 'OK RJ, sorry about the throat.'

RJ responded with a smile of his own and croaked 'My fault, not yours CD.'

Chapter Nine

The next morning was dry but cool as they set out on their run, MJ led the way and set a good pace, the morning air was fresh and the scent of the pine trees was invigorating. As they ran, Conrad was surprised to find that his companions were in very good shape, for MJ maintained the pace until the end.

Having showered and breakfasted, the trio sat around the table on which was placed a tray with a jug of iced water and three glasses. There were also a number of files piled on the table to the right of MJ's chair. Once they were settled, MJ stood up with a file in his hand and addressed them both. 'Gentlemen, as you are aware we have a mission to perform. I can now inform you that the mission is extremely dangerous and will undoubtedly result in the loss of life.' He paused for a moment then continued. 'Our objective is to attempt to infiltrate or eliminate a covert operational cell believed to have recently been established in Paris acting for and funded by the OS (Organisation Speciale). According to information received from our intelligence sources, the OS along with others, have been branded a terrorist organization with a reputation for brutality.

Their leader is Ahmed Ben Bella, a seasoned soldier of Algerian origin, decorated several times for bravery. He is intelligent but ruthless. He seems to be able to be in different places at the same time! The OS is said to have tortured both men and women in horrific ways during its formative years. It has also made several abortive attempts on the life of

President De Gaulle and is supposed to have tentacles throughout Europe. As I said before, our intelligence service believe that they have a unit based in Paris and are planning something 'big', which they believe to be an assault on S.H.A.P.E., Headquarters (Supreme Headquarters Allied Powers Europe) on the outskirts of Paris.'

Reaching for the jug of water, he slowly filled a glass and took a sip. He continued 'Our intelligence people inform us that the latest information they have is now two weeks old and that they cannot make contact with our field agent.' He paused again, thus allowing the seriousness of his statement to register. Resuming he said 'Should an attack on S.H.A.P.E., the worlds 'Police Force' actually happen then every terrorist group in the world will think that they could take on the western world and succeed, the propaganda fallout would be immense.' He looked at the faces of his two colleagues for a moment expecting some reaction, but there was none. He paused for a sip of water before continuing. 'This must not, will not happen, those are my instructions.' He looked down at them, 'Any questions so far?'

Conrad said, 'Yes MJ what the hell am I doing here? This sounds like a military operation, not just a three man band job.'

Smiling, MJ replied 'I shall come to that shortly, however I will just add that this is not, as you put it a "three man band job" there are in fact hundreds of people behind us, many with specialist skills, who, just like you, are being briefed at this very moment, such is the importance of the mission. The cost of this operation will, I am sure, run into millions of pounds; any more questions?'

'Yes,' Conrad said 'you have mentioned a whole team of people behind us, many with specialist skills, no doubt these people are regular soldiers and officers, who no doubt are being paid far more than my £1. 5. 0d. per week, less of course boot polish, blanco, toothpaste and toiletries, and a haircut every three weeks, so I ask you again, what am I doing here?'

Before MJ could answer, RJ spoke with disbelief in his voice 'Is that all you are paid CD?'

Conrad turned to face RJ. 'You amaze me,' he said, 'how many pay parades have you attended in your career as an Officer and how many times have you seen the pittance handed out, followed by a thank you sir and a salute of thanks from the grateful soldier?'

Both officers looked at Conrad, RJ replied 'Actually, none CD, from Sandhurst I went straight into Intelligence and we have very few National Servicemen in Intelligence as far as I am aware.'

'In that case I take back what I just said, although I would have thought that you would have known about pay for soldiers, if only by hearsay,' Conrad replied. 'Well I do now CD,' and he began to laugh, followed by both MJ and CD.'

'You make a fair point CD and I will look into it,' MJ announced, 'although when this is all over you could write your memoirs and make a fortune.' They all laughed again then tapping the table MJ said 'Now back to business gentlemen.'

At 13:00hrs, they stopped for some lunch and then recommenced working at 14:00hrs, finishing at 17:00hrs. This became the daily routine for the first week. In the evenings, they watched films of some of the operations involving the OS including the theft of 25 Million French Francs. They also spent hours trying to pronounce the names of the principal terrorists and their right hand men, plus anyone else that appeared on the films, no matter what their status. However, apart from the leader, Ahmed Ben Bella, most of the names were virtually unpronounceable.

The second week of instruction followed on from the first week just as MJ had said it would. Each morning began with a brisk five mile run through the woods, followed by a shower, breakfast, revision, and further lectures. More reels of film regarding the activities of the OS followed, some were quite unsavoury to say the least. By now the trio had learned to pronounce the previously unpronounceable names. After some discussion, it was decided that in order to retain their new found command of foreign names, the trio should on a day to day basis adopt the name of a certain individual and the other two would address him by that title.

On the Thursday and Friday of the second week, MJ schooled Conrad in the basics of spoken French; MJ spoke French, German and Italian fluently. Eventually after many hours of cramming, MJ decided that with a degree of good fortune, Conrad could make himself understood in a social environment, where there was a degree of background noise. However in his notes to his superiors on the general progress of CD code name 'Ave Maria' as Conrad was now being referred to in dispatches, MJ expressed concerns that due to the shortage of time allocated to him to 'process' 'Ave Maria' he felt that his lack of basic French could be detrimental to the success of the mission.

Two days later, he received a brief note from Major Harris via a midnight courier. The message was short and to the point, it read: **'I disagree with you regarding the French, in fact I see it as a distinct advantage, continue'.**
Harris.

The third week started as the previous two weeks had done with a five mile run through the woods followed by a shower, breakfast, and then the classroom. Today however, as they each pulled out a chair and settled themselves around the table, there was a tension in the atmosphere that was almost tangible.

For a few moments no one spoke. then slowly, MJ arose from his chair, and addressed them 'Gentlemen, I have an announcement to make; following our previous discussions regarding the mission, I am pleased to inform you that the powers that be have seen fit to elevate CD to the rank of acting Captain for the duration of our programme, with immediate effect. Payment commensurate to that rank will be held in a separate account, details of which will be made available in due course, so as not to conflict with any paymaster's records that currently exist.' After a slight pause he continued 'speaking personally I am delighted by the decision.'

RJ endorsed his words by clapping his hands vigorously and uttering 'Hear, hear.' Both MJ and RJ looked at CD who slowly rose from his chair and with a little difficulty said, 'I do not know what to say, other than I am amazed at what has happened to me these past few days. However, I detect the influence of you MJ behind this sudden, incredible promotion.' As if to answer CD, MJ simply lowered his head slightly, once, when he raised it he was smiling.

Conrad sat down and MJ took control again. 'Gentlemen, we now come to the most crucial part of the training programme, the final element,' he paused, 'I was unsure whether to announce this crucial phase of our training before or after I informed you of CD's promotion. I decided on the promotion first and address any cynicism which may follow the announcement of the latter.' He looked at Conrad for a moment and then continued. 'The final phase of our all too brief time together deals with the art of "Life and Death," in the case of the enemy it means 'Death' by whatever method is appropriate, and in your case CD it means, I sincerely hope, 'Survival'.' He paused again and looked at Conrad who returned his gaze, without blinking, but said nothing.

'For the rest of this week, we are going to practice the various ways of killing the enemy, silently, or by explosives. We will learn how to make our own bombs from ingredients which are readily available from most shops on any street in any village or town. We shall go into the woods during the day and at night, and stalk each other, with the intention to kill, I would stress that this is not to be treated as a game, it is serious business.' He paused and reached out for the usual jug of water and filled a glass, after taking a sip he continued and focused on Conrad. 'CD do you think that you could kill someone? And I do not mean with your hands in a fight, which I am sure you could do quite easily, having seen you in action, (he allowed a smile to briefly soften his face) but with perhaps a knife or a gun, or some other method?'

For a moment, Conrad remained silent, then he replied 'By the enemy I take it you mean someone or somebody with whom my country is at war with? Should that be the case then I would have no qualms about eliminating anyone, for I revere my country with its wonderful history and achievements.'

For a few moments both MJ and RJ looked at Conrad then MJ spoke. 'CD you never cease to surprise me, I never thought that you felt so deeply about England.'

Conrad replied with half a smile on his face, 'In that case MJ, you have a great deal to learn about me.'

With a genuine smile on his face, MJ replied 'It would seem so CD.'

The next few days simply flew by, Conrad learned how to make bombs from; Weed Killer and Sugar; Charcoal and Sulphur; and then, he was introduced to the wonders of 'Nitroglycerine.'

During that period they experimented with the various materials and 'blew up' all kinds of 'objectives', from rotting tree's to piles of stone and including the remains of a railway line that had previously carried freight through the woods.

Having completed the 'crash' course in demolition, it was in the woods where Conrad came into his own. He was like a 'will of the wisp,' no one heard him approach them, every time the scenario was Conrad against 'them,' Conrad prevailed. He 'strangled' MJ with a Garrotte (two wooden toggles with a piece of piano wire between) and he 'killed' RJ with a left- handed thrust through the heart with a stiletto, whilst his right hand was clamped over his mouth stifling any noise. Every time, it was Conrad and one of the others against the third one of the group, Conrad struck first, and decisively. When it was Conrad against 'them', he shot them both with his special edition Smith and Wesson '45', complete with silencer, which they each carried as part of their specialist equipment.

No matter what permutation MJ tried, when it came down to stealth, Conrad was the master.

On Friday morning, the last day of their association and after their usual five mile run, shower and breakfast, MJ announced that before they departed later in the day, they would have a farewell dinner together. He also announced that their mission now had an official code name, which was 'Ave Maria.' He explained how it would work. 'CD, should anyone approach you, they should say to you somewhere in the conversation 'Maria,' you will respond with 'Ave,' should you require to test someone, you will mention 'Maria,' and they will respond with 'Ave,', 'Maria' is the trigger for both parties, is that clear?' Both CD and RJ answered 'Yes.'

'Should you be approached by someone who does not use the 'trigger' they are most probably the enemy, so beware, and of course the reverse applies.'

He paused for a moment then continued 'You will be contacted by Lt. Chis Mullon (CM). Once you are settled in at headquarters CD he will be your contact, he is one of my team and a good man. He will be in the British logistics office sited near to a security post.' He continued 'During dinner if you have any last minute questions to ask do so, for tomorrow morning we all return to the barracks at Woking, prior to CD's posting to S.H.A.P.E., Headquarters.'

The dinner turned out to be a sombre affair, for as often happens between men, after a close working relationship, mutual feelings of respect, admiration and camaraderie develop, despite all attempts to remain 'professional', and detached. Such was the case this evening. Eventually they all retired to bed, each with their own thoughts. However before MJ could sleep he had one more task to perform, he sent a coded radio message to Major Harris which simply said:

'Woods mission a complete success, agent is best for stealth I have ever seen.'

MJ

The next morning after the usual five mile run and breakfast, they departed their home for the last three weeks without a backward glance.

Two hours after the trio had left, two old army ten ton trucks lumbered down the path and stopped outside the hut. A corporal and five privates of the Royal Corps of Engineers climbed down from the trucks and surveyed the hut. The corporal had a bunch of papers in his hand and began to read them. 'Take down, load and return everything to stores and make good the general area, including re-turf and replant as required' he said out loud. Before he could say anything more, there was a shout from inside the hut 'Fucking hell corp come and see this, it's not fucking surprising there's no money for new equipment, all the fucking money is being spent on Officer fucking holiday homes, it's a fucking disgrace if you ask me.' The body to the voice appeared in the doorway clutching half a dozen bottles of the left over wine.

The Corporal took a bottle from the Private and looked at the label, 'It's French,' he said 'Chatanerve-Da-Pap' he added.

The Private looked at his Corporal and said 'Fucking hell corp. I didn't know you could read and speak French.'

The Corporal basking in the attention of his Squad puffed out his chest and replied 'That's because you're an ignorant Welshman Jenkins, what's never had an Army edification.'

Striding into the hut, the Corporal along with Jenkins went to where the wine had been kept, 'Let's see how many bottles have been left behind.' In all they had twenty bottles of various wines and spirits. 'What do we do with them corp?' Jenkins asked.

The Corporal looked at Jenkins for a moment then replied 'Bring in the men Jenkins for a demo on how to live off the land.'

Once the men were gathered round him, the Corporal addressed them. 'Now men, we 'as here a situation that will provide us with a few extra rations, which we deserve, provided we is careful. It looks to me that we've 'ad some officers here with no doubt some women livin' it up for some time, while we do all the bloody work.' Everyone nodded their heads in agreement. 'Now what we 'as to do is to be smarter than they think we are, and here my experience and know-how come into play. I know that the quartermaster will need to balance his records, for what goes out, has to come back, unless its broken, so there's twenty bottles, and six of us, that means three bottles each, two full bottles returned, and a pile of glass, cos on the way back on these 'ere bumpy roads, they gets broken, agreed?'

'Agreed,' they all shouted.

'Right then,' said the Corporal. 'Demolition is thirsty work so before we start we'd best wet our whistle.'

As they began to break open a bottle each, Jenkin said out loud 'I've got to hand it to you corp., you sure know you're fucking way around the Army.' Smiling broadly, the Corporal simply tapped his nose, and winked.

Chapter Ten

The tired old steam-belching locomotive pulled into the Gare du Nord Railway Station in Paris and deposited its cosmopolitan civilian and military personnel, en route to the many and varied destinations Europe had to offer the traveller in the early 1960s. Amongst the hundreds of passengers alighting from this mammoth of steam-powered travel, was Lance Corporal Conrad Davenport, (incognito Captain Davenport, unarmed combat expert, explosive expert, and killer in waiting) fresh from the Royal Military Police Depot in Woking, Surrey, England.

As he strode down the platform his kit bag in one hand and some small hand luggage in the other, his eyes searched both the people and his current surroundings. As he neared the end of the platform, he saw a Land Rover with the markings Royal Military Police painted on it and two MPs standing by its side. Handing his rail warrant to the guard, he went up to the Rover 'Are you waiting for me?' he enquired of one of the MPs.

'Only if you are Corporal Davenport,' was the reply.

'Then you are waiting for me,' Conrad replied, smiling and held out his hand.

'Welcome aboard, my name's Conley, Alan Conley,' they shook hands, 'and this is Clive Richards, who is about to be de-mobbed (released from his military obligations).' They exchanged handshakes then Conrad climbed into the back of the vehicle, taking his kit bag from Conley once he was inside, whilst Richards sat behind the wheel.

Once Conley was in the passenger seat, Richards started the engine and proceeded to ease the vehicle into the main road, thence to do battle with the hundreds of cars that seemed to fly at them from every direction. The noise was deafening, for it seemed that every driver drove with one hand on the steering wheel, whilst the other hand was on the car's horn or klaxon or whatever.

So this is Paris, Conrad thought with a wry smile.

The journey to the camp was eventful to say the least. The Land Rover kept jerking and swerving as the driver tried to avoid collisions with other vehicles and coming through to the rear of the vehicle was a continuous flow of expletives as both driver and passenger gave their view of the driving capabilities of the other road users. However, after a journey of about an hour, all three arrived safely at the camp, which was almost in darkness, save for a few lights in one or two buildings and the odd street lamp. As far as Conrad could see in the dim light, a seven foot high wire fence surrounded the camp.

Conrad was taken into the MPs barracks and handed over to the night duty Sergeant, who entered his name into the daily occurrence book then took him into one of the billets and pointed to an old iron bed with springs that had a pronounced sag in the middle, no doubt due to the number of bodies it had supported over the years. The Duty Sergeant said 'Drop your gear here while I go and try and find some bedding for you, in the meantime I'll take you into the bar and introduce you to whoever is in there.'

'You have your own bar?' exclaimed Conrad.

'Yes,' replied the Sergeant, 'as MPs we do not socialise with others, unless by invitation, just in case we have to lock them up, for whatever reason: there were half a dozen British MPs. in the bar together with a couple of Americans. It was explained to Conrad that the American MPs did not have spirits in their Mess, only beers and so they were constant visitors to the British bar where all forms of drink was dispensed.

Everyone made Conrad welcome and offered to buy him a drink, in the end he settled for a glass of fresh orange juice, much to the surprise of the group; Conrad explained that he had had little or nothing to eat or drink since lunch time, therefore the orange juice would be fine. At this, the barman produced from under the bar counter, a cheese sandwich and a packet of crisps, 'Here Conrad, have this, I'm afraid our Mess is closed now, so that's all I can offer you.'

Conrad thanked him for the offer but said 'No thank you, I have some chocolate in my kit bag, so I will manage until morning.' Just then the Sergeant opened the bar door and indicated to Conrad that he should follow him; gulping down his drink, he exited the bar.

Having closed the bar door behind him, Conrad followed the Sergeant back to the billet, on the bed was a pile of blankets and some sheets. 'Here you are Davenport, home sweet home, make up your bed and I will try and rustle up some food for you, it won't be much but it will get you by. In the morning you have the RSM's (Regimental Sergeant Major) orders at 09:30hrs followed by the OCs (Officer Commanding) interview at 10:00hrs, be in white webbing and red hat, and be smart for both parades.' With that he turned and left the room before Conrad could say a word.

About an hour later just as Conrad was putting away the last of his kit, the Sergeant appeared 'Finished Davenport?'

'Just about Sergeant.'

'Right come with me.' He led the way back to the orderly room and there on a table in a corner was a plate of bacon and egg, with some beans, a slice of toast and a pot of tea. Conrad looked at the meal and said 'the men in the bar said our Mess was closed Sergeant.'

'It is,' he replied smiling, 'but not the Sergeants Mess, eat up.' Just then the telephone rang and the Sergeant turned to answer it. 'Orderly Sergeant Newlyn speaking,' there was a pause then 'Yes sir, he's here now having a bite to eat, would you like a word?'

'Right sir, very good sir, anything else sir?'

'Very good sir, goodnight to you sir.'

Sergeant Newlyn replaced the receiver and stood by the phone for a few moments, his hand on top of the receiver; he turned and looked at Conrad, who was just wiping his lips with his handkerchief, having consumed the last of the beans. 'That was the OC Major Haines' Newlyn informed him 'he said to ask you if you had a letter for him from Woking?'

Conrad put away his handkerchief before replying. 'Yes, I have Sergeant; Major Darnie gave it to me this morning just before I left the Depot with instructions to hand it to Major Haines personally.'

Sergeant Newlyn looked at Conrad then after a while said 'Right Davenport, you'd best wash up and get some sleep, no doubt I shall see you later.'

Conrad stood up, went to the door, turned and said 'Thanks for the meal Sergeant, I really enjoyed it.' Then he left closing the door behind him.

The next morning Conrad was awake at 05:00 hrs as usual. Rising from his bed he went to the nearest window and looked out, dawn had just broken and a pale autumn sun was slowly beginning to rise above the horizon. As it did so, pictures of incredible beauty appeared before his eyes as if by magic. Lifelike images coloured in red, orange, yellow, crimson, gold, purple and blue appeared before his eyes, whilst doing so the life-giving heat from the sun's rays slowly began to seep into everything it touched, thus starting yet another day of life in Mother Nature's ever spectacular daily diary which no artist could ever paint. Conrad stood there gazing at the magnificent panorama which was unfolding before him, as he did so his mind went back to a statement made by his boyhood hero Sir Winston Spencer Churchill when showing his wife Clementine the view from the balcony of his beloved home Chartwell. As they surveyed the exquisite vista of the English countryside laid out before them, Winston said 'This,' spreading his hands wide 'is why I bought Chartwell and if necessary, I will die for it.' Whilst

Conrad's vista was not England, he could understand the feelings and emotions of the great man.

Reluctantly he turned away from God's supreme canvas in the sky, a canvass that perhaps only the divine artist Michelangelo could duplicate. As he returned to his bed, he stopped and looked down at his feet. Instead of being cold, for he must have been stood at the window for at least thirty minutes, they were in fact warm. He reached down and touched the floor and found to his surprise that it was warm! Later in the day he discovered that all the floors at S.H.A.P.E., headquarters had under floor electric heating. he would also come to realise that standing on them for twelve hours or more in British army boots and winter dress sometimes without a break, was far from comfortable, to say the least! Picking up his towel and toiletries from his bed, he went to the ablutions and prepared himself for the inspections with the RSM and the OC.

Chapter Eleven

Back in England at the Royal Military Police Depot in Woking, Major Darnie telephoned Major Harris on his secure line and said simply, "'Maria' has arrived safely and I am informed that he has in his possession my letter to Major Haines, as per your instructions.' There was a short pause then 'Thank you Major, I appreciate the assistance you have afforded me, let us hope that 'Maria' can achieve the impossible, for all our sakes,' then the line went dead.

Having replaced the receiver on its cradle, Major Harris sat and thought for a while, the palms of his hands pressed together with his fingertips under his chin. After a few minutes of meditation, he pressed his intercom button and whispered to his secretary 'Mary, ask Captain Johns to come in please.'

A few moments later, there was a knock on the door, 'Enter!' The door opened and in strode Captain Johns, dressed in an immaculate pinstripe suit, white shirt and regimental tie. Closing the door he turned and clicking his heels of his highly polished shoes together, the only recognition required with the Major, greeted his superior 'Good morning sir.'

'Morning Marcus, take a seat,' replied Harris, pointing to a very well upholstered red leather 'Chesterfield' settee. 'Coffee, Marcus?' (Marcus loved it when the Major addressed him by his Christian name, for it was well known within Army Intelligence that Harris had Marcus earmarked to succeed him when he retired).

'No thank you sir.'

'Right, in that case let's get down to the matter in hand.'

Opening a brown manila file with 'TOP SECRET' stamped across it diagonally in large red letters, he looked at the first page and began to read. After a while he closed the file, pulled a lever on the side of his chair and as the back of the chair went into a reclined position he lay back and looked at Marcus, palms together, fingers under his chin again.

Eventually he spoke. 'If I understand you correctly Marcus, both you and RJ wish to volunteer as 'cover' for agent 'Maria' for the duration of this mission, is that right?'

The immediate response was 'Yes sir.'

'Why?' Harris replied.

Marcus sat for a few moments before replying. When he did so he spoke slowly and deliberately as if to emphasise every word. 'Sir, I believe that we have, by chance, found in 'Maria' someone who has all the attributes, both mentally and physically, to be an agent of immense value to the service in the future, should he come through this mission unscathed. I have watched him at close quarters and both I and RJ especially RJ (he said with a smile on his face, a smile that was returned by the Major) can vouch for him, and his potential.'

He paused for a moment then continued. 'But what sets him apart from anyone I have ever known previously, is his belief that 'Britain is best', and therefore worth dying for. Add to that his admiration for all things Churchillian and we have something very special.' Again he paused before adding, 'and from a budgetary point of view, he has cost the department virtually nothing to recruit, therefore RJ and I respectfully request that we be allowed to join him in the field during this operation.'

There followed a long silence as Major Harris pondered on what he had heard, eventually he said, 'Very well Marcus, you and RJ are hereby seconded to operation 'Ave Maria' as of now. You will assume control of the day to day workings of the operation of course and will report only to me. Should you encounter any problems with anyone, call me on the usual number and I will attend to the matter.'

A smile lit up Marcus's face at the news, 'Thank you sir,' he replied simply.

After a lengthy pause Harris asked, 'Have you any idea of your cost requirement for the mission?'

'No sir, I have had little or no time for costing' he replied.

'Very well, in that case I will instruct the Paymaster to allocate an initial budget of two million pounds, should you require anymore, call me, the usual procedure for drawing down the funds will of course apply.' He looked at Marcus for a few moments then asked 'anything else Marcus?'

There was a brief pause then, 'No sir, I think you have covered everything as usual,' he said with a smile.

They both stood up and shook hands, looking at each other as they did so, then Major Harris said, 'Oh, there is one other matter Marcus, do try and furnish me with at least a few bills or receipts when this is all over so that the paper pushers and the accountants have some idea where the tax payer's money goes.' There was a mischievous smile on his face as he spoke.

Marcus clicked his heels together and with a smile on his face replied, 'I will do my best sir, but getting receipts for bullets and explosives is not easy, tends to make the suppliers a little apprehensive, don't you know.' He mimicked one of Harris's least liked administration staff who just lived for receipts for any expenditure.

Harris laughed then opened his office door for Marcus, as he left he said 'Be lucky Marcus,' then he closed the door, and returned to his desk.

As the door closed, Mary looked up from her desk and noted the exchange between both men. 'The Major certainly has a soft spot for you Captain Johns, he almost treats you like a son!'

'We go back a long way Mary, look after him, for he's a very special person.' With that he bent down and kissed her lightly on her cheek, then left the office.

Back at his desk, Major Harris picked up his telephone and began to make several calls. When he had finished, he replaced the receiver, then he looked at the pile of reports gathering in his 'In Tray' from agents all around the world, with a sigh he reached out for the first one.

Two hours later having finished reading the last of the reports, he summoned Mary via the intercom. She entered the room almost at once, a note pad and pen in her hand. As she approached his desk she noted the drawn expression on his face as she looked down at him and wondered to herself what kind of pressures were resting on his shoulders. He motioned her to a chair and for the next hour dictated a series of responses relating to the various reports he had just read. When he was finished, Mary rose from the chair and went back to her office and began the task of sending out replies.

Having cleared his desk, Harris picked up his phone and dialled the number of his favourite club. 'The Garrick Club, can I help you!' a voice said. He booked a table for 8.00 pm that evening then picked up his briefcase, locked his desk and left his office. As he passed by Mary he said, 'I'm off now Mary, you will make sure those replies go out today, won't you?'

'Yes Major, I've almost finished them' she replied.

As he left the office, he paused outside the door and reflected on just how lucky he was to have someone as loyal and efficient as Mary on his staff, for no matter what the work load might be, she never left her desk until everything of any importance had been attended to.

Once outside the office building, Major Harris hailed a passing taxi, as he climbed into the back he simply said 'Garrick Street, please.'

As the taxi pulled away from the curb side and into the flow of traffic, the telephone rang in the Major's office. Picking up the telephone after the second ring, Mary said, 'Major Harris's office, can I help you?'

'Hello Mary, Angela here, is Major Harris available? The Minister (Minister of Defence) would like a word with him?'

'Hello Angela, nice to hear from you. I'm sorry but Major Harris left the office about five minutes ago and did not say where he was going.' (this was a prearranged understanding between Harris and Mary going back many years).

There was a pause then, 'Well Mary, should Major Harris call in, would you please ask him to call the Minister at his earliest convenience.'

'Certainly Angela,' the line went dead, no pleasantries or the usual courtesies, which would normally be a part of a telephone conversation for there existed a very 'frosty' relationship between the transient Political Department of the Ministry of Defence, and that of the dedicated Permanent Military Head of Operations.

Mary slowly replaced the receiver on the cradle and then returned to the task of completing the responses to the various agents. Having done so, she called 'The Garrick Club' and left a brief message for the Major which read; **'Min.' called after you left, wished to talk. Mary!**

Having finally cleared her desk of all the days' important matters, she locked her desk drawers and all the filing cabinets, retrieved her hat and overcoat from the coat rack in the ladies room then paused for a moment on the threshold of the office door and looked back. Satisfied that all was tidy and secure, she turned out the lights, locked the door and took the lift to the ground floor. As she approached the security desk, the day and night shift guards were exchanging places. Once that was completed, she handed over the office keys to the new Guard and signed the release book as she did so. Pulling on a pair of leather gloves, she addressed the Guard 'Goodnight Joe.'

'Goodnight Miss.' Then she left the building.

Once outside, she took a couple of deep breaths of fresh air then hailed a taxi just as the Major had done an hour or so previously. Within a few moments of standing on the edge of the pavement, a black cab came to a halt beside her. Opening the rear door, she stepped inside and said 'Hatton Garden, please 'cabbie'.'

The driver flipped down the charge arm on the tariff clock and responded with 'Right you are Miss,' in a cheerful voice, then he signalled to the oncoming traffic that it was his intention to turn right into the main flow and did so. Horns sounded in protest, but miraculously space was found for the extra vehicle. The taxi driver bobbed in and out of the traffic and proceeded through the labyrinth of streets that is now modern London. With a squeal of brakes, the taxi finally pulled up outside its destination. 'That's two pounds eighteen shillings and nine pence please Miss,' the 'cabbie' announced.

Mary opened her purse and handed over three pounds, 'Keep the change,' she said as she alighted from the cab.

'Thank you Miss,' the 'cabbie' called out as he pulled away.

For a few moments, Mary watched the cab as it weaved its way down the road then turning, she walked the few yards to the front door of the four storey building and climbed the stairs to her apartment on the first floor. She rummaged in her bag for her keys then having found the right one, she inserted it into the lock, opened the door and disappeared inside.

An hour and a half later, Mary emerged from her bathroom, she was wet, pink and naked, a totally different person from the one that had entered the flat previously. In her hand, she carried a large white bath towel which she began to use to dry her long dark hair which hung down to her waist (in the office, her hair was tied up in an old fashioned bun, which gave no indication as to its length, or its texture). As she towelled her hair dry, her full and voluptuous breasts, again not noticeable in the office due to the loose fitting blouses she invariably wore, now stood out proud and firm and with every movement of her arms and towel, swayed provocatively from side to side. She was stunning!

Having finished drying and grooming herself, she applied some deep red lipstick to her sensuous lips then she carefully selected a pair of black nylons from a drawer and slowly eased each one over her long shapely legs. Satisfied that the seams were straight, she then went to her wardrobe for a gown. After some deliberation, she selected a black satin evening dress with a plunging neck line. To compliment her dress she slipped on a pair of delicate black, leather shoes and then applied just a dab of the wondrous Chanel No.5 perfume at the parting of her breasts. As she looked at herself in the long mirror fixed to the inside of the wardrobe door, she decided that the image staring back at her would turn any man's head and she smiled. Going to her bedside table, she picked up the telephone and dialled a number from memory and left a brief message. She then selected a silk stole from a drawer which she draped around her shoulders and left the flat, locking the door as she did so. Slowly, she descended the stairs, her high heels making a rhythmic clicking noise as she did so. Then exiting the building, she disappeared into the neon illuminated London night.

Chapter Twelve

At 09:25hrs, Conrad stood in the tiny corridor outside the RSM's office awaiting his interview. At one minute past the appointed hour, the RSM's door opened and the orderly Sergeant of the day called him to attention, inspected him and then quick marched him into the office, closing the door as he did so. 'Detail halt,' shouted the Sergeant, 'Right turn, stand easy.'

The small office contained a desk and filing cabinet. On the desk, stood two telephones and a collection of pens and pencils, all contained in small round tubs. A closed, brown manila file lay on the desk in front of RSM Drummond.

The RSM was a small man, no more than five feet six inches tall, he was immaculately dressed, with his badges of rank gleaming on his khaki uniform. A silver-topped swagger stick lay on the desk near his right hand. At the top of the arms of his tunic, the S.H.A.P.E. emblem of touching sword points in gold and silver on a green background, was prominent, with the words 'VIGILIA PRETIUM LIBERTATIS', (Eternal Vigilance is the Price of Freedom) in black, forming an arch over the swords.

For a few moments the RSM sat and looked at Conrad. When he finally spoke he said, 'From your file Davenport, (he tapped the folder), it seems that you passed out with merit, it also says that you are quite an athlete and that you would make a good regular soldier.' He paused for a moment then continued, 'have you thought about becoming a regular soldier instead of remaining a National Serviceman?'

'No Sir,' Conrad replied. 'I've hardly had any time to myself of late Sir.'

The RSM nodded his head as if understanding, he continued. 'Well Davenport, let me tell you something about S.H.A.P.E. This is the most prestigious posting in the British Army.' He paused for a moment then continued, 'it is also the most demanding, therefore we only want the best people here such is the nature of our work.' He paused for a moment then carried on. 'From time to time, we escort and protect the world's leaders when they visit here; we carry arms whilst doing so. You may be instructed to kill someone whilst protecting a V.I.P.' He paused again then carried on 'would that be a problem for you Davenport?'

Conrad looked down at him and replied 'No Sir.'

The RSM never let his gaze leave Conrad's face, he continued. 'In the past, one or two NCOs have buckled under the workload, the pressures and the discipline which is necessary to operate in this International arena.' Again he paused, before continuing, 'you will be working hand in glove with the American and French Military Police, therefore you will conduct yourself as befits a British soldier, which, incidentally is the best in the world. But first and foremost, you will conduct yourself as befits a British Military Policeman, again the best in the world.'

He continued. 'You will find some of the people at S.H.A.P.E., believe that the British are no longer a world power, this of course is nonsense. Britain is still a great nation and along with our American allies, we rule the world.' At this point, the RSM was almost shouting and Conrad found himself liking the man, for there was something almost Churchillian about him. Conrad wondered just what the RSM would say if he knew that the person standing in front of him whom he was lecturing, actually out ranked him!

At this point, the RSM rose from his chair and came and stood in front of Conrad and looked him up and down prior to inspecting his dress. Satisfied he said, 'Show me your hands.' Conrad held out his hands, the RSM inspected them then having satisfied himself that they were clean and the nails were neatly trimmed he said, 'Personal hygiene is very important Davenport, remember that, so is personal discipline, for without discipline the human race is no better than the animals in the field, do you understand?' He stared at Conrad.

'Yes Sir,' Conrad replied.

The RSM returned to his desk and sat down, 'Right Davenport, it's time for you to meet the OC,' he said looking at his watch, 'Sergeant Newlyn, take Davenport to Major Haines.'

The Sergeant snapped to attention, 'Yes sir,' he said. 'Detail attenshun, right turn, quick march.'

Once outside the RSM's office, the Sergeant shouted 'Detail halt, right turn, stand easy.' The Sergeant looked at Conrad and smiled and said, 'That went well; he usually tells new NCOs to get a haircut and report back to him.'

Conrad returned the smile. 'He was very well turned out.' Conrad replied. 'And I liked his views on Britain, I feel the same.'

Sergeant Newlyn looked at Conrad for a moment or two and a frown fleetingly creased his face, 'Wait until you have been here a few weeks, you may change your mind.' He looked at his watch, 'Almost time for the OC,' he said.

A few moments later, he knocked on the OC's door, there was a pause before a voice said 'Enter.' Sergeant Newlyn opened the door, brought Conrad to attention as before and then marched him in quick time, into the office. 'Detail halt, right turn, stand easy. Lance Corporal Davenport reporting, sir, direct from Inkerman Barracks, Woking, sir,' he announced and then he also stood at ease.

Major Haines was a portly man, about the same height as RSM Drummond, but not as smart in his outward appearance although his Sam Browne (a brown highly polished leather belt, with a cross shoulder strap, worn by officers and invented by General Sir Samuel James Browne, 1824-1901) gleamed.

The Major and Conrad eyed each other for a few moments before the Major turned his attention to his Sergeant. 'Sergeant Newlyn, I have just remembered that yesterday I promised my wife that I would arrange for some transport to take her to the Palace at Versailles and then collect her in the late afternoon, would you call and try and arrange something with the MT pool (motor transport pool / pool of vehicles) for me, otherwise my life will not be worth living.'

The Sergeant sprang to attention and, smiling, said; 'Leave it to me sir, I will have Mrs Haines transported to the Palace in an unmarked staff car driven by one of our best drivers and then have her collected later, as she wishes.' With that he turned and left the room.

As the door closed, Major Haines opened the file in front of him. After apparently reading a few pages, he slowly closed it then looked up at Conrad. 'So Corporal Davenport, according to your file,' he said tapping it with his fore finger 'you are a man of many talents, someone to be wary of.' This was said with a wry smile on his face. Conrad returned the Major's gaze but said nothing. 'Modest as well,' he added. Conrad remained silent. 'Do you have something for me?' he suddenly asked.

Conrad reached inside his jacket and retrieved the letter he had been carrying and handing it over, then stood back. Major Haines opened the envelope and quickly read its contents. Having done so, he then placed the letter in the top drawer of his desk and locked it.

After a few moments, he opened the file again and began to flip through the pages. Without looking up he asked, 'Have you heard from 'Maria' lately?' Conrad was caught off guard for a moment, before replying '"Ave" no sir.'

Major Haines stood up, extended his hand and said 'Captain Davenport.' They shook hands and for a brief moment they locked eyes with each other then the Major said

'Take a seat, we have a great deal to discuss before Sergeant Newlyn returns from the fool's errand I sent him on.'

Twenty minutes later there was a knock on the door, Conrad stood up and adopted the same stance prior to the Sergeant's departure. 'Enter' said the Major, the door opened and in strode Sergeant Newlyn. He came to attention in front of the Major, who instructed him to stand at ease. Major Haines looked at the Sergeant and said meekly, 'Everything all right Sergeant?'

Sergeant Newlyn looked at the Major and then at Conrad, at a nod from the Major he said simply, 'Fine Sir, only the visit to Versailles was planned for tomorrow, and not today.'

Major Haines put a hand to his head in mock surprise and said, 'I'm terribly sorry Sergeant, I must have got my dates mixed up.'

Smiling, Sergeant Newlyn replied, 'Not to worry sir, all in a day's work.'

'Whilst you've been away Sergeant, I have explained to Corporal Davenport all that is required of him when on duty at S.H.A.P.E. Headquarters, including the fact that only Generals, Officers of our own Corps and those of similar rank in the American Military Police, are saluted inside the building.' There was a pause then the Major added looking at his watch, 'Sergeant Newlyn, can you make sure that Corporal Davenport gets some S.H.A.P.E. flashes (badges of identification fixed to the tops of the sleeves of jackets) put on his battle dress prior to going on duty.'

'Certainly, sir,' replied Newlyn.

The Major rose from his chair and faced them both. In a solemn voice he said, 'I have a very high regard for the majority of the National Servicemen with whom I have been associated over the years and I am sure that you, Corporal Davenport, will only enhance that regard.' With that, he picked up his hat and his stick, thus signalling that the interview was now terminated.

Sergeant Newlyn came to attention immediately and barked 'Detail atten .shun, right turn, quick march.' Newlyn opened the door and they marched outside. 'Detail halt, right turn". Major Haines left his office and passed in front of them touching his cap with his stick as both Sergeant Newlyn and Conrad saluted him. Once out of earshot, Newlyn said, 'Best bloody Officer I've ever worked with, I just hope he's not losing his marbles under all the pressure he has had to contend with. That slip today about his wife's trip, well, I have to say, that's not like him.' he said, seriously shaking his head. Conrad just smiled.

They both walked down the highly polished corridor to Conrad's barrack room. There Conrad handed over his two battledress jackets and Sergeant Newlyn had them taken to the tailors (French, as were the barbers, or butchers as some called them) on site to have the flashes sown on.

He returned an hour and a half later with the finished articles. 'Here you are Davenport,' he said throwing the jackets at Conrad, 'You are now a part of the most powerful organisation on earth... get them pressed and whiten your stripes then I will see you in the bar at 13.00 hrs., and then you can buy me a drink,' he said smiling, as he closed the barrack room door behind him.

At 12.55 hrs. Conrad walked into the bar and was introduced to all the NCOs gathered there by the Mess barman, Nobby Noakes. No sooner had all the introductions been completed when the Mess door opened and in walked Sergeant Newlyn. 'What's your poison Sarge?' someone called out from the bar.

'You, Connerley,' the Sergeant replied smiling. Newlyn was well liked by all the NCOs, mainly because he was both fair and reasonable. 'If you are buying Connerley, I'll have a Jack Daniels, a double, of course, on the rocks,' he added. The sound of merrymaking echoed around the small intimate bar.

From within the group someone said, 'The Sarge has caught you out again Connerley, so pay up, or do you need a sub (a cash advance or a marker for credit)?'

An indignant Connerley spoke out in a soft Irish voice, 'You can keep your sub, English, the day an Irishman cannot buy a drink has not yet dawned, give the Sarge what he wants Nobby,' he said smiling.

Another voice called out, 'Paddy, has no-one explained to you that you can't buy drinks with potatoes.' At this, the whole group erupted with uncontrollable laughter, including Connerley.

Conrad noted with interest the happy smiling faces and the obvious camaraderie which existed amongst the men. Another voice with a Birmingham accent called out, 'Is that a 'King Edward' (type of potato) down the front of your trousers Paddy?' Another burst of laughter rolled around the room.

When the laughter had died down Connerley said, 'No Brummie, that's not a 'King Edward', that's pure fillet steak.' Once more the group burst into laughter.

Sergeant Newlyn came to where Conrad was standing and said 'As you can see Davenport, we have a very good spirit here. All the men here are National Servicemen just like you, who would I am sure, prefer to be at home. But they are here and making the best out of a poor situation. When you meet the American's, you will understand what I mean.'

Conrad looked at the Sergeant and replied, 'I'm sure you are right about preferring to be at home Sergeant.'

Newlyn raised his hand and stopped him, then in a soft voice addressed him, 'In the bar or Mess, Davenport, call it what you wish, we are less formal, unless of course the RSM or the OC are socialising with us, in which case we address them both as 'Sir,' but as they are not here, 'Sarge' will suffice.'

Just then, the Mess door opened and in walked two young men in civilian clothes, the front one called out, 'Hi guys, how yuh all doin?' He was obviously American!

'Nobby, line up the drinks my man, Uncle Sam's come to quench your thirsts.' Laughter again rippled around the bar,

'Hi Biggsy,' someone called out.

'Hi babe, how yuh all doin?'

Sergeant Newlyn whispered to Conrad, 'Your lesson regarding the American's has arrived sooner than I thought.'

Conrad looked at the Sergeant with a puzzled frown on his face. Newlyn explained, 'Biggsy is an American Pfc, (Private first class) the lowest rank, a National Serviceman just like you. However unlike you, he gets paid $40.00 per month against your £1.15.00d per week which includes your stripe and education allowance, marksman's allowance and oversees allowance. He also gets concessions on goods he buys from their PX as do all the Americans.'

'What's a PX?'

'It's a huge store that sells virtually everything for the American servicemen and women, and it's cheap,' Newlyn replied. The Sergeant was now in full flow, 'No buying of cleaning materials for their uniforms either, their webbing is all plastic and just requires a wipe with a damp cloth, their uniforms are made of gabardine and require virtually no pressing, and some even brought their cars over with them, in short they have money to burn!' He paused before continuing 'and yet you cannot help but like most of them, they are generous to a fault, and if they like you, they will do anything for you, as you are about to discover.'

Just then 'Biggsy' approached them, he had a small round honest face with a big smile, a typical American crew cut hairstyle and was wearing an immaculate white shirt which was open at the neck, with a razor sharp crease down each sleeve. The cuff of each sleeve was folded back once and pressed into position, he wore a pair of grey slacks and a pair of black leather slip-on shoes. He was very smart. 'Hi Dude, Biggsy's my name,' he said addressing Conrad, at the same time extending his hand 'I hear you're new in today man.' Conrad took his hand and shook it, Biggsy yelped, 'Jesus man you nearly crushed my fucking fingers man.'

'Sorry,' apologised Conrad, at the same time taking a liking to him.

Shaking his hand he called out, 'Nobby my man, have you got the new 'bloke' and the 'Sarge' here a drink?' Nobby shook his head. 'Then give my friends what they want god damn it, Jesus, a man could die of thirst in here.' Reaching into his hip pocket, he pulled out his bill fold (wallet) which was bulging with dollar bills, 'Nobby my man, you better get another round in for the guys, before you forget how to god damn serve.' Laughter and bonhomie once again rolled around the bar as the effervescent 'Biggsy' took command.

Fortified with another drink, Sergeant Newlyn turned to Conrad and with a smile on his face whispered, 'See what I mean Davenport?'

Conrad whispered back, 'Do they really get paid so much? And did you notice the amount of money in his wallet; he must have had the best part of $200.00 dollars in it.'

Sergeant Newlyn looked at Conrad for a moment before replying slowly, 'My word Davenport, you're observant and yes, they do.' Conrad immediately cautioned himself to be more wary in any future social exchanges.

An hour later, both Conrad and Sergeant Newlyn left the Mess much to the concern of 'Biggsy', who was buying yet another round of drinks for his 'bloke buddies' as he called them.

Outside in the corridor, Sergeant Newlyn announced, 'Tomorrow you will be stationed on Post 7 as supernumerary to Lance Corporal Williams; he will show you what to do. The Post starts at 07:00 hrs, so you will need to be outside the orderly Sergeants' office at 06:30 hrs, for inspection, prior to being transported to S.H.A.P.E., Headquarters. You will be relieved for meal breaks as, when, and if, we can arrange it. The shift (duration on duty) finishes at 19.00hrs, that's twelve hours, not the hours you were told you would be working once you had joined a unit, after passing out at Woking, am I right?'

Conrad nodded and said, 'Correct Sergeant.'

Newlyn looked at Conrad and after a pause said 'Welcome to the world of Supreme Headquarters Allied Powers Europe, Davenport.'

Conrad returned to his room and began preparing his uniform for the morning. Once it was completed to his satisfaction, he lay on his bed contemplating the future, and waited for tea time to arrive. At 16.30 hrs he opened his locker doors and retrieved his knife, fork, spoon and mug then along with a few other MPs, he made his way to the dining hall. Once inside, he picked up a tray at the start of the food queue and looked around the dining hall noticing as he did so how clean it was compared to the first Mess he had encountered back in Oswestry.

'Oswestry,' he mused, that seemed a million miles away from where he was now.

As he thought about those far off days, he was suddenly brought back to reality with 'What's it to be mate?'

Conrad shook his head and looked at the speaker, a young stocky red faced man about his own age, dressed in white and with a large white hat on his head faced him. 'Sorry,' Conrad replied 'I was miles away.'

'I wish I fucking was,' retorted the cook in a soft voice.

Smiling, Conrad quickly looked at the large blackboard behind the range of cookers which displayed the day's menu. After a few moments he said, 'Sausage, egg, chips and beans (Heinz, of course) please.' The cook picked up a plate from a pile standing on a warming tray, and began to dispense his food. As he passed down the line, Conrad picked up a pot of tea and an apple for his dessert, courtesy of America.

Finding an empty table, he sat down and began to eat.

'Mind if I join you?' asked a soft Irish voice.

Conrad raised his head and looked up into the eyes of Lance Corporal Connerley. 'Not at all providing you keep your fillet steak where it belongs.'

Connerley burst out laughing. When he stopped, he responded with 'I think I can arrange that.' He sat down then held out his hand, 'Michael Connerley,' he said.

'Conrad Davenport,' replied Conrad, they shook hands and began to eat.

'So this is your first day at S.H.A.P.E. Conrad!'

Conrad looked up. 'Yes,' he replied.

There was a pause then Connerley said in his soft Irish lilting voice 'Well let me give you some advice, don't cross the fuckin rass man (RSM), he's an evil little bastard, the divil himself is inside him.'

Conrad looked at Connerley and noticed that whilst he had jet black hair, it was laced all over with white streaks and yet he was only Conrad's age. Connerley didn't miss Conrad's brief look at his hair, nor the rise in his eyebrows. Having finished his food he said, 'When I came to S.H.A.P.E., I had a head of black hair my mother was proud of. But the little fuckin' bastard has worn me down, four fuckin' haircuts I had the day I arrived and me with only five fuckin' shillings in my fuckin' pocket at the time and me a fuckin' National Serviceman with not a pot to piss in. And then the little bastard puts me on fatigues painting the fuckin' stones outside his office with a fuckin' tooth brush, a fuckin' tooth brush!' At this point, Conrad was almost on the verge of hysterics, only by gripping his legs under the table with his hands, did he manage to control the laughter welling up inside him.

At this point, Connerley's complexion had turned white, he continued. 'Day after fuckin' day the little divil hounded me, everyting I did was fuckin' wrong, every fuckin' ting'. Then one day I woke and found all deese fuckin' white hairs in me hed, and I fuckin' cracked, I went storming into the divil's office and said, pointing to me hed, you've done this you little bastard, and then I realised that I was still in me pyjamas, and me dick was hanging out.' He went on, 'Of course the divil wanted me court marshalled but the OC stopped im, instead he gave me two weeks camp leave and instructed the camp doctor to have a look at me every day and all because of that little bastard RSM Drummond, may 'is fuckin' soul rot in hell.' At this point, Conrad was on the verge of breaking down and exploding with laugher when Connerley, with a sad, straight face said, 'One day I'm going to kill the fuckin' divil so I am.' That was it, Conrad could not contain himself any longer and began laughing. 'What are you laughing at Conrad? Av I said someting funny?'

Conrad slowly stopped laughing before he replied. 'No Michael, it's just your wonderful Irish accent that's making me laugh.'

Connerley gazed at him for a moment before replying slowly, 'Is that so.' With that, he got up from the table ... left the Mess and never spoke to Conrad again.

Having finished his meal, Conrad sat back in his chair and somberly reflected on what had transpired between them and he wondered what demons were racing around in the poor man's head. After a while, the hairs on the back of his neck began to rise, and he had an awful premonition that something serious was going to happen to Connerley.

'Anyone's seat mate?'

Conrad looked up, into the smiling face of a soldier wearing the insignia of the RMP on his uniform. 'No, help yourself,' Conrad said, 'I'm just about to leave.'

'The name's James, Barry James,' the stranger said as he sat down and offered his hand.

'Pleased to meet you,' Conrad replied, 'Conrad Davenport,' and he in turn offered his hand.

'Saw you talking to Connerley so I figured you were RMP,' James said.

Nothing further was said, whilst James ate his food. Having finished his meal, he looked at Conrad and said quite casually, 'Something bad is going to happen to Michael, I just know it. He can't take the strain anymore, plus, the RSM doesn't like him because he's Irish and weak, which is bad news, because if there's one man you don't want to cross, it's the RSM.'

'What's so bad about the RSM?' Conrad asked.

'He's from the old school of discipline and blind obedience to orders. anything less including weakness, he cannot and will not tolerate.' He paused then continued, 'Having already broken Connerley,' he paused before continuing, 'I suppose you know what happened to him?'

Conrad nodded, 'Michael just told me.'

James nodded then continued, 'Well he sees Connerley as being both weak and unstable and therefore a liability and here at S.H.A.P.E. you cannot have weak and unstable people around, the stakes are too high.' Both men sat looking at each other but said nothing, then James rising to his feet announced, 'Time to go, another twelve hour bloody shift to do and all for peanuts.'

Conrad also rose and said 'I'll walk back with you, I'm on duty at seven in the morning so I think I'll have an early night.' They left the Mess hall together and made their way back to the barrack room, once inside they washed their cutlery etc., and went their separate ways.

Five weeks later, Michael Fergus Connerley was found hanging in the showers.

Sometime later a brown envelope dropped onto the doormat of Mr & Mrs Connerley's neat and tidy house in Northern Ireland. The author of the letter explained in a detached matter of fact manner that their son, Michael Fergus Connerley, had apparently slipped on a bar of soap whilst taking a shower and as a result, had suffered a broken neck. Despite all the attentions of the doctors and the best medical facilities available, it was impossible to save the life of your son.

The letter went on to say that Michael was a likeable member of a select group of men, and had performed his duties to the very highest standards expected of a member of the Royal Military Police. It concluded, 'You can be proud of your son.'

Chapter Thirteen

The next morning, Conrad was up, shaved, dressed and breakfasted by 06.00hrs, he then made his bed and left his area clean and tidy prior to reporting for duty. At 06.30hrs, he and several other NCOs stood outside the orderly Sergeant's office ready for inspection, prior to being transported the couple of miles up the road to S.H.A.P.E. Headquarters. Their transport was an old Land Rover with the registration number 64-BP-48 - the vehicle looked like a relic from the Second World War!

Supreme Headquarters Allied Powers Europe was a sprawl of single storey buildings, criss-crossed with corridors. The flags of all the member nations fluttered on top of white painted poles as you approached the main entrance, it was an imposing sight. Just inside the entrance was a large security reception desk which was usually manned by American MPs, and a gendarme. Everyone entering the building checked in here, Guards were positioned adjacent to the desk and were armed, apart from the British, who carried the bullets for their weapons in pouches on their belts, unless instructed otherwise!

Huge American cars with enormous tail fins, deposited their occupants usually Generals and their Aides, in their multi-coloured uniforms at the main entrance. As they came to a halt, the cars' large chrome radio aerials waved backwards and forwards, almost like serpents swaying to music. Many other makes of cars, Chevrolets, Ford's,

Jaguars, Peugeots, Citroen's, Mercedes-Benz and others, conveyed other ranks in a regular stream. To see them come and go was like watching an epic Hollywood film with a cast of thousands. Except this was the real thing.

Almost at the end of the corridor leading from the main desk, was Post 7 and this was where Conrad and Williams headed. Arriving there, they relieved a tired fellow MP who had been there all night. Having signed over the day book to Williams, the night NCO wearily made his way to the end of the corridor and climbed on board the waiting transport which had previously brought Conrad and the rest of the day shift to work. Once all the night shift was on board, the old trusty Land Rover returned to barracks.

After an hour or so, the corridor began to ring to the sound of feet as more and more people appeared for the start of yet another day's work. As they all approached the small desk which was Post 7, all but the Generals stopped and showed their passes before being allowed to proceed. Many did not like doing so, but the majority recognised that it was necessary. Strangely, it always seemed to be the lesser ranks that caused the problems, however the sight of a hand moving and hovering over the butt of a gun seemed to have the desired effect and all complied.

A couple of hours later, Conrad noticed that his feet seemed to be warmer than normal and bending down touched the floor, it was warm. 'Under floor heating,' said Williams, 'it's a bitch after four or five hours when your feet begin to swell, so keep moving your toes inside your boots, it seems to help.' Just then a wave of people began to approach them from the direction of the main entrance, Williams nudged Conrad and whispered, 'Christ it's General Norstad, the Supreme Commander and a load of VIPs by the look of it, this wasn't in the daily orders … when they get to within five feet, snap to attention and salute, hold it until the General has passed, and then stand easy.'

The party approached and the two NCOs came to attention as one and saluted, the General returned their salute with a quick flick of his hand then he paused and came over to them, the silver stars on his shoulders gleaming. 'Good morning Corporals,' he said, in a soft cultured voice.

Both Conrad and Williams dropped their salute but remained at attention, 'Good morning sir,' they chimed. 'How long have you been at S.H.A.P.E.?' he said looking at Williams.

'Nine months sir,' he replied.

'An old hand eh?'

'Yes sir,' replied Williams. Looking at Conrad, the General nodded his head. 'This is my first day here sir.'

'Really!' exclaimed the General 'and what do you think of what you have seen so far?'

'It's very impressive sir and very expensive to operate I would imagine.'

The General smiled and replied, 'If only you knew, however Corporal … such is the Price of Freedom. Keep up the good work.' With that he turned away and both Williams and Conrad saluted him again, the General nodded, raised his hand to the peak of his hat momentarily then went on his way followed by his entourage.

'Bloody hell,' exclaimed Williams. 'Since I've been here, the General must have walked past me dozens of times and never said a word. Then today he stops and talks to both of us and you, only on your first day here.'

Conrad smiled at Williams and answered simply, 'Luck of the draw I suppose.'

The hours dragged on and the heat in the corridor intensified as both a watery sun broke through the clouds and more and more people used the corridor. 'Will you be OK here while I just nip to the toilets?' asked Williams.

'Sure,' replied Conrad.

A few moments later, several people came wandering down the corridor heading towards Conrad. One by one they showed their passes and continued on their way. The last one, a British Lieutenant said something as he passed Conrad, 'I beg your pardon sir, I did not catch what you said.'

The Officer stopped and turned and faced Conrad, 'I said 'How's Maria, Corporal.'

Conrad looked at him for a moment then the muscles in his stomach contracted and he felt the cold hand of fear suddenly grip him. So it's real, he thought, there really is a mission and then the enormity of his situation hit him, just as though he had been struck by a hammer. 'Ave.' he replied, slightly dazed. There was no further reaction from the Officer, other than casually slipping a piece of folded paper into his hand as he walked away from Conrad and continued his journey down the corridor.

Looking down at the tiny piece of paper, he wondered what message it contained. 'What have you got there?' a voice said.

Conrad looked up, Williams was stood in front of him. 'Love letter,' he replied, smiling.

Williams nodded, 'Oh right, you can go for a walk if you wish, I'll hold the fort.' Conrad was grateful for the break and made his way to the toilets. Entering one of the cubicles he locked the door behind him and then sat on the toilet seat and tentatively opened the folded piece of paper.

The letter simply said that as from Sunday, his name would appear on the daily duty roster as being seconded to a special security post at Fontainebleau (a small town in north central France) where most of the highest ranking Officers from S.H.A.P.E. Headquarters lived together with their families, it was also the headquarters of N.A.T.O., (North Atlantic Treaty Organisation from 1954 to 1966) for an indefinite period. The letter went on to say that he should report for this duty in uniform, at 09:00hrs but have a bag containing any or all of his civilian clothes and shoes with him. There would be a letter to this effect in the orderly Sergeant's office issued by Major Haines, with his stamp 'special orders' on the envelope on Saturday morning, this will appear to be just another special duty. The final sentence instructed him to destroy the letter by flushing it down the toilet, in pieces, once he had memorised the contents. Smiling to himself, Conrad looked expecting to see a face peering down at him. Of course there was none. Then he realised, that having just received a highly confidential letter in a public place, the only private area to read it, would be the toilet just around the corner from Post 7. The letters CM was the only clue to the author of the letter. He read the letter a second time then proceeded to tear it into pieces, then he flushed it down the toilet as instructed. As a precaution, he relieved himself of any surplus matter and liquid and then flushed the toilet again. Having satisfied himself that no evidence remained of his visit, he checked his appearance in the mirror on the wall of the toilet then left.

As he approached Post 7, he noticed Williams surrounded by people and hurried to assist him. Once the rush had been dealt with Williams said, a little aggrieved, 'When I said go for a walk, I didn't expect you to be away for forty minutes.'

'Sorry,' Conrad replied, 'I didn't realise I had been so long.'

Williams smiled and retorted, 'OK, no problem.'

The rest of the day passed uneventfully and at 19:00hrs they were relieved of duty by the night shift NCO and at 19.20hrs they were back at the barracks. In the orderly Sergeants office, they signed 'off duty' in the day book, handed over their weapons and the six rounds (bullets) they carried in their pouches, to the orderly Sergeant, who carefully locked them away then they left the office. As they turned to walk down the corridor Williams said, 'Grab your irons Conrad, for with a bit of luck we may just be in time to get some hot grub.'

They quickly made their way to the Mess hall and were relieved to find that it was still open. Picking up a tray, they looked at what was available. They both selected meat and potato pie with a thick crust, beans, peas and gravy. Much to their surprise, they were also offered a couple of sausages each as they reached the end of the food counter. Filling their mugs from the tea urn, they settled down at the first empty table and began to eat their 'feast'.

Having almost finished their meal, a voice rang out 'Seconds anyone?' Conrad and Williams looked at each other and smiled then in unison they called out 'Here.' Then they jumped up and hurried to the counter. Having received almost the same amount of food again, they sat down once more and proceeded to attack their plates, with vigour.

When they had finally gorged themselves, they both sat back in their chairs and relaxed, then Williams said 'Well what a bloody day this has been, first 'The General' stops and talks to us, a first then the Mess still has some hot grub left and then we get double rations, (helpings) which rarely happens, I can assure you.' Just then a gong sounded from the direction of the kitchen, 'Time to leave,' said Williams. They both got up and left the Mess. Once outside, they slowly made their way back to the barrack room, as they entered Williams said 'Better just check with the OS (Orderly Sergeant) to see what shift if any we are on tomorrow'. They quickly washed their eating utensils, and then put them in their lockers out of sight, an MP rule, then walked down to the office. Williams knocked on the door and a voice called out 'Enter.'

They went inside and Williams took the lead, 'Just thought we'd check tomorrow's roster Sergeant.'

Sergeant Newlyn looked up at his board, 'Rest day Williams then Post 16 on Sunday,' turning to Conrad he said, 'Rest day tomorrow Davenport then special duties on secondment at Fontainebleau on Sunday, but I don't know for how long, which is unusual. There's a letter for you from the Major.' He passed a brown envelope with 'Special Orders' stamped on the front to Conrad, 'I presume this must contain your instructions, any idea what it's about?'

Conrad looked at him and replied 'None Sergeant, I've only been here a couple of days.'

The Sergeant continued to look at Conrad then he said 'That's the strange thing, I can't ever remember sending a new NCO out on his own before,' he paused then added, 'mind you, we are short staffed here so perhaps the Major has said / told Fontainebleau that he can only spare a new NCO in which case I imagine that you will be paired with one or two of our American MP friends, its most irregular though.' With that he half turned away and said over his shoulder, 'Better be off now before I find you two some work to do.'

'We're gone Sergeant, we're gone,' Williams said quickly closing the door behind them.

Smiling at Williams's remark, Newlyn sat behind his desk and pondered the situation. He came to the conclusion that there was something big going on, that was being kept from him, probably a high level visit by someone from the States. It had been rumoured that the American President, John Fitzgerald Kennedy (JFK), might be paying a visit soon. He suddenly sat bolt upright in his chair, 'Bloody hell,' he said out loud 'that's it, JFK and his entourage are coming and the Americans are testing their security, that's the reason for the special orders!' He pondered for a moment or two as he thought about the logistics of such a visit and then said out loud to himself, 'Oh bloody hell, more sleepless nights for everyone!'

Lying on his bed, Conrad slowly opened the envelope and extracted the single sheet of plain white paper. The letter began:

A driver from the British MT (Military Transport pool) will collect you. He will report to the RMP OS and will have papers signed by Major Haines, releasing you from daily duties in order to fulfil highly classified exercises at N.A.T.O. Headquarters, Fontainebleau.

You should have in your possession your civilian clothing and toiletries.

You should not attempt to converse with the driver of the vehicle, for he will not respond.

You should not attempt to write to family and friends before your departure. Any correspondence will be vetted as per the terms and conditions of the OFFICIAL SECRETS ACTS.

You will not divulge the contents of this letter to ANYONE!

Having memorised the contents of this letter, you will destroy same in the usual way.

May your God be with you!

CM.

At 23:50hrs, the bedside telephone of Major Harris's London apartment burst into life. A soft sleepy voice said 'Do you never stop working darling?'

An equally sleepy voice replied 'It would seem not.' Turning onto his side, Harris reached out for the receiver and brought the device to his ear 'Harris,' he said. A warm soft hand fastened itself on his most delicate tissue and remained there. Although both parties thought that they had sated each other previously during their love making, however, the most basic of all human urges began to assert itself again.

'Operation 'Ave Maria' is under way, Sir,' a voice said.

'Any complications?'

'None that I know of Sir,' the voice replied.

'Thank you!' Harris replied, and returned the receiver to its cradle.

A soft voice with a slight giggle murmured in his ear, 'It would seem that I did not totally drain you previously darling,' her hand still massaging him. He turned and looked at her, the back of his fingertips began to slowly trace a path from her neck down to her thighs. Then his hands once again began to explore every part of her body. 'How could I ever get enough of you,' he said huskily. With that, the two became one again and abandoned themselves to the pleasures of the flesh!

Chapter Fourteen

On Sunday morning, Conrad was waiting for his driver outside the barracks at 08.55hrs.

At 09.05hrs, a black Citroen car came to a stop alongside Conrad, 'Sorry I'm late,' said the driver stepping out of the car, 'had a problem with your Orderly Sergeant regarding paperwork.'

'That's ok,' Conrad said, smiling. The driver took Conrad's bag and placed it on the back seat. He beckoned Conrad to join it then closed the door. Taking up his position behind the wheel, he engaged first gear and slowly pulled away.

Conrad settled back into the plush, black, leather seats and looked around the interior of the car. The windows were covered with pull down blinds. He started to release one but was stopped by the driver, 'Sorry' he said, 'the blinds must stay in place, it's all about security.' Raising his eyebrows and shaking his head, Conrad closed his eyes for a moment and let his senses absorb the faint smell of cigar smoke and wax polish which emanated from the car's interior. He decided that this was probably an Officer's staff car, not a general all- purpose vehicle. He opened his eyes as he felt a change in the vibrations of the engine.

Judging by the whirring sound of the tyres, he assumed that they must now be travelling at speed on the AutoRoute (Motorway) in the direction of Fontainebleau. The car eventually came to a halt with a squeal of brakes, followed by a cloud of dust. As the dust cloud settled, both Conrad and the driver alighted from the vehicle. With his bag in his hand, Conrad stood for a few moments and took in his surroundings. They were in a forest, a forest so dense that the pale autumn sun could barely penetrate the foliage. Scattered around were a few single storey buildings, surrounded by a wire fence which glinted in the weak sunshine. In the far distance, there appeared to be far more substantial buildings, one of which stood out amongst the rest. So this is the Forest of Fontainebleau, he said to himself and I suppose the large building must be the Palace of Fontainebleau, and the residence of General Norstad.

A slight noise in the trees brought Conrad back to the present, dropping his bag he automatically adopted a crouched position and looked around him in anticipation of an attack. A voice called out, 'Easy CD. Driver you can now return to your Unit.' Realising that there was something out of the ordinary going on, the man jumped into the driver's seat and set the car in motion. With wheels spinning and dust billowing all around it, he propelled the car back down the road as though pursued by a pack of banshees.

Once the dust had settled again, the 'voice' left the cover of the trees and came into the clearing vacated by the car – there was no Conrad in sight. Standing in the open dressed in his camouflage uniform, the 'voice', suddenly realised that he was now a target. The hairs on the back of his neck began to rise; sweat began to break out on his forehead and under his armpits. Suddenly his hands became clammy, and sweat began to run down his back. He stood there for several minutes, turning his head from side to side, trying to locate Conrad, but without success. The silence was deafening! 'You're dead.'

The 'voice' almost jumped out of his skin, spinning round he was confronted by Conrad. 'Jesus Christ, you almost gave me heart failure.'

Conrad looked at him and with a degree of contempt in his voice asked 'And just who the hell are you?' Before the unfortunate man could answer, the branches of a dense cluster of rhododendron bushes crackled and broke, and out stepped the figures of MJ and RJ (Captain Marcus Johns and Lieutenant Robin Jackman) dressed in camouflage uniforms, just like the hapless individual facing Conrad. Both MJ and RJ strode up to Conrad and took him by the hand shaking it vigorously. 'Good to see you again,' they chorused in unison.

Conrad was taken aback by their sudden appearance, so much so that for a few moments he did not utter a word then his face broke into a grin and he said, 'What are you two reprobates doing here?'

As usual, MJ was the first to speak, 'Well CD after you left the UK, MH. (Major Harris) called us into his office and informed us that because you were the worst pupil ever to have passed through his hands either directly or indirectly, he had decided to send us out here to watch over you, as a punishment.'

Conrad looked at them both then began to laugh 'Kiss my arse,' he said, then he put his arms around both their shoulders and the three men, facing each other, enjoyed a few rare moments of masculine intimacy that can last for a moment, an hour, a day or a lifetime in the memories of those involved.

Their special moment was brought to an end by a subtle cough, all three turned and faced the fourth member of the party, 'Sorry CM,' MJ said, waving him over to where the three of them stood. 'Gentlemen, let me introduce Chris Mullon CM of British Intelligence, based at S.H.A.P.E. Headquarters.'

CM came across and shook hands with each of them, when he came to Conrad he extended his hand tentatively. As he shook it, Conrad said, 'Had I not been whom you thought I was, you could now be dead, never expose yourself until you know who you are dealing with, did you forget the code word?'

A dejected CM. replied 'I never thought to use it, because I have seen you on duty.' For a moment or two there was an embarrassed silence then MJ said, 'Well I think we can all learn lessons from today, so let us now move on from here and meet the last member of the team.'

Picking up Conrad's bag from behind the tree where he had dropped it earlier, they walked through the forest a couple of hundred yards until they came to a small single storey building in a clearing surrounded by banks of rhododendrons and brambles. Leading the way, MJ walked up to the door and gave three knocks in quick succession, from inside a female voice said 'Enter'. MJ opened the door and led the way inside.

The room was in darkness but as the last of the party crossed the threshold and closed the door, the lights were suddenly switched on, and confronting them was a young woman holding a pistol. Recognising MJ she put the weapon in a pocket in her loose fitting dress and said 'You are late, I was getting worried.'

'Sorry, we had a slight problem en route.' Turning to the group he said, 'Gentlemen, let me introduce you to Iesha Legrande, IL, the final member of our very select party, she speaks Algerian, French and English.' All shook hands briefly and mumbled various forms of greetings.

When Conrad took her hand he said simply, 'What's a nice girl like you doing in a place like this?' And then he smiled at her.

Holding his hand, she replied in a soft sultry voice with a French accent, 'I don't know, many times I ask same question.'

The prolonged holding of hands did not go unnoticed by MJ. Putting his hand in front of his mouth, he coughed discreetly and said 'Right folks let's have something to eat and then get down to business, we have many things to discuss.'

Three hours later, their plans were completed. CM would return to S.H.A.P.E. Headquarters and monitor any intelligence which came in via the various networks and if relative, would pass it down to the team, via undercover agents. Conrad and IL. would take up residence in an apartment already rented in her name on the edge of the Place De La Madeleine in Paris, and as far as the outside world was concerned, they were lovers living together. MJ and RJ would be 'floaters' (working individually as a back-up for the team) and responsible for the passing of information back to Headquarters.

As they all sat back in their chairs and relaxed with a drink, MJ said 'CD a minute of your time please,' and beckoned him to follow him into one of the bedrooms. Once inside he closed the door before saying, 'I have something for you.' With that he bent down and flipped open the catches on a small suitcase reclining on the bed. Slowly he extracted several clips of ammo (rounds / bullets) and laid them out on the bed. 'There are twenty clips here CD so unless you go on the rampage and kill half the inhabitants of Paris, you should have sufficient fire power for your needs, if not let me know and I will provide more.' For a few moments he looked at Conrad before continuing. 'Now this is the serious part CD, should you be taken, God forbid, you have the ultimate escape facility at your disposal.' With that he passed over a small round box.

Conrad took it and looked inside. With a frown on his face he asked, 'What do I need with a few buttons?'

Looking at him MJ replied with a degree of tenderness he had not intended to display, 'CD those are not buttons, they are Cyanide tablets disguised as buttons, need I say any more?' There was a long pause before anyone spoke, then MJ said 'Sew them onto your clothes CD and it's worth remembering that they can also be used against the enemy.' Again a long pause then, 'just for the record CD your cover story will be that you have gone AWOL. (Absent Without Leave) and have sympathy for the Algerian movement.'

The two young men looked at each other for what seemed like an eternity, the hours spent together sweating and straining in the woods and classroom had forged a bond between them that until this moment in time they had not realised had existed. Breaking the spell between them MJ continued, 'This is the point of no return CD, you can pull out now and no-one will blame you. If you continue, I must inform you that you will be at risk day in and day out, therefore, TRUST NO-ONE.'

'We go on,' Conrad said emphatically, but with a slight huskiness in his voice and he turned to leave the room.

'Conrad, sorry, CD, you will need this,' he said holding out a large envelope.

Conrad turned back and faced him and with a smile on his face, he pointed and wagged his index finger at MJ before saying 'Your first mistake MJ, see it doesn't happen again, what is it?' he enquired.

Laughing MJ said 'It's expenses, Twenty-five thousand NF (New Francs) you will need it for whatever,' he said shrugging his shoulders. 'One has to live.'

Conrad took the envelope and looked inside it, he had never seen so much money before in his life. 'A large amount of money MJ,' he said.

'There's plenty more if you require it' was the casual reply. 'Before I have to go to this apartment in Paris, do I have time to go for a run? I've had no exercise since I came to France.'

Looking at his watch MJ replied, 'Certainly, Oh, before I forget, not that you would of course, do stagger the times and places when you phone into base, otherwise you could be compromised.'

Looking at MJ, Conrad replied smiling, 'You're right MJ I would never have forgotten to do that.' Laughing together, they left the room and rejoined the others.

Conrad went straight to his bag which he had left by the entrance and began to extract his tracksuit and a pair of running shoes. As he did so, MJ spoke 'Right folks, it's time for us all to go our separate ways, we all know what to do so there is nothing more to say. CD is going for a run so will you tidy up here IL then drive the pair of you to the apartment?'

Nodding her head she asked, 'Can I join you on the run?'

Conrad's head came up from rummaging in the bag, 'Can you run?'

'Yes,' came the frosty reply.

Conrad looked at MJ who simply shrugged his shoulders and smiled, 'Right then, let's get started.'

The others departed without further comment and Conrad went into a bedroom to change. When he returned five minutes later, IL was waiting, dressed in a baggy crimson tracksuit top and a pair of white shorts and shoes – she was a totally different person to the one in the loose fitting dress of a few minutes ago. She had long shapely legs and slim hips, her hair which had been pulled back from her head and tied at the back with a ribbon, now cascaded a long way past her shoulders in long auburn curls, she had applied some lipstick and she looked beautiful. 'What's that perfume you are wearing, it smells wonderful?'

'What else would a French girl wear but Chanel No.5,' she said smiling at him. The seduction of Conrad had begun but he was not aware of it.

'Right,' Conrad said 'lead the way Mademoiselle and let's go for a run in the woods.'

They set off at a leisurely pace with IL in front, after a few miles she turned and with sweat running down her face said, 'Would you like to lead now?'

He replied, 'No thank you, I'm enjoying the view.'

She turned and began to run on again then after a few yards, she stopped and turned around having suddenly realised what he had meant by 'enjoying the view,' and with a smile on her face said, 'You're a very naughty boy CD.'

'And you're a very attractive lady IL,' he replied.

With that, he went past her and began to stride out. 'Wait for me,' she panted, as she began to follow him.

A little while later, they arrived back at the house hot and sweating. They both had a shower, dressed and began to clean the place. Eventually, they were satisfied that they had removed all evidence of anyone having been there. From the kitchen Conrad called out, 'Do you have any food at your apartment IL because there's a fridge full in here.'

'I am having some, but if you like things there, bring it.' He was beginning to like her accented English, with the occasional misuse of words. 'Ok, I'll fill a bag.'

Finally, they left the house and made their way to the back of the building to one of the many clearings in the forest and there before them stood a strange looking little car. It was a box with four rather large wheels and with two large headlights fixed to a bar, it looked like a frog. Down the side was evidence of a coming together with other cars, in fact as he walked around it, there wasn't a panel on the car free from damage. Having completed his inspection, he looked at IL. 'What is it?' he asked.

With obvious affection for the beast she replied, 'This is Dolly, my car.' (Citroen 2CV)

'Does it work?'

'Jump in and will I show you.'

They put the food and their belongings on the back seat and then Conrad gingerly eased his way into the passenger seat. A strange lever protruded from the front of the dash board. 'What's that,' he asked.

'Ziss moves the gears,' she said. Then waggling the thing about whilst at the same time turning the ignition key, the contraption seemed to go up and down, belching smoke as it did so then it suddenly shot forward heading for the nearest tree. Conrad sat in his seat terrified as the tree filled the windscreen, then the strange craft lurched to one side and they headed away from the forest, down a rough track and eventually joined the AutoRoute to Paris.

The journey to the apartment was a nightmare; vehicles came out from every road along the route without a signal. Hands seemed to be permanently on the horns, hooters, sirens and anything else that made a sound. At traffic lights, the drivers revved their engines like mad men ready for the lights to change. Then when they did, they all surged forward like a tide of Wildebeest trying to cross the river. Drivers waved their fists at each other, as one cut in front of another in the mad dash forward, uttering all kinds of obscenities at each other as they did so.

Throughout the journey, IL sat composed and at ease, even though they almost touched several vehicles including what Conrad thought was a thirty ton truck. However, nothing could have prepared him for the utter madness around the Arc De Triomphe at the centre of the Etoile, at the top of the Champs Elysees. Here utter madness reigned. Lane after lane of traffic merged in a mad dash for a few extra feet of road. The noise of horns was deafening. Cars shot from one lane to another, apparently oblivious to the requirements of all those around them. And yet, amidst all this chaos, the traffic seemed to flow smoothly.

'Don't you just love Paris?' IL said looking at Conrad.

A much shaken Conrad replied 'It's certainly different to Yorkshire.'

'What is Yorshur?' she asked frowning.

'It's where I live' he replied, 'and it's YORKSHIRE.' he said very slowly.

'Yorkshire.'

'Very good and close enough,' he said as the little contraption came to a halt outside a large multi-storey building. Easing himself out of the car, he noted that his shirt was soaked in sweat around the arms. They walked from the car carrying their various packages up a few steps and into the foyer of the building. There they were greeted by the concierge 'Bon soir Mademoiselle,'

'Bon soir Monsieur,' she replied as they went to the lift. Once inside she pressed No.4 on the control panel and the old lift began to groan its way up from the basement to where they stood. The doors creaked open and they both stepped inside. After a few moments it came to a halt and the doors once again creaked open.

They stepped out into a narrow corridor then turned right. A few yards down the corridor she stopped and inserted a key into the lock of door 118 and stepped inside. The apartment was nicely appointed and furnished and consisted of a large living room where they now stood, a kitchen, small dining area, a bathroom and two bedrooms. 'Very nice, very nice indeed in fact,' he said as he walked around the rooms, opening doors and peering inside each one. The inspection complete he said 'Where shall I put my gear?' IL pointed to a door, 'But there's no bed in there.'

'You will have to use the, how you say it, cooch over there,' she said pointing to the corner of the room. Conrad looked in the direction of her arm and noticed an old black leather settee. He went over and tested it, it seemed well sprung and comfortable.

Returning to the middle of the room he said, 'Ok that's fine, I've slept on worse things. By the way it's COUCH, not COOCH.'

She laughed and said 'Thank you teacher, I will try and remember that for future.'

'Is there any hot water IL? After that drive I could do with refreshing myself.'

'You not like my driving?' she chided him.

'It wasn't your driving; it was all those idiots around us.'

He could hear her laughing from the kitchen and then she said 'There should be plenty water, just let it run for minute or two.'

When he had finished showering, he changed into a white shirt, dark slacks and shoes, no tie. He went into the living room and was amazed to find that the table was already laid for two, with a red napkin by each set of cutlery and two red candles burning in the middle of the table. A glass of red wine stood by each napkin. He called out 'The table looks lovely.'

'Thank you,' she replied from the kitchen.

He wandered over and pushed open the kitchen door, 'Can I help you?' he stood riveted on the spot. She was facing him, a wisp of hair hanging down over one eye. She was wearing a white pleated skirt with a crimson blouse and around her middle she wore a black belt but it was the blouse that Conrad could not take his eyes off. It had a plunging neckline which would have left no doubt in the mind of anyone that saw her, that she was nothing less than voluptuous.

Realising that he was staring, he began to blush. He looked down and started to back away. As he did so, he collided with the kitchen door which was ajar. 'Dinners almost ready,' she announced, 'why don't you sit down?' He looked up at her and saw that she was smiling at him. Extricating himself from the door, he went to the table and pulled out a chair. A few moments later she entered carrying some dishes which she arranged around the table on heatproof mats. 'Be careful the dishes are hot,' she warned. He did not reply for he was fighting his emotions in an attempt to regain control of himself. She came back into the room carrying a large bowl which she placed in the middle of the table a few inches below the candles. 'I hope you like my cooking,' she purred as she lifted the lid off the bowl. A cloud of steam arose from its contents. 'This is Libyan soup with Couscous and vegetables.'

'What's Couscous?'

'It's a North African dish of crushed wheat or coarse flour,' she replied.

The meal was delicious and by the time they had finished he was sweating profusely. 'Was the food too hot for you?' she enquired as she bent to retrieve his plate.

'No,' he replied hoarsely, 'It's your blouse that's making me sweat, could you close it please?' She looked at him and smiled but made no attempt to adjust the offending garment.

She washed the dinner pots and he dried. In the confines of the small kitchen they touched each other occasionally. Each time they did so, it was like a small electric shock to him. Once again he was becoming embarrassed for no matter how he tried, he could not prevent the enlargement taking place in his lower body. He just hoped that she had not noticed.

With the chores out of the way, they both returned to the living room and sat down. After a while he stretched himself and said 'It's been a long day IL if you don't mind I think I'll turn in.' She looked at him and smiled. 'Do you have a blanket for the couch?'

Getting up from her chair she stood in front of him and said softly, 'You can share my bed if you wish.'

He looked at her for what seemed an age then slowly he said 'I've never done this before, I'm not sure what to do.'

She looked at him and raised her eyebrows in surprise and then tenderly she said, 'You mean you never slept with woman before?'

He shook his head. 'No,' he replied.

She kissed him softly on his lips and whispered 'Well the other part of you seems eager to meet me.'

Looking puzzled he said 'What do you mean?'

She simply pointed down, he lowered his eyes and his embarrassment was complete for his manhood was straining to be released. He tried to apologise but she put her fingers to his lips, stifling his words. Then still smiling at him, she took him by the hand and led him into her bedroom.

The room was in semi-darkness as they entered, she refrained from putting on the lights in case they caused Conrad further embarrassment. She approached the bed then turned to face him. For a moment or two they both looked at each other and then he slipped his arms around her and drew her to him and kissed her gently. She immediately responded and their embrace became more and more vital and demanding. She could feel his hardness hot and pulsing through the thin fabric of his slacks and her desire for him became overwhelming. Still locked in a passionate embrace, she began pulling his shirt from his slacks This done she struggled with his belt buckle. By now Conrad was swept away on a tide of passion for this beautiful woman and like her, he was trying to remove her blouse from her skirt and belt. Their hands were everywhere fumbling with each other's various pieces of dress in an attempt to remove all the barriers between them and their passion.

Panting, she eased Conrad away, removed her clothes quickly then helped Conrad with his. Now, naked as they were when they first came into the world, they both looked at each other, desire almost dripping from them. Conrad was the first to speak, 'I have never seen a naked woman before and you are truly beautiful,' he said huskily, his eyes fixed on her breasts.

'Thank you,' she replied seductively then she bent down to the bed and pulled back the clothes, beckoning to him as she did so.

Once in bed, they embraced and fondled each other as lovers have done since time began then, in a voice he could barely hear she said, 'You are wet, do you want me?'

'Yes, oh yes,' he replied, desperation in his voice. Quickly and expertly, she guided him into her, she was warm and moist and pliant. Suddenly bright lights began to flash and explode in his brain, sensations he had never known before surged through his body and he trembled from head to toe. The sensations wracking him were transmitted to her and she cried out time and time again when his pent up seed exploded inside her.

Sometime later when their passion had subsided, he looked at her and gently brushing aside some wisps of damp hair from her face said, 'I never dreamt that making love could be so wonderful, every part of my body is still on fire. I hope I did not hurt you for I do not know what came over me.'

There was a long pause before she replied languidly, 'No my darling you did not hurt me, you were gentle and kind and I love you and him!'

They embraced each other tenderly several times before she finally curled up against him and sleep overcame them. Before dawn broke they loved each other again and again.

The bedside telephone once again rang out in Major Harris's London apartment, extricating himself from the person next to him he picked up the receiver, 'Harris' he said.

The voice at the other end said, 'Sorry for the late hour sir, couldn't get through until now, 'Operation Ave Maria' is now functional and will commence duties as from tomorrow.'

'Any complications?' (his standard response).

There was a pause then 'Info from headquarters would indicate that JFK will now be at S.H.A.P.E. Headquarters on 02-06-1961 Sir, which does not give us much time to fulfil the mission.'

There was a long pause then Harris said, 'Very well, do what you can to expedite matters but, if possible, do not compromise the principal agent, for I have another project for the two of you in the near future.'

'Very good sir.'

'Do you have sufficient funding?'

'Yes, thank you sir.'

'Very well, keep me posted and look after yourself.' With that he replaced the handset and returned to his bed partner, 'Sorry my dear, state affairs and all that.' Tenderly he kissed the nape of her neck before pulling the counterpane over them. A moment later he placed his left arm around her waist and within moments they were both sound asleep again.

Chapter Fifteen

As the weak rays of the sun filtered through the bedroom curtains of the apartment, the lovers slowly and painfully tried to extricate their arms from each other, as they did so they both shook their arms in order to restore the circulation to their blood starved limbs.

During the night they had both decided to address each other by their Christian names (or others) when in the apartment in view of their relationship, but only if alone. As Iesha finished stretching her arms, her large breasts jostled from side to side then stood out proud from her body. Watching her, Conrad marvelled at the beauty and symmetry of the female form. Noticing Conrad staring at her, she came and stood in front of him, 'And just what are you thinking?' she said putting her arms around his waist.

Smiling Conrad looked at her and placing his hands on her shoulders replied, 'I was thinking how very beautiful you are,' and kissed her on her forehead 'and,' he continued 'it's time you made me some food woman, otherwise I will have no strength to attend to you later.'

'Later!' she exclaimed, looking at him, 'I think 'HE', may want to 'attend' me sooner, you naughty boy.'

Conrad began to chuckle now that he was no longer embarrassed when basic instincts took charge of his body, 'That's because you are a very naughty teacher,' he replied. They both hugged each other and then collapsed on the bed laughing.

After they had eaten, they washed the pots and pans, put them away and cleaned the apartment. Having finished all the chores they decided to go for a walk. Outside the air was fresh and invigorating. As they strolled arm in arm down the various avenues with their little coffee shops and bars Iesha said hugging him tighter than before, 'Isn't Paris exciting, I just love it?'

Conrad looked at her and replied, 'It certainly beats Bridlington.'

Looking at him she replied 'What is Bri dington?'

'Brid-ling-ton!' he replied, 'it's where I live.'

Iesha nodded her head and replied 'I see.'

They stayed out most of the day and when they returned to the apartment, they were both in a sombre mood for they both knew that now, they had to put their personal feelings to one side and concentrate on the business in hand, the OS.

From intelligence gathered over several months, it was confirmed that some members of the OS cell operating in Paris had been seen at one of the city's popular night spots, namely the Caveau (cavern club) 5, Rue de la Huchette, once the haunt of Sidney Bechet, but latterly the night spot where Maxim Saury performed and entertained the multicultural peoples of Paris. It was therefore decided that the Caveau would be Conrad's first port of call.

That evening after they had both bathed and refreshed themselves, they had a light meal and then at 9.00pm they left the apartment and made their way to the Caveau. Conrad had with him an ample supply of NF and was dressed in what could only be described as 'Bohemian' clothing which they had purchased that afternoon whilst out walking. Conrad was not too happy with his attire, but saw the reasoning behind Iesha's thinking that as he was on the 'run', it would be sensible to have at least some form of disguise and thus blend in with the surroundings. She also suggested that he did not shave on a regular basis, which he reluctantly agreed to.

They arrived at the Caveau (Conrad called it the Cavern) at about 10.00pm. To say that the place was 'swinging' would be an understatement. It was jammed with people of all ages and different colours and the sound was deafening. A thick layer of cigarette smoke clung to the ceiling to a depth of three or four feet. The group on the small stage were playing songs of the late very popular, Sidney Bechet, the American multitalented coloured musician who had lived in Paris for many years, prior to his death at the age of sixty-two, including the very popular "Petite Fleur". As they finished the number, thunderous applause rang out together with shouts of "Encore," "Encore," as the group slowly left the stage for a much needed break.

For Conrad, the sudden lull in the noise level was a pleasant relief, he squeezed Iesha's hand gently and said, 'This is quite a place, pity about the music.'

'What do you mean?' she replied, smiling.

Conrad answered 'Well this place would make a wonderful setting for some of Richard Wagner's works.'

'Who's he?' she asked.

Somewhat surprised he replied, 'Richard Wagner was a German composer who produced some very sombre but moving music; he was also Adolf Hitler's favourite composer.' Just then the next group on stage appeared and conversation became a shouting exercise.

As it was impossible to see more than twenty yards in any direction, Conrad squeezed Iesha's hand again and motioned that they should move around the room. Nodding she followed him, bumping into many couples as they did so. Finally having covered the whole area they stood with their backs to the wall adjacent to the stage. Leaning down so his lips were close to Iesha's ear he said 'I cannot see anyone here that I recognise, can you?' For an answer she simply shook her head. Looking at his watch it registered 02:40am, squeezing her hand again he pointed to his watch, 'Shall we go?' he shouted.

Looking up at him she replied in a loud voice 'One more dance, darling Please.'

For the next few minutes they clung to each other as the group played music of a more relaxed tempo than previously, as if to mark the end of the evening's revelry. Once again, Conrad's body misbehaved and slowly Iesha raised her head and looked at him. 'Shall we go?'

Looking down at her he lightly kissed her nose and answered, 'Please.' Without further comment, she simply pressed her lower body even closer against that of Conrad's and with a loving smile on her face, felt his desire for her.

The journey back to the apartment was uneventful and as soon as they had closed and locked the door, they began disrobing each other frantically, as they made their way to the bedroom. No sooner had they divested each other of all their garments they fell onto the bed still clutching each other and became as one.

The next day they returned to the club and Conrad spent several more fruitless hours looking for anyone who faintly resembled the people he had seen on screen back in England, but without success.

They continued this exercise day after day and they even staggered the times they arrived at the Caveau but each time they drew a blank and they began to get down hearted and the money was beginning to run out.

Whilst out running one day, he stopped at a public telephone and dialled CM on his secure line. He informed him that progress was virtually non-existent and that he required further funding. He told CM which one of the five secure 'post boxes' they used to make the deposit and put the telephone down. The call lasted a mere forty seconds, which was all the time that was allowed by prior agreement between him and MJ. Should anyone try and make contact with base and exceed forty seconds, without a password, it would be deemed that the enemy had infiltrated the system and that Conrad had been compromised.

As he left the telephone, he looked around him and was about to set off running when he noticed a man with a paper standing on the street corner, he looked odd and out of place and the warning lights began to flash in Conrad's mind. He set off running slowly in the opposite direction to the man and at the first corner in the road he turned sharply and waited. A few moments later, he heard the padding of feet and as the man turned the corner, Conrad hit him in the throat with the edge of his hand. The man gasped and crumpled to the ground. Conrad bent over him and began to search his body for any weapons, taking his time as he did so, lest he miss anything.

His search produced a stiletto devoid of any markings of approximately 12" long, in a leather sheath strapped to the man's leg plus an old German 9mm. Luger automatic. The man had a swarthy complexion and long dirty unkempt hair; in fact he looked and smelt as though he had not washed for some considerable time, for a peculiar odour emanated from his body. A further more rigorous body search produced no form of identification. As a matter of routine caution, he checked the gun and found it to be fully loaded. Looking around him he noticed that the road was deserted and house after house was boarded-up; litter drifted around the street on a slight breeze and furthermore there was not a soul in sight, ideal conditions for what he had to do when the man awakened.

As he squatted by the would-be assailant, he took off the man's jacket and laid it to one side then he removed his shirt which he tore into strips. As he did so he noticed the number of scars on the man's upper body and wondered why he was so marked. Binding his arms securely behind his back, he also fastened the man's knees and feet together, then sat back and waited for him to recover.

He did not have long to wait.

When he opened his eyes, he saw Conrad facing him with his own Luger automatic pointed directly at his chest. His jacket or what remained of it, for it had by torn to shreds by Conrad in his search for some form of identity, lay in a pile on the floor between Conrad's legs. When the man had recovered sufficiently enough to speak, his upper naked body was shaking with cold. Conrad asked him in French, 'Why were you following me?' The man said nothing. Conrad repeated the question this time in Arabic. Still no response, he asked the question again, this time in English again no response. Shaking his head from side to side slightly, he pursed his lips whilst wagging his finger in front of the man's face. He repeated the question again, slowly but again, no reply. With a final shake of his head Conrad lowered the gun until it pointed directly at the man's groin. Then slowly his right index finger curled around the trigger and began to squeeze. Sweat began to appear on the man's forehead then, just at the point when he thought that the gun would fire, he screamed in French 'Don't shoot, don't shoot.' Conrad wavered for a moment then slowly lowered the gun and waited.

Sobbing with relief the man began to talk, he had been told to follow the 'English' and find out where he lived, because he has been asking questions in the Caveau Club and spending money. 'Who told you to follow me?' Conrad said raising the gun again. By now the man was shaking with both cold and fear, tears were running down his face joining with the mucus from his nose, his eyes bulged in their sockets, as he looked back at the face of the man before him. Conrad sat impassively, watching him. 'Who told you to follow me?' He repeated.

'The Algerians,' he sobbed spitting out mucus and tears as he tried to speak.

'What Algerians?' Conrad demanded.

The man was by now clearly terrified. Conrad once again pointed the gun and waited for the answer. With his eyeballs rolling in their sockets he replied, 'The OAS Algerians.'

'Who are they?' Conrad asked.

'The Algerian Army,' he replied.

'Do they meet at the Club Caveau?' The man nodded his head slowly as it sank to his chest. Conrad looked at him for a while then said 'I think you have told me the truth, so I will not take your life, remember that.'

The man raised his head and looked at Conrad 'I am already dead English, if you do not kill me, the OAS will.'

His shoulders began to heave as the man realised his predicament.

Conrad stood up picking up the stiletto as he did so then he hacked through the pieces of shirt which bound the man's knees and feet. Facing him he said, 'What is your name?' The man replied 'Aly Al Mahmour.'

'Well Aly Al Mahmour, I bid you good bye,' Conrad raised the gun and pulled the trigger. There was a click as the firing pin fell on an empty chamber. The wretched Aly looked at Conrad and realised that he had been fooled. With hate in his eyes he shouted, 'Bastard English,' then coughed as more body liquid entered his mouth.

Picking up the stiletto, Conrad continued on his way as if nothing had happened. At the first manhole / storm drain he came to, he dropped the knife down it but kept the Luger. The journey back to the apartment was uneventful, but as per his training, he continuously checked both his surroundings and the people he chanced to see. In view of what had just happened, he had decided to place himself on high alert, whenever he was on the street.

As he approached the apartment block, he paused in the doorway of a cafe and carefully observed the passers-by. After two or three minutes of surveying the road, he was confident that no one was following him so he crossed the road and entered the building. Once outside the door of the apartment, he gave the prearranged knock and waited for the door to be opened. Nothing happened. He knocked again … Nothing. Drawing the Luger from his pocket, he released the safety catch and noiselessly primed it (engaged the first round) then tried the door handle. The door opened silently as he depressed the handle. The room was in darkness. He eased himself inside then slowly closed the door behind him.

Suddenly the room was filled with light and Iesha stood before him in a flimsy black negligée. 'Darling why the gun?' Ignoring her remarks he turned and quickly locked the door.

'You left the door unlocked!' he said accusingly 'I could have been anyone, including the OAS.'

'I thought I would surprise you on return,' she purred seductively as she approached him. Conrad's throat began to dry as he watched her glide towards him and his initial anger that she had not adhered to previously agreed basic security precautions evaporated into the Parisian air.

On tip toes, she pulled his mouth down onto hers and kissed him longingly, at the same time pressing her lower body against his. Conrad's response was instantaneous and a shudder of delight ran through Iesha as she felt him once more respond to her actions. They clung together for a while then easing him away from her she said breathlessly, 'You like?' pointing at the negligee.

'It's beautiful,' he replied. 'But not as beautiful as you.'

She came into his arms again and they embraced. When they eventually parted Conrad whispered 'Anyway I prefer you without clothes.'

With mischief written all over her face she retorted, 'You naughty boy,' then turned and ran into the bedroom throwing off the negligee in the process. He quickly followed her hopping from one leg to another pulling off his trousers as he did so. At one point in his eagerness to reach the bedroom he fell over as his foot caught in the bottom of his trousers. This brought squeals of laughter from Iesha as she watched his ungainly progress towards her. Finally reaching the bed, he looked down at her then pulling off a sheet, he held it at arm's length like a giant cloak, he paused a moment then as if enacting a scene from a Dracula film, he bared his teeth and covered her.

For the next two hours they fondled and loved each other until they were both exhausted then they fell asleep, locked together in each other's arms. When they awoke the room was in darkness, Conrad looked at his watch and saw that the time was 16.40hrs, slowly he extricated himself from Iesha and made his way to the bathroom. Having cleaned his teeth, he then showered and was just about to leave when Iesha joined him. They washed each other and laughed as each fondled the other making lewd comments about each other's body, as they did so. Finally they stumbled out of the shower, dried each other then returned to the bedroom and dressed. After they had dined, Conrad told Iesha what had happened that morning. He also stressed the need for strict personal security, no more leaving the door unlocked whilst he or she was out. Having dined, they went into the living room and Iesha switched on the radio.

Light music drifted from the small plastic radio filling the room and then the programme was interrupted by a news flash. Conrad could not follow the French announcer's rapid speech, however Iesha could. When the report had finished she said, 'A man believed to be an Algerian had been found floating face down in the Seine, his upper body which was naked, had many scars and his hands were tied behind his back, with what appeared to be parts of his own clothing. The Police think that the man may have been a drug dealer and ask members of the public for any information they might have regarding this incident to come forward. All information would be treated with the utmost confidence.'

She looked at him concern showing on her face. 'What do you think really happened to the man?' she asked.

After a brief pause he replied, 'Well, he either made his way to the Seine after I left him and threw himself in or, someone found him, questioned him and then dumped him in the river.' Another pause then, 'However, I think the latter is the most likely answer. So, if I am right, that now means that they now know who I am to some degree and that I am aware of their interest in me, therefore the action starts as of today.'

They discussed the situation for some time and decided to stay away from the Caveau until after Christmas which was now only a few days away. They came to their decision reasoning that the body in the Seine would be in the papers for the next few days and would attract a higher police presence than normal, furthermore the OS if involved, would, as a matter of security, lay low for a while.

For the remainder of the evening, there was a sombre atmosphere in the apartment, as both realised their fragile position. As midnight approached they decided to retire having heard no further news regarding the body in the river.

The next morning, Conrad left the apartment whilst it was still dark and made his way to his 'Post Box'. He found a spot behind an old building where he could watch the area whilst concealed from casual passers-by. He waited for almost an hour, but saw no-one use the road. However, his major concern was the fact that as the air temperature was only slightly above freezing point, someone with sharp eyes could have noticed his regular breathing when the warm air he exhaled, condensed with the colder morning air.

Eventually, he satisfied himself that it was safe to proceed, so leaving his sanctuary he crossed the road and entered the piece of waste ground which harboured the secret depository. Once again, he casually looked around him before stooping, and removing the package that awaited him. Without looking at the package, he quickly put it inside the bulky pullover he wore over his tracksuit, and set off back to the apartment.

At irregular intervals he stopped, as though gasping for breath, whilst doing so, he casually and discreetly looked about him. He saw no-one that looked suspicious, there were no cars in view and nothing he could see or feel, gave him any cause for alarm. Satisfied that all was well he continued on his way, albeit cautiously.

As he approached the apartment building he went into one of the street side cafe's and ordered a coffee. The weary waiter passed him a cup and Conrad sat by a window table and sipped the hot, strong liquid, whilst casually watching the road. After twenty minutes or so, he finished the coffee and left, but instead of crossing the road and entering the apartment, he turned to his left, walked down the road a few hundred yards, crossed over, and approached the apartment from the opposite direction. Satisfied that he was not being followed, he went inside. 'Bon jour Monsieur' said the weary old concierge, looking over his glasses at Conrad, 'Bon jour Monsieur,' replied Conrad 'ça va' but before the man could answer, Conrad was in the lift and closing the doors.

Once inside the apartment he locked the door and engaged the newly installed door bolts he had fitted a few days ago for extra security. After removing the package he had been carrying under his clothing, he went into the bathroom and carefully positioned it almost at the bottom of the dirty clothes bin; casually he dropped some clothes on top of it. Having satisfied himself that all seemed to look natural he undressed and stepped into the shower.

Ten minutes later, pink and glowing with life and vitality he emerged from the steaming shower cubicle. Picking up a couple of white towels from the towel rail, he wrapped one around his waist, and began drying himself with the other. A few moments later the bathroom door opened and Iesha walked in, her only clothing being a pair of black flimsy panties. As she did so, Conrad was towelling his back, both arms were fully extended, almost as though he was being crucified. Every muscle in his athletic body rippled as he slowly towelled himself dry.

Man and woman looked at each other, each thinking their own thoughts, but neither one spoke. Slowly he lowered the towel as Iesha came towards him. Wrapping her arms around him, she clung to him; her warm breasts pressed against him, but still she did not speak. Once again, Conrad's body responded to her almost naked presence. Almost inaudibly she whispered 'I love you and every part of you.' Before he could reply, her hand gently pulled aside the towel, and then she began to slowly slide down his body.

With her hands gently resting on the soft swell of his buttocks, her mouth slowly encased his manhood. Bright lights flashed before his eyes. Every nerve and fibre of his being suddenly came to life, wave after wave of fantastic sensations raged through his body as her lips and tongue played with him. Trembling like a leaf in the breeze he slowly began to sink to his knees, with Iesha still clinging to him. As his climax rapidly approached, he tried to ease her away from him but she would not be denied. Unable to prevent himself crying out at the pure ecstasy of the moment, he abandoned himself to the desires of this beautiful, loving, sensuous woman.

Sometime later, Iesha left his body and without saying a word went to the kitchen, she reappeared a few moments later with two glasses of chilled wine. Passing a glass to Conrad, she settled herself between his legs, and leaned back against his chest and began to sip the cool amber coloured wine. No words were exchanged for none were necessary.

Chapter Sixteen

The package, when they opened it held four separate items; the first contained a large amount of money, the other three, contained less savoury items. Most of the money he gave to Iesha for safe keeping and food. The rest he put into an old French leather wallet he had bought from a market stall when out shopping with Iesha one day. He then put the wallet into the back pocket of his trousers.

The second packet was small but deadly. It consisted of ten cigarettes each with a filter tip, in a very light case. The case had no markings which could be traced to its place of origin. Each of the cigarettes had a feint red line around them, approximately a third and two thirds down their length. 'Why would they send me cigarettes?' Conrad asked, 'they know I don't smoke?'

'There's a note,' replied Iesha pointing to the bottom of the packet.

Passing the piece of paper to him, he began to read. 'I know you don't smoke but these are special cigarettes. Inside each one, where the red bands are, there is a tiny propellant which when the cigarette is being smoked, will fire a tiny pellet of highly concentrated CURARE at whatever is in front of it. Contact will hardly be felt, but they (man or beast) will be dead within seconds, due to asphyxiation.' He looked at Iesha then he continued, 'when the second band is reached, the propellant will fire another pellet, but this time not forwards, but backwards, into the mouth of the smoker, with the same deadly effect.'

The third packet produced a small lint lined tin of syringes, the note simply said, "CD these are filled with scopolamine and morphine. From your army training you will know what that means (induces twilight sleep, an aid when questioning) be careful with them." MJ.

The fourth packet was the smallest of all, it had a sheet of paper wrapped around it, which when removed revealed a tiny steel phial, on the outside of the phial was written one word, CYANIDE. Inside were five tiny capsules. In a soft voice he said 'More cyanide, I must have enough to eliminate half the inhabitants of Paris.'

Sitting back in his chair he perused the contents on the table; finally he said, 'Well MJ a very Merry Christmas to you, wherever you are!' Turning to Iesha he said, 'Let's hope I never have to use these presents MJ has sent me.'

Iesha smiled feebly and replied, 'I hope not too.'

An air of melancholy descended on the apartment as the day wore on, until Conrad suggested that they go for a walk in the weak winter sunshine. This cheered her up and she went to get ready. When she returned she had put on a large pale blue coat with a fur collar with a belt tied around the middle. Her hair cascaded onto and down over her shoulders, she looked stunning, she had also put on her favourite perfume, Chanel No. 5.

Conrad having put away the 'presents', went into the bedroom and put on a white polo neck pullover and a black leather jacket, another purchase he had made when he bought the wallet then he joined her.

Instead of using the lift, they went down the stairs and out through a service door, one of Conrad's security measures and into the cold winter air. They walked arm in arm for an hour or so then they went into a small street side cafe. Iesha went to the counter for some coffee. While she was away, Conrad sat down at a corner table and surveyed the street in both directions. By the time she returned, he was content that there was nothing out there that gave him any cause to be alarmed.

'This is, how you say, cosy,' she whispered in English, so that no one would overhear.

Smiling he replied 'Very cosy.' They sat and sipped their coffee just like everyone else in the intimate little cafe. Holding hands, they looked out of the window at the passing traffic and the groups of people walking up and down the pavement going about their business.

Suddenly, the plate glass window of a shop across from them and no more than fifty yards or so higher up the road from the cafe, disintegrated, glass and flames belched out from the ill-fated building. Passers-by were blown off their feet, maimed and killed, as pieces of wood and bricks were hurled into the air. Shards of glass flew everywhere. Pieces of flesh and bone rained down from the sky, a grotesque final resting place for the poor innocent people who had just happened to be passing when the explosion occurred. Some of the debris hit the cafe windows including a severed hand, which left a thin trail of blood as it slipped obscenely down the window which thankfully remained intact. A huge column of smoke and dust slowly drifted upwards in the cold winter air… debris now littered the street and cries of pain could be heard clearly inside the cafe from those poor souls still alive outside. Then someone from within the cafe screamed, 'Bastard OS' and the hypnotic spell of seeing but not believing that which one's eyes had recorded was broken, and there was a dash for the door.

'That was a bomb,' Conrad said 'let's get away from here, now.'

'We can't leave all those injured people,' Iesha protested.

'if we stay we will be interviewed by the police, is that what you suggest?' Realising that he was right, she squeezed his hand and they joined the queue leaving the cafe. Expletives filled the air!

The scene in the street was like something from a Second World War film – bodies, parts of bodies, bricks, timber, parts of clothes and the odd shoe lay about the street, but the most sickening sight of all was the remains of a blood stained pram (baby carriage), there was no sign of the parents nor of the precious child. 'You Bastards!' Conrad shouted out loud as he steered Iesha away from the scene, 'You will pay for this carnage.'

They had not walked more than a hundred yards when in the distance they heard the distinctive sound of a host of police sirens speeding towards them. Conrad steered Iesha into a small dark alley between two buildings and awaited the arrival of the cars. Almost immediately, three black Citroens with lights flashing and sirens wailing came down the road, followed by an ambulance, heading for the disaster area. As soon as they had passed, Conrad and Iesha left their hiding place and quickly made their way back to the apartment. They entered the apartment the way they had left it then having secured the door they slowly sat down on the couch. Neither spoke. Holding hands they remained silent for several minutes as a personal mark of respect for those that they had just seen maimed, or blown to pieces at the hands of the cowardly terrorists.

Eventually Iesha said slowly and with deep feeling, 'Sometimes I detest the human race and today is one of those times. What harm did the baby ever do to anyone that it should die like it did? Where was God? Why did he allow this to happen?' She began to cry, the tears rolled down her cheeks and her shoulders began to shake as her sobbing intensified.

Gently placing his arm around her shoulders he whispered, 'I don't believe in God and today has proved my belief but I swear to you and the baby and all those people in the street that I will do all I can to find out who carried out this evil deed today and when I do, they will suffer.'

Lifting her tear stained face to his, she kissed him gently on his cheek and hugged him. He returned the gesture and for a few moments nothing more was said. A little while later she whispered, 'I keep wondering if the baby was a boy or a girl.'

Looking puzzled he said, 'Does it really matter if it was a boy or a girl, an innocent baby lost its life today?'

'Of course not,' she replied 'I was just thinking that we could have been the ones in the street walking our son or daughter.'

Looking even more puzzled than before he replied, 'I'm sorry dear but I don't understand what you mean.' Gently easing away from him she dried her eyes with one of his handkerchiefs then looking up at him, she whispered, 'I am carrying our son or daughter.'

Chapter Seventeen

It was Christmas Eve in London and Major Harris was fastening the bow tie of his evening dress when the telephone rang. 'Harris,' he said as usual.

There was a click and then 'Good evening sir, I hope I haven't disturbed you?'

'Good evening MJ,' the Major replied 'And no, you have not disturbed me but I am preparing to go out to dinner with a member of the cabinet, a boring devil to say the least, however, as budget times are approaching, one has to inform these transient people just what is required of them whilst still in office. Fortunately, this particular minister always provides a very expensive table at the tax payer's expense of course which helps to relieve the tedium of having to listen to his whining over the running costs of my SCD (Special Covert Department).' MJ laughed down the phone, 'Sounds like a bad way to spend Christmas Eve Sir.'

'I must admit that I could think of several more pleasant ways to pass this evening, however duty, etc. etc. demands otherwise,' he replied.

For the next fifteen minutes, MJ brought the Major up to date with the events in Paris, including the body in the river and the bomb blast near to where CD and IL were staying. He concluded his report by saying that CD had collected the package of money and other items and that no further action would take place until the New Year. 'Very well MJ keep in touch and a Merry Christmas to you and your team.'

'Thank you sir,' and before he could say another word, the receiver was replaced on its cradle and the connection was terminated.

***

'What did you say?' asked Conrad.

'I said I am carrying our son or daughter,' Iesha replied.

'But you told me that you could not have children,' Conrad replied shaking his head.

'So doctors told me,' she replied looking at him with affection. 'Obviously you do not do what doctors say, you naughty boy.' Stepping forward she placed her arms around his neck and laid her head against his chest. Instinctively Conrad embraced her. They held each other for several minutes, each occupied with their own thoughts.

Finally Conrad eased himself away from her and looked down at her glowing tear-stained face which he now gently cradled in his hands. All the emotions known to mankind – admiration, affection, contentment, desire, longing seemed to be encapsulated in one small, simple word, love, as she returned his gaze.

Tenderly, he kissed her lips then picking her up he carried her into the bedroom and laid her on the bed.

Several hours later they had decided that at the start of the New Year, Iesha would request that she be relieved of her duties due to her condition and if possible, dismissed from the Armed Services, even if it meant buying her release.

The next few days seemed to flash by; Christmas Eve was an experience never to be forgotten. Disguising themselves as a middle aged couple they left the hotel by the rear door and hailed a taxi. Iesha instructed the driver to take them to the magnificent cathedral of Notre Dame. Once inside the stone colossus, Conrad's mind was taken back to his childhood days when, with his mother, they went to see the wonderful black and white film, "The Hunchback of Notre Dame" a film inspired by Victor Hugo's classic novel "Notre Dame de Paris," featuring Charles Laughton as the deformed bell-ringer Quasimodo, who appeared throughout the film swinging from the many columns that supported the cathedral, plus anything else that would bear his weight, whilst at the same time rescuing the beautiful Esmeralda from a death by burning at the stake. As he looked around the magnificent building, he fully expected to see the deformed figure of Quasimodo looking down at him. Smiling to himself, he looked around at the truly awe inspiring building and he was deeply moved. The angelic voices of the children singing in the choir brought tears to his eyes. Silently he pledged himself to defend all that was good in mankind and to eradicate wherever possible, all that was evil.

Standing in the great man-made temple his spirits were lifted like never before, as a thousand voices sang out the Christmas message, "Peace on earth and good will to all men". In the magnificence of Notre Dame, Conrad could not understand just how stupid and decadent mankind could be. For after almost two thousand years of history and civilisation to look back on and learn from, we continue to make the same mistakes. As he lowered his eyes from the ceiling, he was confronted by Iesha's gaze, 'Is it not wonderful?' she whispered, 'It truly is,' he replied. 'How man could create something as beautiful as this and yet be responsible for so much destruction, pain and suffering throughout the world, I fail to understand?'

With arms wrapped around each other, they stood transfixed, in the great arena of Notre Dame, as wave after wave of glorious, uplifting, melodious sound washed over them. People all around pressed hands, handkerchiefs and even coat sleeves to their faces, in order to mask the flow of emotion that poured from the very heart of every man, woman and child gathered in this magnificent edifice to God.

In the early hours of the morning, they left the sanctuary of the cathedral and stopped the first taxi they saw. Once again Iesha gave directions, but avoided giving the driver their true destination, instead she directed him to an area almost a mile away from their apartment. Having paid him, they casually watched him as he drove away. Satisfied that they were safe, they proceeded to walk the rest of the way to the apartment, still disguised as an elderly couple.

Once inside the apartment, they divested themselves of their disguises then Conrad went to the fridge and produced a bottle of Champagne and two flutes. As the cork burst from the bottle, he quickly filled their glasses then linking arms they sipped the golden liquid and wished each other a Merry Christmas. Having had two glasses of Champagne each, he went back to the kitchen. After a few moments he returned with a small package which was fastened to a large pale blue envelope, bearing the initials IL. With eyes shining, she eagerly opened the envelope and removed the Christmas card, having read it she threw her arms around his neck and kissed him. When they had parted, she gently removed the decorative outer wrapping paper from the package, which revealed a small blue velvet box. Carefully she raised the lid. Inside was a gold ring with three small diamonds set in the middle. Every facet of the diamonds caught the artificial light of the room and sparkled uncontrollably, every turn of the ring seemed to create a new light pattern, each brighter than the previous one. Iesha lifted her eyes to his and was about to speak when he said, 'It's an engagement ring.' Tears began to roll down her cheeks as she clung to him as she realised what the ring meant. When she had stopped sobbing he gently asked, 'Will you wear my ring?'

'Of course will,' she replied and once again Conrad chuckled at her slight error of speech. When she had dried her eyes, she went to the bedroom and when she returned she carried a huge envelope with a small package tied to it. On the front of the envelope it said in her bold hand writing, "To My Man." Like Iesha before him, he opened the envelope first and found inside a very French Christmas Card!! Then gingerly he opened the small package and discovered a bright red box similar in size to the one he had given her. And like hers it also contained a ring. This ring was also of gold and had a shoulder which had her first name initial surrounded by Conrad's initial 'C' engraved on it.

Before he could speak she said softly, 'Will you wear my ring?'

'You know I will,' he replied. They sat listening to the radio whilst they finished the Champagne then they tidied the apartment before going to bed.

The tranquillity of the Christmas period passed by all too quickly when reality reared its ugly head on the morning of the 2nd. January 1961 as Conrad entered the main room of the apartment and found pushed under the door a small white envelope. Carefully he opened it and withdrew the piece of flimsy paper it contained. The message was precise and to the point, 'Sorry, but its back to work.' MJ.

Whilst out on his run collecting his 'mail', he thought of all the evil things he had seen of late and decided that he would try to persuade Iesha to stay behind when he went to the Caveau Club that evening. He knew full well that she would object to such a proposal, as she was under military orders to assist him. His visits to his post boxes produced nothing. However on his return, he just happened to glance in a shop window, his reflection shocked him, for he now had a substantial growth of hair all over his face and his head hair touched his shoulders. He looked he decided like a tramp.

Upon his return, he showered then had a breakfast of orange juice, scrambled eggs, bacon, toast and coffee that Iesha had prepared for him. When he had finished the meal, he delicately mentioned his concerns about her continuing to help him at the Caveau Club. As he suspected she refused to let him go without her, if only as she put it, 'As some insurance, in case you getting into trouble.'

'Get into trouble,' he replied smiling.

'My Eenglish is no good?' she said emphasising Eenglish.

'Your Eenglish, as you say it, is very good and well you know it,' he replied laughing. Eventually he gave in and agreed that they would go together.

Before leaving, Conrad checked that his arsenal of weapons were about his person and not obvious to any passer-by then he checked Iesha's gun, cleaned it and then handed it back to her. Once again they left the apartment block via the rear stairs and service door then walked for some time before hailing a taxi. Once again Iesha gave instructions where they wanted to be dropped off. Once outside the Caveau Club they paid the taxi driver and went inside. The atmosphere was electric, bodies of all shapes and sizes danced to the vibrant music of Maxim Saury and his band and as usual a thick layer of smoke drifted above the heads of the swaying people making visibility difficult.

Slowly, they eased their way around the edge of the room, as they did so Conrad bought two glasses of orange juice. They continued to edge their way around the floor when Conrad suddenly stopped, causing Iesha to bump into him. 'What's the matter?' she said.

Conrad slowly turned around to face her. 'Over there at the corner table by the stage, they are all here, Ben Mussa (often mistaken for Ahmed Ben Bella, who was in prison for they were like two peas in a pod) Hisham-al-Ghoul, Ali-al-Bachra, Sadiq-al-Shaht, and Ally Bashra, all OS, top people. It would appear that they also have some 'heavies' with them, about four as far as I can make out in this smoke.' The hairs on the back of his neck began to rise. Adrenaline began to pump through his veins and a feeling of controlled excitement settled over him as slowly they approached the group of terrorists. By now Conrad was swaying on his feet as if drunk, whilst Iesha clung to his left arm and scolded him in French for being so.

Slowly he took out one of the special cigarettes, with his right hand and lit it. Pausing in order to gauge the rate of burn of the cigarette, he came alongside one of the now obvious 'heavies'. As he slowly passed by, the man slipped his right hand into his pocket and left it there then as Conrad shuffled past, he turned away and resumed his conversation with the rest of the group. Conrad noted that the cigarette had burnt down almost to the first red line, so casually he pointed the deadly cigarette at the man's neck. There was the faintest of sounds, almost like a deep sigh and a slight movement in his fingers and then he had shuffled past the group. Casually, he half turned as if looking for someone. The man's hand was slowly scratching the back of his neck then after a few seconds he began to sway from side to side, very slowly his knees began to buckle then he fell face down onto the floor. He was dead! The whole process took a mere twelve seconds. Casually Conrad and Iesha walked away from them but not before Conrad had dropped the rest of the deadly cigarette on the floor and crushed it with his foot, before leaving the scene of the 'crime'.

Once outside, they hailed the first taxi they saw and left the Caveau. Inside the cab Conrad whispered 'So, the cigarettes actually work.' Shaking his head slightly in disbelief, he smiled at her then in order to bring a degree of levity into the conversation he whispered, 'I always said smoking was bad for your health.' They both began to laugh softly. The driver behind his glass window could not hear them but could see them through his rear view mirror, he supposed that they were just a couple of lovers on their way home, it was perhaps as well that he was not aware that he was transporting such a deadly cargo across Paris.

After a slight lull in conversation, Conrad began to chuckle. Iesha looked at him and enquired what was amusing him. He replied, 'In the Second World War, the French resistance used to leave exploding rats in their once safe houses so that when the German soldiers raided them, they found the rats and as they kicked them or whatever they did to get rid of them, the rats exploded killing many of the soldiers.'

He was now rocking with laughter and Iesha became infected by it and joined in. In between his bursts of laughter he paused and said to her, 'Instead of exploding rats, we have killer cigarettes.' He then burst into laughter again. Iesha now understood the reason for his laughter and began to laugh again. After a while they calmed down and just sat quietly holding hands. The driver who was a typical Gallic sentimentalist had from time to time been looking in his mirror, to check on his young passengers, began to smile to himself at their obvious happiness, 'Oh to be young and in love with not a care in the world,' he said to himself languidly, then his smile changed to one of gloom and he pouted his lips, as he thought of what awaited him when he arrived home. Taking a deep breath, he shrugged his shoulders and muttered to himself "C'est la vie."

As usual, they stopped the taxi some distance from their apartment and made their way back on foot, checking every so often that they were not being followed. Satisfied that they were safe, they once again entered the building via the rear entrance.

Once inside, Conrad locked and bolted the doors, whilst Iesha went to the kitchen to make something to eat. She returned a few minutes later with a large plate of sandwiches on a tray, together with a bottle of wine and two glasses. 'That didn't take long,' he remarked.

'I made them before we left,' she replied.

They sat down and enjoyed the food. Since he had been living with Iesha, she had introduced him to some of the pleasures of wine drinking, she had explained how various wines were made and stored, prior to being bottled and marketed. Much to his surprise, he had begun to enjoy wine with his food, instead of either tea or coffee. Throughout their meal, they made no mention of the fact that earlier Conrad had killed someone in cold blood.

Having finished the sandwiches and cleared away the plates, they returned to the main room and sat quietly sipping their wine. Eventually Iesha brought up the subject of the dead man and asked how he felt, his reply surprised her. 'I feel fine, for today my country has one less terrorist to worry about and the poor people and the baby who died in the road have to some degree been avenged. Furthermore, before many more days have passed, the cell we saw in the Caveau, will cease to exist; now I know that the cigarettes work.'

'So you feel no remorsee?'

'It's remorse dear,' he answered smiling, 'and no I don't, none whatsoever, this is war and they are the enemy and we will defeat them,' he replied.

Snuggling up to him she said, 'I am glad that you are not disturbed by this evening, for I know you are a sensitive man and I thought you might be upset.' He gently squeezed her shoulder and looking at her repeated, 'Its war and we will defeat them.' They eventually went to bed and slept soundly for the next six hours.

Sometime later he went for a run and on his return he bought a newspaper. Once inside the apartment he secured the door as always then asked Iesha to check the paper and see if there was any mention of the death in the club. 'There was just a brief passage which said that a man had died of a heart attack. No name was given and no address was mentioned,' she said looking up from the paper. 'How very strange' he replied, 'obviously they want to keep themselves out of the spotlight.' They both agreed to stay away from the Caveau Club that evening and to stagger the times they did attend in future.

That evening, Iesha made a meal of steak, garlic potatoes, kidney beans in a cream sauce and diced carrots, with an excellent bottle of red wine to assist the digestion. She called out to Conrad who was taking a shower 'Food in five,'

'Ok,' he replied. When he had dried he came and sat at the table and filled the glasses then awaited her entrance. She appeared carrying two plates, which she placed at each end of the table. When he looked up from his plate to say thank you, he just stared at her. She was wearing the revealing blouse she had worn some time ago which had aroused him and caused him great embarrassment. 'You look beautiful,' he said, 'but I cannot eat this delicious food, with you looking as you do.'

She began to laugh. 'If you don't eat your, how you say, mains? You cannot have your dessert.'

'If dessert is what I think it is, can we have dessert first and mains, as you put it later?'

'No you can't you naughty boy,' she replied wagging her finger at him.

They lingered over the food and wine and then turned off the main lights, leaving only a small reading lamp for illumination. Conrad went to the old gramophone they had and put on an LP by the American artist, Andy Williams, one of Iesha's favourite singers. As the soft melodious music began to fill the room, they melted into each other's arms and moved slowly around the floor. Waves of Chanel No.5 assailed his senses as Iesha pressed herself against him. Once again as they shuffled around the floor, the most basic of all instincts gripped him and he had to adjust his clothing. In a husky voice she whispered in his ear, 'It seems 'he' needs something,' without replying, still holding her, he steered her into the bedroom, and they both sank slowly onto the bed.

Sometime later as both glowed with life and vitality, they eased away from each other, their bodies glistening after their love making. Iesha was the first to speak. 'That was wonderful,' she said 'my whole body is on fire.'

Looking at her he replied rather lamely 'Mine too.'

They lay looking at each other for a few moments then Iesha arose and went to the kitchen, pausing to restart the gramophone as she did so. She returned carrying a glass of cold white wine in each hand, giving one to Conrad she sat down next to him 'Here's to us,' she said as she touched his glass with hers.

'To us,' he replied touching her glass in return. Faintly from the main room came the strains of 'How Long Has This Been Going On' as the record began to repeat itself. Giggling like a couple of teenagers, they drained their glasses then after smoothing the crumpled bed sheets, they pulled the bedclothes over themselves and fell into a deep contented sleep, wrapped in each other's arms.

The telephone at the side of Major Harris's bed rang four times before it was answered by a sleepy voice 'Harris.'

'MJ sir, sorry about the hour, couldn't reach you before.'

'Been away,' was the reply, there was a brief pause then;

'We have a kill a guard to Ben Bella.'

Harris came alive. 'Any damage to our agent?'

'Not a scratch sir.'

'Wonderful, anything else?'

'No Sir.'

'Very well MJ keep me posted.'

'Of course Sir.' Harris replaced his receiver thus cutting the connection. He lay back on his pillow and let his thoughts race. A soft hand touched his bare chest and began to play with the hairs then it slowly began to work its way down his body. Turning his head in order to face the owner of the hand he said affectionately, 'You are insatiable,' he said smiling in the dark.

'So you keep telling me,' came the sleepy reply. Switching on a small bedside table lamp, he began to leave the bed. 'Where are you going?' she cried.

'Fear not my dear, I am just going to retrieve a bottle of Champagne from the fridge, before we resume our anatomy class.'

'Champagne, you know I cannot resist Champagne!'

'Precisely my dear,' then with a lecherous look on his face he said, 'Prepare yourself for my return.'

Chapter Eighteen

The next morning Conrad was up and out on his run before Iesha awoke. He had checked all his post boxes except one, all were empty. On his way to the last, he suddenly became aware of a cyclist he had seen previously that morning. Rounding the corner of a building which he knew had several recesses in which to conceal himself, he stepped into one and waited. The cyclist came round the corner and stopped. He looked up and down the road several times before alighting from the bicycle, pulling from his pocket a gun as he did so. Cautiously, his head turning from side to side, he surveyed the road. As he approached Conrad's hiding place, he looked to his left as a car passed by at the end of the road. Something hard struck him on the back of his head and he slumped to the ground.

When the man had recovered his senses, he discovered that he was bound hand and foot by strips of his own shirt. Facing him was a shaggy faced individual holding a gun inches away from his head. 'Your name?' Conrad demanded.

The man spat in his face. Slowly wiping away the spittle, Conrad noted that the tell tale signs of fear were slowly but surely beginning to form on the man's face. His eyes were bulging and a thin film of sweat began to break out on his forehead, also his tongue began to traverse his lips, slowly at first, then increasing as he began to realise the seriousness of his situation. He then began to shake uncontrollably. Reaching inside his tracksuit top, he removed a small box from a belt he had made himself which contained various elements of his personal armoury. The box contained two of the special syringes he had been supplied with. Removing one, he held it up in the air and depressed the plunger slightly until some of the liquid oozed out of the end of the needle. He then bent down and took the man's arm and slowly lowered the syringe, until the needle touched his skin.

'What are you doing?' the man screamed in French, spittle and mucus dribbling down his chin.

In a matter-of-fact voice Conrad replied, 'I'm going to kill you unless you tell me who you are and why you are following me,' he replied in the same language.

Almost at the point of hysteria, the man's bowels discharged their vile contents and the man in his shame and degradation blurted out, 'I am Aly-Bin-Sur, I saw you in the Caveau Club two nights ago when my friend Aly-El-Habib suddenly died. Then I saw you out running today and decided to follow you.' Whilst the man was talking, Conrad had been studying his face and although he was not one hundred per cent sure, he thought that he recognised him as one of the 'heavies' surrounding Ben Bella.

'So you saw me in the street and decided to follow me, with a gun, why?' The point of the needle pressed ever so slightly against the man's skin thus prompting him to continue.

'I thought you might be "Interpol,"' he sobbed. Looking at the poor wretch before him, fluid and matter oozing from every orifice, Conrad decided that this was a chance encounter; therefore his cover had not been compromised.

Looking at the wretch before him he pondered what to do with him. Reaching inside his tracksuit top again, he pulled out his cigarette case and lighter; opening the case he carefully removed one of the deadly cigarettes. Slowly as though savouring the thought of tasting the tobacco, he placed a cigarette in his mouth and flicked open his lighter. Whilst doing so he casually watched the reactions of his adversary. Taking two puffs of the cigarette, he raised his eyes to the skies as if in ecstasy and waited. Looking down at his hand, he noted that the first red line on the cigarette had almost been reached. His opponent was looking at the cigarette with a craving born of years of drug taking. Pointing the cigarette away from the man before him, he felt a slight tremor between his fingers as the first of the deadly projectiles was ejected. A few moments later with a silly smile on his face, Conrad offered the remains of the cigarette to Aly-Bin-Sur who in desperation readily accepted it. On the fourth deep inhalation, the second red line on the cigarette had disappeared. A few moments later the man known as Aly-Bin-Sur was dead.

Before leaving the scene of the execution, Conrad made sure that he had left no evidence on or around the body that could subsequently be traced back to him. Pocketing the man's gun, plus a belt of ammunition from around his waist, he satisfied himself that he had left no form of identification on the body, having done so he left Aly-Bin-Sur in his own filth and set off at a mile eating lope back to the apartment.

Approaching the apartment building, he stepped into the doorway of a shop and bent down to apparently attend to his shoe laces, spending more time than would be the norm, for such a small task. Finally, he straightened up and stepped out onto the pavement. Casually, he began to perform a few exercises whilst at the same time glancing up and down the road. Satisfied that there appeared to be no-one following him, either by car or on foot, he set off at a slow jog. As a security measure, he went straight past the front entrance of the apartment building, then a few hundred yards down the road, he turned right then on a road almost parallel to the one he had just travelled down. He doubled back and once again approached the building from the rear, and went inside.

Using the stairs as opposed to the lift, he bounded up them two at a time, such was his level of fitness, until he reached the fourth floor then barely panting, he softly padded down the corridor to the door of the apartment. Giving the customary identification knocks, he waited for Iesha to admit him. There was a long pause and he was about to repeat the knocks when he heard the locks and bolts click open. Easing himself inside the half open door he was confronted by Iesha draped in a white towel. 'Sorry I was so long answering,' she said, 'I was just having a shower when you knocked.'

'I was beginning to think that something had happened to you, whilst I had been away,' he replied as he locked and barred the door.

Turning to face him again she said, 'You look hot and sweaty.'

'I am,' he replied, 'have you finished showering?'

'Not quite,' she replied.

'Then in that case we can bathe together,' and with a quick tug on the towel, it fell from her body and settled around her feet.

After looking down at her nakedness, she then slowly raised her head and faced Conrad, with a look of horror on her face she said in mock surprise, 'Oh, you are a very naughty boy! What am I to do with you?'

Looking at her he replied with a 'deadpan' face and a solemn voice 'I don't know Miss, but I dare say I could think of something.' Laughing, he reached out to grab her but she dodged his outstretched hands and quickly turning, she ran to the bathroom, giggling as she did so, closely followed by Conrad.

Sometime later after they had dined, they both sat down and reviewed the current situation. Iesha produced the various pictures of the major members of the cell that were known to them. Picking up one of the pictures she turned it over and read the notes on the back, then passed it to Conrad. 'Hisham-al-Ghoul,' he said softly as he looked at the picture, 'One of Ahmed Ben Bella's right hand men, a planner, fund raiser and apparently quite ruthless. I would like to remove him from the cell,' he said with feeling.

After a long pause Iesha said, 'I thought we were supposed to get inside the OS cell, not kill them one by one.'

'That was the plan at the beginning of the mission, but later when MJ informed me that because JFK was due to visit France and meet with President Charles de Gaulle, earlier than first thought, I told him that we did not have enough time to do so. The powers that be then decided that we attempt to 'break' the cell, as opposed to get inside it. So here we are, exterminators, as opposed to infiltrators. However, the important thing is to defeat them, one way or another.'

After a couple of hours, Iesha decided that she would have to go out and do some shopping as they were getting low on provisions. Before she left, he checked her small hand gun she carried and warned her to be careful. 'Don't worry,' she said, 'I shall be fine, see you soon.'

Opening the door for her, he kissed her tenderly before she departed then locked and bolted the door before returning to the table. Once settled he sifted through the pictures again before finally picking up the one's of Ahmed Ben Bella and Hisham-al-Ghoul then in the quiet of the room he said softly 'To the pair of you beware, for I am on your trail, and your days are numbered. When you wage war on innocent men, women and especially children, you deserve no mercy. And I will afford you none. You and your kind are not fit to be called members of the human race, and I despise you, and all that you stand for.'

A couple of hours later Iesha returned with a large bag of food including two large sticks of golden brown, crispy French bread, which Conrad loved. Having put all the food away, Iesha went to the bedroom and changed into something casual, before returning to the kitchen to prepare a meal. Almost two hours later, she came into the living room carrying a large bowl of Carbonnade de Boeuf a la Flamande, with croutons, which is a traditional Flemish dish, consisting of pieces of braising steak cut into squares, onions, garlic, thyme, bay leaves, mustard, olive oil, beer and Gruyere cheese, complimented with thick pieces of warm French bread and a dish of deep yellow butter. A bottle of mature red wine completed the meal. The aromas were intoxicating.

As Iesha began to serve the food, Conrad lit the two red candles he had placed on the table then turned off the electric lights. Sitting down together, they tucked into the meal. The food of course was delicious as usual and during the course of the meal, he complimented her several times. Responding to his praises she replied in a mock servile manner, 'Thank you sir, I am happy to please you,' bowing her head slightly as she spoke. Laughing together they finished the meal then Conrad transferred the soiled dishes and cutlery to the kitchen, returning a few minutes later carrying two cups of strong dark coffee, just as Iesha liked it. As he laid the cups on the table, Iesha placed a record on the old gramophone and the plaintive voice of the 'little sparrow', Edith Piaf, France's darling began to fill the room, singing perhaps her most popular, and best remembered song "Je ne regrette rien".

As he sat with Iesha cradled in his arm, he was deeply moved by the emotion and feeling that the little singer's voice could produce, especially from such a frail body. No doubt her life of extreme hardship, suffering, abuse and failed relationships, had in some strange way blessed her with a voice so rustic, yet so unique, that it could reach out and touch millions of people the world over. No doubt many of the people that bought her records, had like her, suffered to a greater or lesser degree and were now trying to rebuild their lives after the Second World War and like her, were desperately trying to find someone or something, to hold on to, and Love!

Sadly, Edith Piaf the 'little sparrow', was denied the one basic lasting union she craved, and she died in 1963 aged 48.

The long playing record eventually came to an end and the needle scratched away monotonously at the vinyl until Conrad eased himself away from Iesha and turned it off. Returning to the couch, they sat quietly together for some time each with their own private thoughts. Conrad sat with eyes partly closed and once again silently pledged himself to do all that he could, to eradicate the warmongers and fanatics, wherever they might be that sought to destroy all that was good and wholesome in the western civilised world.

Eventually he rose from the couch, stretched himself and announced 'It's time to go to work folks.' He then went directly to the bedroom. Once inside he strapped on his belt of special 'weapons' then covered them with his usual loose fitting clothing. Although Iesha was military she did not like to see Conrad putting on his 'killing things' as she called them, and so she stayed out of the room until he had finished dressing. Once he had completed his wardrobe, he returned to the main room and waited for Iesha to change into her evening clothes.

Leaving the building by the rear service door, they slowly made their way to the main road via the back streets. Once they were well away from the vicinity of the apartment, they hailed the first taxi that came their way. The taxi came to a sudden halt just passed where they were standing. Conrad opened the door and climbed inside whilst Iesha gave the taxi driver instructions then she climbed in the back alongside him and they both settled back into the leather seats. The taxi reeked of cheap cigarette smoke and they both wrinkled their noses in disgust.

The driver was a big surly looking fellow with a large ginger moustache, stained in the middle no doubt from smoking too many cigarettes, he looked at them from time to time in his rear view mirror, but throughout the journey said nothing. The taxi eventually came to a halt outside the club and they both alighted, Iesha first then Conrad. They paid the driver and then slowly walked into the nightclub. As usual the club was full of people all enjoying themselves, but as Conrad looked around the floor he could not see any members of the Algerian cell.

Going to the bar he bought two glasses of orange juice, and returned to where he had left Iesha. Handing her a glass they both leaned back against the wall and casually surveyed the faces before them. After almost half an hour he turned to Iesha and whispered, 'I cannot see any of the cell members anywhere, can you?' In response Iesha simply shook her head and continued to scan the floor.

Just before midnight, the doors opened and a group of six men entered the club and went and sat at a table in one of the poorest illuminated parts of the building. The revellers paid no attention to them but both Conrad and Iesha knew instinctively that these were the Algerians they had been waiting for. Due to the subdued lighting and the smoke haze, plus the distance between them, it was difficult to make out their individual faces. Whispering in Iesha's ear his intentions, they slipped onto the dance floor and slowly began to make their way around the edge of the floor to where the group was seated. Eventually they approached them. As they did so, a young couple occupying a table a few yards away from the group stood up and joined the masses on the floor. Seizing the opportunity to get close, Conrad steered Iesha to the vacant table where they both sat half-facing the terrorists. Conrad ordered two more drinks from a passing waiter, and then waited.

Within a few minutes of sitting down, the heads of the terrorists began to turn and look at Iesha, which was exactly what Conrad had anticipated would happen. In doing so, he could now see their faces clearly and he immediately recognised Ahmed Ben Bella (Ben Mussa) and Hisham-al-Ghoul. The rest he had never seen before. Conrad and Iesha remained calmly in their seats holding hands, whilst a steady stream of lewd comments and laughter reached their ears from the nearby table. Looking at Iesha, Conrad smiled and squeezed her hand to reassure her and carried on talking.

Several minutes later, one of the group stood up and began to approach their table, he was a big man with a short cropped beard. As he approached, Conrad picked up one of his 'special' cigarettes which he had previously placed on the table in anticipation of such a situation and applied his lighter to it, drawing deeply on the cigarette as he did so. A moment later, he blew the smoke into the air in a nonchalant manner, apparently unconcerned by the man now only a few feet away from him.

The terrorist faced Iesha and unashamedly stared at her ample bosom then nodding his head in the direction of the dance floor, he reached out to take her hand. Iesha shook her head and turned to speak to Conrad at the same time drawing her chair closer to his. The terrorist stood there for a few moments with an evil smile on his face then looking back at his fellow scum, he made some gesture which neither Conrad nor Iesha could see, but which produced a chorus of laughter from them. He then turned to face Conrad and Iesha again. He moved forward a few paces to her new seating position and reached down to take her hand. As he did so, something touched the side of his neck, instinctively he put up his hand as if to ward off a fly and rubbed the offending spot. As he did so, Conrad slowly raised himself from his chair, said a few words in French to the terrorist and then pushed him with both hands and sent him reeling into the table he had recently vacated.

Taken by surprise by the strength of Conrad's push, the terrorist fell amongst his fellow conspirators and slumped to the floor amidst a tirade of abuse from those around the table who had been expecting some good 'sport'. When they eventually sorted themselves out and sat down again, they discovered to their dismay that their comrade was dead.

A few yards away from the terrorists table, Iesha and Conrad shuffled around the edge of the dance floor, apparently unaware of what had happened a few moments earlier, however they noticed that as soon as the terrorists discovered what had happened, both Ben Mussa and Hisham-al-Ghoul immediately got up and left. Surprisingly, not one of the revellers near the scene seemed to have noticed the disturbance.

The music stopped and they went back to their seats. As they approached their table, two of the three terrorists were supporting the dead one and slowly making their way to the exit, whilst the third one walked just in front of them, so close in fact that he almost blocked any sight of the dead man. To all intents and purposes the man appeared to be drunk and they were escorting him from the building. As they drew level with Conrad, the one in front glared at him and muttered something which Conrad could not understand, however he presumed it was not complimentary.

Before they passed-by, Conrad said in French to them 'What's the matter with him he looks dead on his feet?' As he did so, he slipped something into the pocket of the man nearest to him supporting the body then he returned to his seat at the table and sat down. Reaching out to the ash tray, he retrieved the unused half of the cigarette and carefully replaced it in his case with the rest, then casually leaned back in his chair and watched them leave, humming to himself Ave Maria.

'What did you put in the pocket of the man?' Iesha asked.

Looking at her he replied, 'My word you are observant, it was a little homemade device which with a bit of luck should activate in about five minutes time, which means we should leave now,' he said looking at his watch, before the Police arrive. With that he got up pulling Iesha gently to her feet as he did so. They reached the exit just in time to see the 'dead drunk' being bundled into the back of a black Citroen car then the driver put the car in gear and set off down the almost deserted road. The car had only travelled about a hundred yards when there was a brilliant flash, closely followed by a loud explosion and the car disappeared in a ball of flames and smoke. Pieces of debris flew everywhere, a mushroom of dense black smoke rose above the inferno that was once a car into the cold early morning Parisian air.

Watching the funeral pyre Conrad whispered to Iesha, 'I just hope that Ahmed Ben Bella and Hisham-al-Ghoul were in the car along with their bodyguards. Now it's time to go before the Police arrive and start asking questions.'

Unfortunately Conrad's hope was not to be granted, for the two leaders had left the club a few moments previously in another car, however the two terrorist leaders saw what had happened to the following vehicle through their rear view mirrors and windows. With a look of incredulity on their faces, they watched as the fireball quickly receded as they sped away.

With a shaky voice tinged with a touch of fear of the unknown, Hisham-al-Ghoul said to his leader 'What is happening, we have just lost four of our best men this evening?' For an answer he received only a blank stare, and a barked order to the driver of the car to drive faster.

As a veteran of many military conflicts, Ben Mussa had felt the cold hand of fear touch his body many times in the past. Normally he knew the source of that fear, usually the enemy he was facing and could therefore do something about it. However, the unknown enemy, which was his perception of the situation, was an entirely different matter and this greatly concerned him.

Having quickly walked away from the explosion, Iesha and Conrad hailed the first taxi they saw and went back to the apartment without saying a word. Once again they took the usual precautions before entering the building then once inside they settled down on the couch, each with a glass of wine and pondered on the events of the evening. 'So what did you put in his pocket?' Iesha asked eventually.

'Just a small homemade device I was shown how to make during my three weeks crash course in counter espionage back in England.'

'But where did you get the materials to make what must have been a bomb?'

'You can buy them on any street, in any town, if you know what to ask for,' he replied.

Conrad declined to answer any questions regarding the device and they lapsed into a period of quiet which was eventually broken by Iesha when she said, 'I have been thinking about the past few weeks and I think you should change your appearance now for with your long beard you do stand out in a crowd, especkily when you attack them.'

Laughing at her mispronunciation of especially, he hugged her and was about to speak when she said, 'Why are you laughing?'

He explained why and they both began to laugh. When they had finished Conrad said to her, 'I wish I could speak French half as well as you speak English.'

'You are getting better,' she said reassuringly. 'Yes but slowly, and I don't have much time,' he replied.

After a while Conrad asked, 'What exactly did you have in mind when you said I should change my appearance?' She paused for a while before answering then replied, 'To begin with I think you should shave of your beard and then change your clothes for something more Parisian.'

'The beard I can understand, but the clothes might be a problem bearing in mind that I have to carry certain items underneath them.'

'I will find you something,' she said enthusiastically. Finishing her wine she said softly looking up at him 'Why don't you shave now, I will help you.'

Looking somewhat puzzled he asked 'Why the hurry?'

Lowering her eyes she replied demurely 'Well, two reasons; one it tickles when we make love, which we haven't done for a while and I want you, secondly, tomorrow's newspapers will I am sure have some description of a man with a large beard who knocked over someone in the Caveau Club just a few minutes before the car blew up.' Conrad was about to speak when she put her finger over his lips and continued, 'And I think the taxi driver that took us to the club will recognise your description, because of your beard.'

Removing her finger she looked at him. With a smile he said, 'The driver wasn't looking at my beard, he was looking at your bosom, however, lead me to the shearing room Mademoiselle and perform your Delilah act.'

An hour later, Conrad emerged from the bathroom patting his face with some of Iesha's scented oils, his face somewhat reddened by the constant application of the razor to his skin. Looking at himself in the mirror, he was surprised to see the difference in his appearance; he lingered for a moment then walked into the bedroom. He stopped just inside the doorway as he surveyed her. She was sitting in the middle of the bed holding a hair brush in her hand. She had apparently just finished brushing her long lustrous locks for they cascaded way down past her shoulders, and shone like thin fibres of amber and bronze in the half light of the room.

She was wearing a see-through negligee which highlighted every curve of her stunning body and the sensuous fragrance of Chanel No.5 filled his nostrils. As he looked at her, desire swept through him and his pulse began to race, throwing the brush onto a nearby bedside chair she beckoned him several times with her index finger seeing how aroused he was becoming. Stumbling to the bed, he turned off the small table lamp and removed his pyjama trousers. As soon as his body touched the bed, her mouth sought his and they melted together as one. His manhood was as rigid as a bar of steel inside her soft pliant body; so intense was their desire for each other that the moment of high passion was quickly upon them and both cried out time and again, as the pure ecstasy of their love making wracked their bodies.

Afterwards when the fires of passion had died down they lay exhausted in each other's arms barely able to move; their bodies coated in sweat. Eventually Iesha rose to leave the bed.

'Where are you going?' he asked dreamily.

'To get a drink,' she replied huskily, 'Would you like one?'

'Please.' Leaving the bed she slowly walked to the door then stopped and turned to look at him. Her large breasts heaved with pride and contentment as she fleetingly ran her fingers across her tummy, knowing that inside her was his child, their child. Conrad looked at her and returned her smile.

When she returned a few moments later with two glasses of cold Chablis, Conrad was sitting up with his head against the headrest and watched her enter the room, her hair which previously had been neatly groomed was now dishevelled and fell about her shoulders in a random manner which he thought made her look even more beautiful.

The next morning whilst out on his run, he checked his post boxes and was pleased to discover that he had some mail; a letter and a small parcel. Putting them inside his waterproof top, he set off on the return journey, stopping on the way to buy some newspapers.

Back at the apartment, he immediately took a shower then had a breakfast of cereal, scrambled eggs, bacon, toast and coffee then he settled down on the couch and opened his mail. The letter was from MJ and contained a brief note confirming the date of the visit of the President of the United States to S.H.A.P.E. Headquarters. It also informed him that in the parcel was something rather special that the 'boffins' back in the UK had produced, which may be of use, but should be handled with extreme care. It ended with "Good hunting",

MJ

Intrigued by the letter, he opened the parcel carefully; there was a note inside the outer cover which read: The small 'eggs' contain a mixture of the aluminium salts of napathenic acid and palmitic acid with a percussion detonator; it ignites easily, and burns at temperatures up to 1000°C. It is particularly useful against humans. It is commonly known as NAPALM. The note went on to explain how to store the 'eggs' and gave some ideas on how they could be used.

Conrad's hands had gone clammy as he thought how he had put the parcel inside his shirt, not knowing what it contained and had run three miles with it jostling against his chest. When he had finally removed all the outer packaging, there in front of him sat six silver 'eggs' on a bed of cotton wool and shock absorbent paper. At the sight of the packaging, he exhaled in relief then went to the kitchen and wiped his hands and face.

Returning to the 'eggs', he carefully picked one up and examined it, having done so he was surprised to find how light it was, no heavier in fact than an ordinary hen's egg. Returning the 'egg' to its 'nest', he read the rest of the note. When he had finished he leaned back on the couch and smiled to himself.

What an arsenal the boffins had now produced for him, for each 'egg', if 'laid' correctly, had the potential to destroy a conventional building of some size, or any other object for that matter due to the intensity of the heat it produced. Elated by his latest weapon, he carefully repackaged the 'eggs' and placed them on top of a tall wardrobe in the bedroom then, as a precaution he placed a note in front of them saying 'Do Not Touch', just in case Iesha came across them when cleaning.

The rest of the day passed by uneventfully, Iesha who had been out shopping most of the day, made a dinner of veal with roast potatoes with garlic, French beans, slivers of carrot in a cream sauce, warm French bread with butter, and a bottle of red wine.

They had decided not to go to the Caveau Club that evening in order not to create a regular pattern, so when they had cleared away all the dishes they retired for the night. No high passion this evening, just a slow lasting loving and then they fell asleep in each other's arms.

Once again the telephone shrieked out in Major Harris's bedroom and as usual he answered it with 'Harris,' there was a pause then 'Sorry for the late hour Major but I could not raise you sooner and I have some important news for you.'

'You don't have to keep apologising MJ, what news?'

'Well sir, it would seem that last evening CD eliminated four of Ben Bella's top men, who are, sorry, were, part of the Paris cell.'

'Good God,' exclaimed Harris, 'how did he manage to do that? Is he all right?'

'Well sir, the exact details are a little patchy, but it seems that there was an incident in the Caveau Club which involved our agent and a group of six men, including Ahmed Ben Bella and Hisham-al-Ghoul. At one point, someone from the group tried to force a woman who was sitting with a man with a large beard onto the dance floor. The man pushed the intruder and he fell back onto the table he had just left. After a couple of minutes two of the group left closely followed by the rest, who were dragging one man as though he was drunk. They got into a car and drove off watched by a man with a large beard and a woman. A few moments later the car blew up, there were no survivors, after a few moments the man and woman walked away, they did not re-enter the club.'

There followed a long pause before the Major spoke. 'Well MJ it seems that our man has surpassed our wildest expectations, how many has he eliminated now?'

'Six Sir and all close to the centre of the cell. The 'elite' must be wondering what has happened.'

'Absolutely,' replied Harris.

Another pause then, 'However a word of caution for our man, the enemy will, I would suspect be having a war council meeting right now and will if I understand them, be putting agents out on the streets looking for our people. So from now on, step up the security, draw down further resources if necessary and inform CD to be on high alert and above all, remember that I have another mission for you both, which is imminent.'

'Very good sir,' another pause then, 'Well done MJ' and before he could respond the telephone went dead.

For several minutes, Marcus stood with the telephone in his hand and pondered on the conversation he had just had with his superior. Slowly he replaced the telephone on its cradle and stood looking at the wall of the telephone booth. 'Well done MJ' he mimicked the Major. 'Well done! I've done sod all, its CD risking his life out there.' Opening the door of the booth, he walked around the corner of the street and entered the first pub he could find.

Striding up to the bar, he hoped that this evening he did not encounter someone with a big mouth spouting about human rights, the IRA or whatever, for he was now rapidly descending into what the professional killing soldiers call. "the danger zone". This is a period when someone very close to a fellow comrade, in a high risk situation, is being exposed to the ultimate sanction and they are unable to assist them personally.

Taking his drink to a far corner of the room, he sat down and raised the glass to his lips. In one gulp he half drained the glass before placing it on the table. Looking at the glass with unseeing eyes he whispered, 'For god's sake Conrad, take care, I'll be with you as soon as I can.' Picking up his glass he downed the rest of its contents. A few moments later he returned to the bar and purchased another drink. Returning to his seat he sat down and placed the glass on the table in front of him and stared at it.

His mind went back to the three weeks they had spent together in the woods surrounding Woking, the lectures, the physical training, the night exercises and especially the way Conrad had defeated him and RJ in the art of stealth and survival. His face slowly eased into a broad smile as he remembered the way Conrad had brought RJ, himself an accomplished exponent in the art of self defence, to his knees, with almost casual ease. He sat looking at his drink as though it was some magic looking glass which would show him where to go and what to do, but of course it didn't. After peering at the glass for several minutes, he suddenly stood up, straightened his clothes and walked purposefully from the pub, leaving the drink untouched.

Having left the warmth and comfort of the public house, he pulled up the collar of his coat against the wind and sleet which had just started to fall and strode down the pavement in search of a taxi. Almost immediately he spotted one across the road and waved it down. Once alongside him the cabbie said cheerfully 'Where you going guv?' At the same time dropping down the charging arm on his fare machine as he did so.

Once inside the cab Marcus said simply 'Heathrow Airport cabbie, as fast as you can.'

The morning after the car incident, Conrad was up and out on his run as usual, the air was crisp and invigorating. When he called at his various 'post boxes', he was surprised to find mail in each one and in each case it was a simple brown envelope. Stuffing them inside his shirt he made his way back to the apartment. Once inside he went through his usual routine and then sat down and opened the letters. Each one had the same message:

"Intelligence suggests that you should now adopt the highest alert status possible... very well done." MJ

Sipping a cup of coffee, he read the messages several times and each time he thought of Iesha. By shaving off his beard, he now looked an entirely different person, but try as he may, he could not think of any obvious way in which he could change her appearance. The answer of course was simplicity itself to him; leave Iesha behind on all future missions; however he knew that she would not accept that proposition. Rising from the couch, he went to the gramophone and placed on the turntable a long playing record of the great Italian tenor Enrico Caruso. Amongst the selection of wonderful songs the great man performed was of course his favourite, Charles Francois Gounod's Ave Maria. Settling back on the couch, he closed his eyes and let the magnificent music of the master composer and the voice of the maestro wash over him; bathing and soothing his very soul with their supreme talents.

As the record progressed, small droplets of moisture gathered at the corners of his eyes and began to slowly trickle down his face, so moved was he by the music.

For the next hour, 2379 Lance Corporal Conrad Davenport (Acting Captain Special Duties) National Serviceman, Bridlington, East Yorkshire, England became a human being once more, instead of a legalised killing machine.

A loud knock on the door brought him back to reality.

Rising slowly, he turned off the gramophone then wiping the tears from his eyes, he went to the door and gave an answering signal of, Knock, knock-knock, then waited, receiving the correct response, he opened the door and Iesha entered carrying two large carrier bags.

Once inside he locked and secured the door then turned to face her. 'You look pleased with yourself,' he said kissing her lightly on her cheek.

'I have surprise for you,' she replied 'wait here while I go and change,' with that she turned and carrying the bags went into the bedroom, closing the door behind her as she did so.

Returning to the couch he sat down and wondered what she was doing.

Fifteen minutes later she called out 'Close your eyes.' He did so and waited, 'Open,' he opened his eyes and was amazed at what he saw.

'Who are you?' he said in amazement, for in front of him stood a long haired blonde woman with a large puffy face and a large mole on her right cheek.

'You like?'

'What have you done?' he said laughing.

'Well I thought that after what has happened the OAS will have people out on the streets looking for a man with a large beard and a woman with long dark hair, so as you have changed your appearance, I thought I should do same.'

'But what have you done to your face?'

'You mean my cheeks,' she replied, he nodded his head. 'Face pads,' she replied and then putting her fingers inside her mouth, she removed one.

'That's amazing,' he said, 'you look a different person.'

'Good, that's what I hoped you would say, now we can go out this evening and continue our work.'

'Wouldn't you prefer to stay here where you are safe?'

She slowly crossed the few feet which separated them then looking up to him she placed her arms around his neck before replying, 'Yes, I would, but we are military people, not civilians and we cannot please ourselves, you know that.'

'Just thought I'd ask you.'

'I know,' she replied. She lowered her head to his chest and whispered something.

'What did you say?'

'I said could we not go to bed for a few hours?'

Conrad eased her away from him and looked at her 'But it's only two o'clock,' he replied.

'So you have something better to do this afternoon?'

'Indeed I don't,' he replied. With that they disappeared into the bedroom.

They emerged a couple of hours later and Iesha immediately went into the kitchen and began to prepare a meal for them both. After they had dined, they sat on the couch each with a cup of coffee in their hands and listened to a record of Sidney Bechet and his band which had been recorded at the Caveau Club only a few months previously.

As the music finished, the needle began to scratch in the grooves of the vinyl disk, almost immediately Conrad arose and went to the gramophone. Removing the record from the turntable, he returned it to its glossy dust cover, switched off the machine then returned to the couch and sat down looking at Iesha as he did so.

'I've been thinking,' he said, 'instead of taking taxis to the club and risk being identified by even more people; it would make good sense if you drove us to the club in your car.'

Iesha thought for a moment before answering, when she did, she replied 'OK providing that I don't have to wait outside while you go in alone.'

Conrad looked mortified at this suggestion and with a straight face replied 'How could you think such a thing, the thought never crossed my mind?' Of course he was lying, the idea of Iesha driving meant that should a desperate situation arise, she at least might be able to exit the scene quickly, without having to seek out a taxi, which might mean the difference between life and death. However, he was surprised that she was so attuned to his way of thinking.

They went to the club and spent four hours wandering around peering in every dark corner looking for some evidence of the Algerians, but could find no trace of them. Finally they left. They returned the next two evenings at different times, but each visit proved to be fruitless.

At 3.00am they decided to leave and return to the apartment. On the way home in the car, Iesha informed Conrad that 'Whilst talking to some of the regulars at the club, on the pretext of looking for 'clients', no-one seemed to remember the events of a few nights ago when a car blew up in the road and even the doorman did not remember the event. It was as though nothing had happened.'

'That's very strange,' he replied. 'Someone has obviously gone to a lot of trouble, and spent a lot of money to 'clean' things up, the point is of course, just how many people are involved?'

Arriving back at the apartment, Conrad made them each a cup of coffee and whilst they sipped the hot liquid they discussed the situation at some length without coming to any positive conclusions. Somewhat dispirited they returned the cups to the kitchen, put out the lights and retired to the bedroom.

The next day Conrad left the apartment and set off on his run, at each of his 'post boxes' he had mail. Back at the apartment he went through his pre-breakfast routine whilst Iesha prepared him some food. Having showered, he entered the living room pink and warm and glowing with health. Iesha entered carrying a large plate of bacon, eggs, sausage, toast and coffee.

As he tucked into the food, her eyes watched his every movement so much so that he paused and looked at her. 'Why are you staring at me?' he asked.

'I was thinking how much I love my man and how lucky I am to have you.'

There was a pause before he replied 'Yes woman. you are lucky to have me and I am pleased that you realise how lucky you are.' Raising the towel she was holding above her head he continued, 'On the other hand, I also realise just how lucky I am to have you, now get into the bedroom, and prepare yourself.'

Breaking into laughter, she responded meekly 'Yes master, but please, be gentle.' With that she pouted her lips and wiggled her way to the bedroom. Pausing in the door way, she turned to face him and began to undo each button on the front of her blouse, very slowly. When the last one had been released, she eased the garment from her shoulders and let it fall to the floor, there was no other fabric protecting her modesty. In slow motion she entered the room then half turning she began to close the door. When it was only a few inches ajar, her right index finger slowly beckoned him to join her.

Well and truly aroused, he rose from the table and slipped into the bathroom. Quickly he washed his hands and face and brushed his teeth before splashing on some deodorant. Then he rushed to the bedroom still aroused and quietly closed the door behind him. Later that morning, they emerged from their 'love nest' and settled down on the couch, each with a cup of coffee to hand. After a few sips, they began to open the mail which Conrad had previously retrieved and which they, at the height of their passion, had temporally forgotten about. Each letter contained the same information:

"Intelligence reports suggest that the Cell has now moved to the Red Light district of Pigalle, near to the Moulin Rouge, an area of small bars and dark narrow alley ways. From now on you MUST adopt extreme caution in everything you do. Intelligence also advises that you have to date dealt the Cell a severe blow to their planned activities, so much so that ABB has returned to Algeria, leaving HAG in charge of operations in Paris. Major Harris sends you his personal good wishes for your work to date.
Congratulations!"
MJ

'Why do they gather in crowded places?' Iesha asked.

'Safety in numbers I would imagine,' Conrad replied.

They fell silent for a few moments then Conrad asked, 'Where's Pigalle? Is it near here, can we drive there?'

In order to answer his questions, Iesha arose and went to a cupboard, returning with a map of Paris. Spreading the map on the table she pointed out the location of the Moulin Rouge with her finger, 'It is a bad area, lots of people go missing in Pigalle, usually they are found floating in the Seine, you will have to be very careful, my love.' Conrad said nothing, but he noted the concern on her face.

'What's the Moulin Rouge?' he asked eventually.

'It's a traditional French cabaret, the words mean 'Red Mill,' it was built in 1889 by Joseph Oller who already owned another well-known night club called the Olympia. It's famous for the large imitation Red Windmill on its roof. The Moulin Rouge is a symbol of French Culture and with its

Bohemian past, it has had a marked influence on Western Europe. It is situated in the Red Light district of Pigalle, on the Boulevard de Clichy, in the 18th, arrondissement, near Monmartre, which was frequented by artists in the 19th century.'

Conrad sat back in amazement at her spontaneous and detailed response to his question. When he replied, there was genuine admiration in his voice, 'Iesha, you never cease to amaze me; that was most impressive, I didn't realise that you were so well informed, have you been studying the history of the Pigalle area?' In response, she just gave him a brief smile and nodded her head.

There followed a long period when neither spoke. Finally Conrad broke the silence. 'After we have dined, I suggest we go and reconnoitre the area, before we actually go into any of the bars and clubs, for we need to know the area just in case we have to make a quick exit. Don't you agree?' Without saying a word, Iesha simply nodded her head in agreement then got up from the couch, went to the kitchen and began to prepare their evening meal. She was clearly very concerned regarding the next stage of their operation against the OAS.

The meal that evening was a sombre affair, Iesha was withdrawn and hardly spoke, she merely picked at her food and her wine glass remained untouched. Conrad was his normal self and ate with great gusto and by the time he had finished his meal, he had drained two glasses of red wine.

Finally, he asked what was troubling her, slowly she raised her head from staring at her plate of almost untouched food and with moisture clearly beginning to show in the corners of her eyes replied, 'I have a bad feeling about going into the heart of Pigalle, it is a bad place, especially at night.'

Conrad reached out and placed his hand over hers and squeezed it gently. 'I understand your feelings,' he said softly, 'but I have to go, you on the other hand do not, so why don't you stay here where you are safe?'

Shaking her head she replied, 'No, I want to be with you in case you need some help, and besides, I wouldn't like to be here alone.'

They held hands for a few moments more and looked at each other then Conrad stood up and gently withdrew his hand, at the same time he reached into his pocket with his other hand and slowly withdrew his handkerchief. Reaching out, he dabbed the corners of her eyes with the clean white linen, 'Don't cry darling,' he said tenderly, 'we shall prevail and now it's time to prepare ourselves for this evening.' Returning the handkerchief to his pocket, he turned away and went into the bedroom.

Once inside the bedroom, he collected his small arsenal of weapons from around the room and laid them on the bed. Selecting the items he thought he might require that evening, he returned the rest to their hiding places then he secreted the chosen items about his body. Finally, he checked the cigarette case and its deadly contents then added three more of the lethal tobacco sticks. Then with the case full, he carefully closed the lid.

Satisfied at last that he had all he needed for the evening's work, he went back into the living room. Iesha had stopped crying by now but still looked distressed; however she put on a brave smile and entered the bedroom without saying a word.

An hour later they exited the apartment via the rear stairs and slipped quietly into the dark street. They walked the couple of hundred yards to where Iesha had parked her car then after a cursory check, climbed inside and Iesha turned the ignition key. After a few coughs and splutters, the little car's engine came to life, belching out a cloud of blue smoke as it did so. After twisting and shaking the gear lever into position, the little car suddenly shot forward, pushing Conrad back in his seat as it did so. 'Careful old girl or we shall all go up in smoke' he said laughing.

They arrived in Pigalle forty minutes later and slowly toured around the various seedy streets, Conrad making notes in his mind as they did so. They slowly turned a corner and were suddenly confronted by a blaze of multicoloured flashing lights, which almost turned the darkness into daylight and there before them stood the world famous Moulin Rouge, in all its brash, garish splendour.

They stopped the car at the side of the road and gazed at this remarkable edifice which had been created to delight all with an interest in the human form. Suddenly Conrad grabbed Iesha and pressed his lips to her cheek, whispering as he did so, 'For God's sake act like a pro, and look down quickly, OAS heavies coming our way.' As he spoke, he fumbled under his baggy coat and removed his gun. With it held securely between his knees, he expertly screwed on the silencer with his left hand and then pretended to apparently fondle the woman.

A few moments' later, two men approached the car, one on either side and peered inside. Conrad's pulse began to quicken as he sensed danger. The one on Conrad's side knocked on the window and gestured to him to open it, the other did the same. Conrad ignored him and went back to apparently nuzzle Iesha's cheek. 'We have trouble I think, be ready to duck,' he whispered.

The man on Conrad's side now banged on the window, slowly Conrad turned away from Iesha and opened the window slightly, 'What do you want?' he said in French. Leering at him, the man responded in French with a strong Algerian accent 'We've been looking for a woman for some time but they are too expensive so we will share yours.' With that, he pulled out a knife. Iesha screamed as her window disintegrated under the blow from a gun and a hand reached inside the car and grabbed her hair. The hairpiece came away in the man's hand and for a fleeting moment, he looked at her in amazement, then he shouted to his companion 'I swear it's the bitch from the Caveau club,' holding aloft the blonde wig. Those were his last words, Conrad shot him in the throat then in the blink of an eye, he turned and did the same to the other one through the partly open window. So efficient was the silencer that the only discernable sound was a soft 'phutt', as each bullet left the barrel of the gun. 'Start the car whilst I get your wig.' Conrad hissed, opening the car door as he did so. Quickly frisking the man he had just shot, he crammed his possessions into his pockets then ran round to the other side of the car and searched the other man. As he did so the car's engine spluttered into life, Iesha kept it revving as Conrad dragged the men into the gutter. Having completed his task, he looked around him and was pleased to note that of the few people on the street, no one seemed to have noticed what had happened. Jumping into the passenger seat he shouted, 'GO, GO,' and slammed the car door. The car eased forward slowly gathering speed, so as not to draw attention to it. As soon as it turned the corner and left the Moulin Rouge behind, Iesha pressed her foot down on the accelerator and quickly increased her speed. From the shadows of one of the shop doorways there emerged a bundle of rags masquerading as a human being who starred after the disappearing car for a moment or two. Mouthing something to himself, he then reached into one of his coat pockets and pulled out a bottle of cheap wine and took a long swallow. Shaking his head as the course fluid hit his throat, he shuffled over to the two bodies and looked down at them. Cautiously he looked around but no one had yet noticed the two bodies lying at the side of the road. Bending down he quickly began to go through their pockets. When he had finished, he stood up and cursed to himself. 'Merde, merde, not a thing of value on them.' As if to console himself, he pulled out the bottle from his coat and took another drink, kicking the nearest body in his frustration.

The bottle went spinning from his hand and shattered on the floor, seemingly from nowhere, three men with hard, swarthy, angular bearded faces, suddenly appeared and surrounded him; each held a gun in their hands. The tallest of the three men came forward and put the barrel of his gun under the chin of the wretch then took a step back and wrinkled his nose in disgust at the smell which emanated from him. Bending down he looked closely at the bodies on the floor, uttering a string of strange sounding expletives, he suddenly straightened up and lashed the poor wretch across the face with the barrel of his gun, drawing both blood and a gasp of pain from the unfortunate beggar.

'You have killed our brothers,' the tall man shrieked and again hit the beggar across the face with his gun. The poor beggar sagged at the knees and slowly slumped to the floor, unconscious. Turning to one of the others he said, 'Call the car and when it arrives put this swine in the boot.'

The one he addressed came to attention immediately; then from a pocket in his coat produced a two-way radio and called someone. 'The car will be here in a few moments brother Hisham,' he announced. Hisham-al-Ghoul did not respond, he simply looked at the beggar on the floor in front of him and then spat on him.

At the entrance of the Moulin Rouge, one of the doormen raised a hand to his head and pressed something to his eye, after a few moments his hand dropped down to his side again and he resumed his statue like pose and looked to his front.

A car with dipped lights slowly pulled into the side of the road, the driver got out and opened the boot, Hisham-al-Ghoul's two henchmen bundled the poor beggar into it, then the driver closed and locked it before returning to the driver's seat. The car pulled away from the kerb and approached the Moulin Rouge before turning left as Conrad and Iesha had done previously. Once again, the doorman raised his hand to his head and pressed something to his eye.

After a few moments, he slowly lowered his hand to his side as he watched the car disappear into the distance.

Half an hour later, two seemingly drunken men approached the entrance and tried to gain admission but were turned away by the doorman. A trained eye watching the scene may have noticed that the doorman passed something to one of the men before they staggered back onto the street.

A hundred yards or so down the road, the two drunkards suddenly became sober and ran into a small alleyway where a car waited. They jumped inside and the driver immediately started the engine then quickly engaging the first gear he set the car in motion. Driving as fast as he could down the narrow streets, they eventually left Pigalle behind and headed for the Auto Route out of Paris.

The car with Hisham-al-Ghoul and his henchmen came to a halt outside what appeared to be a disused building a few hundred yards off the Boulevard de Clichy. Alighting, the driver and Hisham-al-Ghoul went to the door and let themselves in.

Turning on the light, revealed a Spartan brick building approximately fifty feet by twenty, with rough wooden tables and chairs down each of the two longer sides. Selecting a table in the middle of the room, the leader sat down then slowly reached inside his jacket pocket and extracted his silver cigarette case. After some deliberation, he chose a black Russian Sobraine with a gold tip from the selection the case contained then with his left hand, he took out his cigarette lighter, a stainless steel American 'Zippo' (one of the best in the world) and slowly began to raise it to his lips. With a casual flick of the fingers of his right hand, he snapped open the top of the lighter and as if by magic, the lighter's special wick burst into life (with this lighter the Americans have made lighting a cigarette with a 'Zippo' an 'art form'). With his cigarette drawing nicely, he exhaled a cloud of pungent smoke into the room then settled himself in the chair and waited for the rest of his men to bring in the 'assassin'. The driver took up a position behind him standing with his arms crossed over his chest in an intimidating manner.

A few moments later, the other members of the group of terrorists entered the building dragging the stinking beggar with them. They dumped him in a chair opposite their leader then took a pace back, wrinkling their noses as they did so. The dried blood on his face added to his wretched appearance.

For a few moments, Hisham-al-Ghoul sat looking at the man before him then demanded, 'Where's the gun which killed our brothers?'

'We found no weapons on him brother Hisham, only lice,' replied one of the bodyguards.

With a look of contempt on his face for the man before him, the terrorist leader demanded 'Who do you work for, why did you kill our two brothers and what did you do with the gun?"

The poor beggar looked back across the table at the man before him and the words tumbled out of his mouth, 'What are you talking about Monsieur, I work for no-one, I don't have a gun, I have killed no-one, I am just a poor beggar living off the streets.'

Hisham-al-Ghoul nodded his head slightly and one of the men behind the beggar struck him on the side of the head with the palm of his hand. The beggar cried out in pain and almost fell out of the chair. With his ears ringing, he attempted to put a hand to his head, but it was knocked aside by the guard who had delivered the blow.

'I will ask you again you piece of merde, just in case you have suddenly remembered.' He repeated the questions and received the same answer, however just before the guard was going to strike him again, his mind suddenly became crystal clear and he remembered how he had discovered the bodies, then he began to babble out the story in a torrent of words.

'Monsieur I tell you the truth, there was a small car at the side of the road with two people in it, two men approached the car one on each side of it then something happened and one of the doors opened and a man got out, he ran round to the driver's side and picked something up off the road and then bent down and dragged something into the kerb. Then the car drove away, slowly at first then faster. I saw all this from a shop doorway and when the car had gone, I crossed the road to see what had happened and I found the two bodies. I bent down to search them in case they had money or goods on them but they had nothing then I realised that the man in the car must have killed them and took all their valuables, for when I did search them, they had nothing on them. I swear that's all I know Monsieur.' The beggar was by now shaking violently, both from fright and a lack of alcohol.

Hisham-al-Ghoul looked at him and recognised the signs of a confirmed alcoholic then he barked out an order and one the guards left the room, he returned a few moments later with a bottle of spirit. At a nod from his leader, the man put the bottle on the table in front of the beggar. The man lifted his tear-stained grimy face and saw the bottle of 'comfort' before him. With his hands shaking he reached out and took hold of the bottle then after struggling to open it, he took a long swallow of the liquid, before replacing it on the table.

'Tell me, what is your name?' purred Hisham-al-Ghoul.

'Jacques Chabrac,' replied the beggar.

'Well Jacques, I believe that you have told me the truth about my men and so no-one in this room will harm you.' Jacques's face lit-up and he reached for the bottle again. After he had taken another long swallow, Hisham gently pushed the bottle to one side and said softly, 'Now Jacques, tell me all you can remember about the car.' For the next thirty minutes he coaxed and extracted all the information he could from the poor wretch then standing up he stretched and said, 'It's been a long day Jacques and I have things to do, so my men will take you back to Pigalle where we found you.' With that, he took out his wallet and selected a few new franc banknotes which he passed to Jacques.

The man's face brightened at the sight of the money and he quickly calculated how many bottles he could buy. 'Thank you Monsieur, you are most kind.'

Hisham brushed aside his thanks then indicated to his men that it was time to take the man back. As they got to the door, Hisham called out something in Algerian to one of the guards who turned and replied in the same language. Then they all left the building.

They took a different route back to Pigalle and drove with the windows down in order to combat the smell of Jacques; they spoke in Algerian all the time.

After twenty minutes or so, the car pulled up at a piece of waste ground and the two guards got out and began to walk towards a wall. 'You want a piss?' one of them called out.

Jacques got out of the car and began to stumble towards them in the dark. In his semi-drunken state he stumbled and fell, banging his head on something hard. Cursing he got to his feet and looked around him, but in the darkness he could not see them. Putting his hand to his head, he felt blood on his face. 'Where are you?' he called out.

'Here, behind you, you filthy pig.' As he turned to face the voice, what was left of the unfortunate Jacques Chabrac's alcohol soaked brain suddenly exploded, as a bullet from a 1935 Army issue Mauser 99 entered his head killing him instantly.

'Don't forget the money,' one of the guards called out.

'I have it,' replied the other, 'now let's get away from here.'

Back at the apartment, Conrad and Iesha looked at the items Conrad had taken from the two terrorists; a couple of Mauser 9mm, some five hundred French Francs, plus two identity cards which proved that they were members of the OS. The names on the identity cards were Mohamed-el-Musa and Mohamed Ait Mustaffa, both Sergeants. 'Not much evidence here,' he said looking at Iesha, 'do they ring any bells with you?'

'No,' she replied shaking her head. 'But don't they look evil?'

Looking at the pictures again, Conrad simply nodded his head in agreement. Then in an attempt to lighten the sombre mood which had pervaded the room, he added with a smile on his face, 'One could be excused for saying that that they look 'dead ugly'.'

To his surprise, Iesha jumped from the couch and snapped at him, 'How can you joke about something as serious as this, you don't seem to realise that we are dealing with evil, dangerous men who will stop at nothing in order to achieve their objectives. Have you forgotten the poor family blown to pieces in the street whilst we sat drinking coffee?'

Conrad got up and went to console her but she turned away from him and began to sob, softly at first, then uncontrollably. With her shoulders heaving she made her way to the bedroom, entered and then closed the door behind her, leaving Conrad staring at the door.

An hour later she re-emerged and went straight to the bathroom and washed her face, then finding no-one in the living room, she went into the kitchen and found Conrad making breakfast. 'How can you think of food at a time like this?' she asked.

'One has to eat,' he replied softly. Looking at her, he could see the strain she was under and again suggested that she abandon the mission, but again she refused.

Having breakfasted on fruit juice, omelettes, toast and coffee they retired for a few hours' sleep. As soon as they climbed into bed, Iesha clung to him like a frightened child, until she went to asleep. Conrad lay with his eyes open and pondered the day's events before he too fell into a deep sleep.

Some miles away at S.H.A.P.E. Headquarters on the outskirts of Paris, in a photographic darkroom Lieutenants Jackman and Mullon (the drunks in Pigalle) removed the film from a camera and passed it to an American technician to develop. A short time later they examined the pictures which the doorman (an undercover agent) had taken, then retired to a secure room and began to sift through the dozens of picture albums, of all known OAS personnel going back to 1954.

Five hours later, Lieutenant Robin Jackman rubbed his weary eyes and exclaimed 'Jesus, do we have some heavy crap here!' For they had, before them, thanks to the skill of the technician and the sophistication of his equipment, almost perfect pictures of Hisham-al-Ghoul, Mohamed-el-Musa and Mohamed Ait Mustafa, the picture of the driver of the car they were still working on. After a few moments of meditation he said, 'I think I had better call MJ and tell him what we have come up with.' With that he hurried from the room and went straight to the nearest secure telephone.

The telephone rang for a few minutes then a voice said 'Hello MJ here.' Jackman quickly passed on all the current intelligence he had and then waited for a response. 'Are you sure about this info RJ?'

'I am,' was the reply.

'Very well, keep up the good work and I will get back to you as soon as possible, let me know of any further developments as soon as you can and RJ we had better make plans to contact 'Maria' and tell him the situation.'

'Very good MJ,' then the line went dead.

An hour later the telephone rang on Major Harris's desk, 'Harris,' he said after a few moments.

'MJ here sir, can you talk?'

'MJ, it's good to hear from you, please continue, how are things?' For the next twenty minutes MJ went through all the information he had, including his conclusions. Then he paused whilst his Superior Officer mulled over all he had heard. After a few moments he replied, 'I agree with you and your conclusions MJ, the situation looks bleak indeed, especially with Ben Bella out of the country.' There was a pause then the Major continued, 'Go to 'CODE RED' status, alert 'Maria' and put as many personnel on the streets as you deem necessary; by the sound of things our man is going to need all the assistance we can give him.'

'Right Sir anything else?'

There was a pause then, 'Nothing else MJ except watch out for yourself.' Then the line went dead.

Immediately after he had finished talking to Major Harris, MJ went to his desk and made some notes regarding their conversation then called RJ and informed him of the mission's new status and arranged to meet him at S.H.A.P.E. Headquarters the next day in order to co-ordinate the next crucial stages of the mission.

With the conversation terminated, RJ replaced the telephone on its cradle then turned to face CM, 'It would seem that we are now at 'CODE RED', so it's all systems go and we now have to inform CD as soon as possible.' Then as an afterthought he added, 'I have a feeling that this could get very messy. Very messy indeed.'

Later that day, Conrad went for his usual run but used a different route from his previous one for the sake of security. He posted the two ID cards together with a note requesting information on them in his main post box. At the other two post boxes, he left a detailed account of what had happened in Pigalle. He also mentioned that Iesha was becoming increasingly concerned about going into the Pigalle district, but despite his suggestion that she should abort the mission, she refused to do so. Having posted his mail, he set off back to the apartment at a fast pace just as a light rain began to fall which soaked him to the skin.

As he ran, he closed his eyes and raised his head to the skies for a moment and let the soft rain fall on his upturned face. A few teardrops crept from the corners of his eyes as he thought of the green fields of home, his family and friends and what they might be doing at this very moment, safe and secure in their own private little worlds. Shaking his head to clear the nostalgia that threatened to swamp him, he brushed the tears from his eyes with his hands and pressed on, as he did so the words of General Norstad, The Supreme Commander Allied Powers Europe came back to him. "Such is the Price of Freedom Corporal."

With a renewed determination that the terrorists must never be allowed to succeed, he raced on arriving back at the apartment well ahead of his best time to date. He stayed indoors with Iesha for the rest of the day, but try as he may, he could not lift the melancholy which seemed to have possessed her.

The next morning he was up bright and early as usual and with Iesha still asleep, he left the apartment to check on his mail. At each of the 'post boxes' he visited there was news, bad news, the words 'CODE RED' jumped out at him from the intelligence reports he held in his hands. The reports stated that the two terrorists Conrad had killed in Pigalle had been identified as some of Ahmed Ben Bella's most trusted and dangerous supporters, both killers and both apparently devoid of any human compassion, who had been with him since the war with France began back in 1954/55. Therefore retribution MUST be expected.

The reports went on to say that during the war, they had been accused of committing several crimes against both men and women, although there was no hard evidence to support these claims. The reports concluded that Extreme Caution should be exercised at all times from now on.

Tearing the reports into small pieces, he set off back to the apartment stopping briefly en route to throw the pieces of paper down a road drain then waited whilst the water in the drain slowly seeped into the paper, obliterating the writing then he set off back to the apartment.

On arrival he went up the back stairs to the apartment and gave the usual knock signal and waited for Iesha to open the door, after a few moments he knocked again and waited, still no response. Suddenly the cold fingers of fear grabbed his stomach and the hairs on the back of his neck began to rise. Drawing his gun from behind his back he reached out and tried the door handle, it turned and to his horror the door opened. Crouching down, he pushed the door gently and peered inside and then his worst nightmare became a reality – the apartment had been ransacked, broken glass, cushions, knives forks, food and clothes littered the floor. He rushed into the bedroom, but there was no Iesha, he slowly opened the bathroom door, but there was no-one inside. Returning to the living room he closed and locked the door then turned to survey the damage.

He carefully inspected each of the rooms looking for traces of blood, but thankfully found none. He then went to his various hiding places where he kept his mixture of weapons and heaved a sigh of relief when he discovered them all to be intact. He sat down and tried to understand what had happened to Iesha. A slight scraping noise at the door made him stiffen and grip his gun tighter. On the floor was a brown envelope which had been pushed under the door, he looked at it for a few moments then slowly approached it. Putting his ear against the door, he listened for any sign of noise on the other side, but there was none. Very quietly, he unlocked the door then gently eased it open and looked outside. There was no-one in the corridor except the old concierge, who was just about to shuffle into the lift.

'Monsieur,' Conrad called out, running down the corridor to the lift, 'have you just pushed a letter under my door?'

The old man turned and faced him, 'Yes Monsieur, it was left this morning shortly after Mademoiselle went out with her friends.'

Now the fears that had been present in his mind for some time really took hold of him. 'What friends?' he asked.

The old man just shrugged his shoulders and stared at him 'I know not Monsieur, I was just told to give you the letter when you returned.'

Conrad looked at the old man, and smiled at him. 'Merci monsieur,' he said waving the envelope.

Chapter Nineteen

At the word 'friends' his worst fears were confirmed, Iesha had been kidnapped and was in the hands of the Algerians. He shuddered to think what they might be doing to her and his unborn child. With a heavy heart, he slowly returned to the apartment and went inside locking the door behind him as he did so.

Carefully, he picked up the envelope and tested its weight in the palm of his hand, he then raised it to his nose and sniffed it, no apparent explosive device inside he concluded. Carefully he ran his fingers over it searching for any undulation within the envelope which might alert him of any form of danger, again there was nothing. Finally, he switched on the light and held the envelope close up to the bulb for visual examination, after a few moments he let out a sigh of relief after deciding that it was harmless. Going to the couch he sat down and with a sharp knife carefully slit open the top of the envelope. With his thumbs and index fingers of each hand holding the other sealed edge, he gently shook the envelope and a single piece of folded paper fell out onto the couch. After pausing for a moment to wipe the sweat from his forehead, he picked it up and slowly unfolded it. The message in large, bold, black letters jumped out at him and hammered at his temples. The message in English was short, it read:

**ENGLISH PIG WE HAVE YOUR WOMAN IF YOU
WANT TO SEE HER BE AT 42 AVE De CLICHY
20.00HRS TONIGHT**

COME UNARMED

Conrad sat looking at the paper in his hands for several
minutes, but not really seeing it then pulling himself together,
he looked at the paper again and began to analyse it. The
writer had a good command of English and so must be
educated, possibly an officer, possibly the leader. There were
no hidden clues in the message, so he was certain that Iesha
had not written it. Why specify 20.00hrs? Why not
immediately? Answer, it's daytime and there might be
witnesses. Come unarmed, this was nonsense, no-one in his
situation would go into his enemy's lair unprepared and they
know it, therefore they are expecting me to be armed.
Location, not being familiar with the area, he went to a
cupboard and rummaged around in it until he found a street
map of Paris, then he returned to the couch and sat down to
inspect it. Avenue de Clichy he discovered was off the Place
de Clichy and not far from the Porte de Clichy, that probably
meant many old, disused buildings, where people could easily
disappear without a trace. Leaning back on the couch, he
closed his eyes for a moment or two trying to visualise the
area in his mind, then said out loud to himself 'Right you
bastards, now I know the game plan, I'll give you a run for
your money.' Opening his eyes he got up and began to
prepare himself for what he had to do for the rest of the day.

His first task was to tidy the apartment, that completed he
went for a long shower in order to remove any trace of body
deodorant that a sensitive nose might detect when being
stalked, then he made himself a hot meal. A cold, calm had
now settled on him as the professional soldier took over and
he slowly and methodically began to set out his plan of
operation for the evening. As he did so, his mind flashed back
to his training days on the crash course in the woods of
Woking and a wry smile touched the corners of his mouth as

he remembered how he had 'slain' each member of the team whilst no-one had laid a finger on him, however, today was real, a life or death situation, not training.

Finally, he gathered together a selection of weapons from his small arsenal then cleaned and double checked them for he was in no doubt that today his life would depend on them functioning perfectly. Satisfied at last that all the items he had chosen were in good working order, he retired to the bedroom and slept for a few hours.

He awoke at 3.00 pm and proceeded to dress for the evening ahead; donning some old clothes he went into the bathroom and prepared himself. When he returned twenty minutes later, he was hardly recognisable. He now had large bushy eyebrows, a beard and spots on his face and he walked with a stoop. Looking at himself in the long mirror in the living room, he gave a faint smile and said to himself softly, 'Well in the dark, I might just pass for a down-and-out wino.'

Going to the kitchen, he picked up an almost empty bottle of wine just to complete his disguise and put it one of the pockets of his coat, then returned to the living room and began secreting his weapons about his body. Finally satisfied, he returned to the kitchen and looked in a jug where Iesha kept her car keys, thankfully they were still there. Relieved at not having to cross Paris in a taxi, he picked them up and slowly made his way to the door. Cautiously, he eased open the door and quickly looked up and down the corridor, there was no-one to be seen, taking one last fleeting look at the apartment which had been his home for many weeks, he softly closed the door and made his way to the stairs.

Had anyone been watching the apartment building they would have noticed a stooped old man holding a bottle leave and stumble down the road, but no-one was watching. Slowly, he made his way to where Iesha had parked the car. As he approached the area, he casually scanned the road but could not see anyone or anything to cause him concern. Stopping a few feet from the car, he sat down on the floor and pretended to take a drink from the bottle and looked around him. After a few moments he decided that all was well then slowly regained his feet and approached the car. Was it booby trapped he asked himself; after a few moments of consideration he decided to do a quick check. Five minutes later having assured himself that the car was safe, he gingerly opened the car door and eased himself into the driver's seat. He sat for a few moments, nothing happened. Then he slowly inserted the ignition key and started the engine. There was no explosion, only coughs and splutters followed by a dense cloud of blue smoke as the little engine finally came to life. As he sat there waiting for Dolly's Citroen 2CV engine to warm up, his mind flashed back to the woods when he had first been introduced to Dolly by Iesha and he smiled to himself, 'Come on old girl' he said out loud 'we have some serious work to do today so don't let me down.'

Having found first gear, he eased the car into the road and set off at a sedate pace, he had not a covered a hundred yards before a car horn blasted him for going too slowly, smiling to himself he continued on his way, unfazed by the driver's attitude.

After many near misses and much arm waving by scores of Parisian drivers en route, he eventually reached the Place de Clichy, he slowly drove around it until he found the exit he required then he proceeded down the Avenue de Clichy and reconnoitred the area. The avenue and many of the buildings were as he had expected and No. 42 was an apparently disused small factory block, built of brick. Because it was now dark and he was one of dozens of cars on the road, he had no fear of Dolly being recognised as he passed by the boarded-up entrance. Two hundred yards or so away from the factory, he parked and locked the car then very slowly began to shuffle down the road, holding the bottle in front of him in one hand and a unlit cigarette in the other. At regular intervals, as he stumbled along, he kept lifting the bottle to his lips as if taking a drink.

With only a hundred or so yards to the factory, he left the avenue and turned down a back alley which he believed to run parallel to the main road. As he wandered along, he was careful not to stand on any of the pieces of broken glass which littered the road in case someone heard him. Suddenly, he went into high alert mode as his senses detected the faint smell of tobacco smoke in the air. As he had anticipated, for anyone on guard duty throughout the world, could be guaranteed to have a smoke in order to relieve the boredom of his situation. The Algerians it seemed were no different. With every step he took, the smell became stronger then he saw a pinpoint of light just ahead of him and then the silhouette of the guard was no more than fifty feet away.

Softly humming something incomprehensible, he stumbled along in the middle of the alleyway and approached the guard who immediately threw away the cigarette and then challenged him. 'What are you doing here old pig, looking for free wine?' And he began to laugh at what he thought was a joke.

Conrad shuffled over to him and raised his right hand holding the unlit cigarette and with his left hand holding the bottle, he offered the guard a drink, then in slurred French he said, 'A drink for a light Monsieur so that I may dream I am a king.'

The guard began to laugh as he fumbled in his pocket for his lighter, 'Keep your piss you old pig,' then he flicked the top of the lighter and produced a strong flame. Conrad immediately recognised the lighter to be a Zippo. He bent his head to the flame and lit the cigarette, after a few moments he exhaled some smoke then shuddered as though in ecstasy. The guard was watching his performance with great interest then after a moment or two, he demanded, 'What have you got in that cigarette?'

'The white lady,' he replied.

'Give it to me,' the guard demanded reaching out to grab his hand. As he did so, he moved slightly to one side and out of direct line of the tip of the cigarette. Conrad felt the usual small tremor between his fingers as the tiny projectile of death was released, but unfortunately it missed its mark.

'Careful monsieur, you will break it,' he wailed then raising the tip to his lips, he gently blew on the end to make sure it was still burning, before slowly handing it over. The man took the remains of the cigarette and eagerly put it between his lips sucking deeply on it. 'Dream of Allah my friend, for soon you will be in paradise,' Conrad whispered.

Just then there was a slight puff of flame from the end of the cigarette and a moment later the guard put his hand up to his throat. His eyes were closed and his lips still held the cigarette… then very slowly, his knees began to buckle, and he slumped to the ground; a few moments later, he was dead.

Conrad quickly dragged the body into a dark corner then searched it; he found some cigarettes and the Zippo, yet another Luger 9mm. pistol and an ID card, which stated that his name was Rashid Aly Ishmael. He pocketed the ID and the Zippo then ejected the bullets from the gun and threw them away in different directions.

He had just put the gun under one of the many piles of rubbish which littered the place when a voice called out softly, 'Ishmael, where are you?'

Melting into the dark shadows, he drew one of his guns from his waist belt and screwed on a silencer, and then he waited for whoever had called out to show himself.

A few moments later, the outlines of two people approached him. 'Ishmael you lazy dog, if you have fallen asleep again Hisham will kill you, where are you? Hisham wants you.' The men were now only a few feet or so away from where he stood. 'Where are you Ishmael you son of a dog?' There was of course no reply. Then the other one said 'I don't like this Mourad, something is wrong, we had better get back and report to Hisham.'

From the dark shadows the silenced gun spat twice in quick succession, knocking the men off their feet without making a sound.

A minute later Conrad emerged from the shadows and went to examine the bodies. Once again he pocketed the ID cards he found on them then discarded their guns.

Checking his watch, he was surprised to find that the time was 19.20hrs, so he slowly began to make his way to the end of the disused site, where a faint light flickered in the darkness.

His keen eyes easily discerned the path the two men had just used and so he very carefully retraced their steps. The distant light gradually grew brighter and he could now see the outline of the building which housed it. He stopped in the shadow of a crumbling wall and surveyed the scene before him. Nothing moved and he began to wonder if there were any more guards on duty and the only noise was the distant sound of the passing cars on the Avenue de Clichy.

Bending down, he picked up a few small pieces of brick and then threw a piece out into the darkness, some twenty feet away from where he stood and then he waited. Nothing happened, he repeated the process several times, but no-one appeared. After a few moments, he decided that all was safe and so he cautiously left his hiding place. After a few minutes, he stood by the old building and looked about him, there was no sign of any movement, nor could he detect any wisps of tobacco smoke in the air. His heart pounded in his chest and adrenalin pumped through his body. All his senses were on full alert and a cold excitement gripped him.

Finally, convinced that there was no-one else out there, he very carefully began to walk around the building looking for an entrance. Halfway round he came upon a door with a broken window in it, it was open. Slowly, he turned the handle and it opened easily without making a noise. The light he had seen which had guided him to his present position was a large old oil lamp, sitting on an old wooden box. He looked around the room and noticed some stairs in the corner of the room; slowly he eased himself around the edge of the room until he reached the foot of them.

As he looked up them, a door at the top suddenly opened and a flood of light illuminated the whole of the staircase and a small landing. At the top was a tallish man with his back to Conrad, he was facing into the room talking to someone, 'Very well I will have a look outside and see if all is well.' He turned and closed the door then began to descend the stairs; fortunately he was not carrying a torch. With the staircase now back in darkness Conrad waited for the man to appear, as soon as his foot touched the floor he shot him in the back of the neck with the silenced gun. Conrad rushed forward to prevent him from falling and making a noise.

For a few moments he remained still and listened; there was no movement from the upstairs room. Carefully he moved to the oil lamp and took out two of his 'eggs' from inside his coat and placed them on the wooden box then replaced the spent bullets and moved back to the foot of the stairs. Very slowly he began to mount them, his soft rubber soled shoes not making a sound.

Once he reached the top he paused and placed his ear to the door and listened. He could make out three voices, two men and a woman; with a surge of pleasure, he realised that it was Iesha's voice, she was alive. He could not hear properly what was being said because they were speaking in Algerian and not French, he looked at his watch and to his surprise noted that it was 20.05hrs, he was late.

As with all doors and this one was no different, there was a keyhole; slowly he lowered himself so that he could see through it. He could just make out two men, one seated smoking, the other standing but very little else and no matter how much he tried, he could not see any sign of Iesha. Just then the man standing half turned and began to walk to the door.

Before Conrad could do anything, the door opened and the two men looked at each other for a fleeting moment then Conrad shot him in the chest. The force of the bullet at such close range knocked the man backwards and before he hit the floor, Conrad entered the room and adopted a crouched position just inside the door, his gun arm swaying back and forth as he covered the area in front of him.

From his position he commanded the whole of the room and in a fraction of a second, his eyes took in every aspect of his surroundings. In the middle of the wall opposite him was a window which let in some pale, defused light from the avenue through its cracked dirty panes of glass. There were two wooden boxes on which stood two oil lamps like the one downstairs which burned brightly and there were two men. One must have been outside the line of sight of the keyhole he thought as he surveyed them. The other sat in a chair with a black cigarette in his hand and a look of amazement on his face. The other stood behind him and a few feet to his side, Iesha was tied to a chair no more than ten feet away from him at the side of the left hand wall facing forward.

The two men suddenly recovered from the shock of seeing Conrad and the man standing moved forward a pace and attempted to draw a gun from his jacket. He never made it; the gun in Conrad's hand coughed once and shot him through the heart. With a look of both surprise and horror on his face he twisted sideways with the impact of the bullet and crashed to the floor.

Conrad's eyes never left the face of the other man who was now on his feet staring at him, hate burning in his eyes. As he faced him, the man said in good English, 'So you are the pig who has been killing my brothers, for doing so, you will die slowly before this night is out.'

Conrad said nothing, he just watched his face. Suddenly there was just a slight flicker in his eyes and he said 'Now' and leapt to his side, he was too slow, Conrad's gun spat once more and the bullet crashed into the man's chest.

'Hisham!' a voice screamed.

Conrad turned his head in the direction of the sound. Iesha stood looking at him and in her hand was a Luger 9mm and it was pointing at him.

He started towards her but she stopped him with a wave of the gun. Confused, he looked at her and asked, 'What's going on? You were tied up when I came in!'

With a wicked smile on her face she leered, 'That was just for show.'

Shaking his head slightly he replied, 'Iesha I do not understand, why are you pointing that gun at me?' And he began to move towards her but again she waved the gun at him and he stopped.

Keeping the gun pointing at him, she moved over to the one she had called Hisham and briefly looked down at him.

There was an ever increasing pool of blood forming around him.

'You have killed my love,' she spat at him, tears rolling down her face 'and now I will avenge him by killing you.' She raised her Luger.

However, due to the excitement of the past few minutes she had forgotten that he also had a gun and it was now pointing directly at her. For what seemed an eternity they gazed at each other, then in a cold emotionless voice he said, 'I think this situation is called a stalemate.'

'Not for long,' she replied, he cocked an eye at her then she continued, 'As soon as the guards realise the time they will be here to deal with you.'

Conrad looked at her and as he did so from the back of his mind came something MJ had said to him back in the woods of Fontainebleau, "From now on, trust no one." Looking at her he said with feigned sadness in his voice, 'What happens to our child you are carrying?'

She looked him with utter contempt and began to laugh, 'There is no child you fool, I was only acting. I detested your every touch of my body,' the venom in her voice was frightening. She continued 'But I am Algerian more than French and you were my mission, so I obeyed my orders and bedded you.'

Looking at her, a great sadness came over him. What kind of blind allegiance to a terrorist organisation made a beautiful woman do what she had done. 'So the things we did together meant nothing to you?'

'Nothing,' was her vitriolic reply.

Still looking at her, he said, 'You called him Hisham, I take it you meant Hisham-al-Ghoul, what exactly was he?'

'Hisham-al-Ghoul was a great Algerian freedom fighter who fought shoulder to shoulder with the great Ahmed Ben Bella, another great Algerian freedom fighter.' As she spoke her voice level increased significantly and a glaze came over her eyes. It was then he realised that she was a fanatic and nothing he said would change that. She continued. 'And Hisham and I have been lovers for seven years.' As she spoke her gun arm began to waver slightly and Conrad realised that if he could keep her talking, he might just be able to get a clear shot at her.

He continued, 'So this killer of innocent women and children is someone you admire, and love.'

'We are at war, don't you understand? What happens to individuals is of no concern to me or the movement in our struggle for freedom, we will fight to the death all those who oppose us.' She was now shouting and almost out of control, the beautiful Iesha he had known was now almost unrecognisable.

For a moment or two the pair of antagonists looked at each other, both members of the human race, created by the same process, but divided by two cultures which were totally incompatible.

Just then there was a slight noise to the right of Conrad and instinctively he turned his head, the man he had shot in the doorway, although dead, was twitching on the floor as his nervous system finally shut down. Looking back he saw a spurt of flame and smoke from the barrel of Iesha's Luger and something tore into his side with tremendous force, causing him to gasp, at the same time his own weapon spat forth its own deadly missile and a once beautiful face disintegrated into a mask of blood, bone and tissue, before falling to the floor with a sickening thud.

After a few moments, Conrad stumbled across to where she lay and looked down at her… tender moments suddenly flooded into his mind as he thought of the times they had spent together. Then with a gentleness which surprised him under the circumstances, he whispered 'I hope you find peace with your God, Iesha,' and then with great difficulty, he placed her by the side of her lover, putting an arm across his chest.

He was losing blood fast, as he made for the door. At the top of the stairs, he paused to look at his wound, there was a large hole in the flesh above his hip and he was beginning to feel nauseous. Taking a deep breath and clutching his side he staggered down the stairs and headed for the outside door, as he did so he bumped into the wooden box supporting the oil lamp and the two 'eggs' he had put there.

As he stumbled to the door, one of the 'eggs' fell off the box and exploded. White hot flame engulfed the room and leapt up the stairs in a fireball and within seconds the building became an incinerator, exploding bullets from the weapons of those left inside sent tracers into the night sky, just like a giant firework display. Then another ball of white hot flame lit-up the night sky as the second 'egg' exploded and night became day.

Conrad collapsed just outside the door as the first 'egg' exploded; he managed to drag himself a few yards away from the building before his strength finally gave out. As he lay on the ground panting for breath, he thought he could hear sirens and voices and then the face of his mother appeared in front of him, misty and distant and very faintly he heard her wonderful mezzo soprano voice singing to him, his favourite song, Ave Maria as she used to when he was a child. He reached out to touch her … but there was no-one there … then he thought he could hear someone speaking kind words in English to him … and then he realised that he was dying.

**

At 04.00 hrs, the bedside telephone in Major Harris's London apartment came to life, on the fifth ring a sleepy voice said 'Harris.'

'Major . It's MJ.'

'I take it you have some important news for me?'

'I do Sir, both good and bad.'

There was a pause then, 'Well in that case give me the bad news first.'

Another pause then, 'Agent Maria has been shot and is critically ill, he's on a life support machine in the Army hospital at Fontainebleau.'

By now Harris was sitting up. 'Will he pull through?'

'I don't know Sir, it's touch and go, he's lost an awful lot of blood.'

'What happened for God's sake?'

MJ explained that since the 'Code Red' alert, he had deployed extra cover on the streets to watch and follow 'Maria'. He explained about the disused building on the Avenue de Clichy and the dead bodies they had found and the subsequent fireball.

When he had finished his report, the Major exclaimed in disbelief 'Jesus Christ MJ It sounds like World War III out there.' There followed a long pause then the Major coughed and said, 'You said you had both good and bad news, what's the good?'

'Well Sir, it seems that this evening 'Maria' has single-handedly eliminated seven members of the OS cell, which means that apart from Ahmed Ben Bella, sorry Ben Mussa (intelligence was now up-dated), the entire cell has been wiped out.' Again there was another long pause, 'Are you still there sir?'

'Of course I am … I'm just trying to comprehend all that you have just said to me.'

'He deserves a medal sir.'

'Absolutely,' replied the Major. The line went quiet for a few moments before the Major spoke again, when he did so his mood had changed from being sombre, to one of jubilation and he said, 'MJ you and all your team have done a remarkable job, I cannot commend you too highly, I shall inform the minister as soon as he arrives at his desk this morning and I am sure that he will want to thank you personally for a job well done.' Before he could say a word the Major continued. 'Keep me informed of our agent's progress and as soon as you have gathered all your intelligence together, bring me a complete operation report, with some receipts.' He laughed at what he thought was a joke 'and then Marcus I shall take you to my club and wine you and dine you.' Then the line went dead.

Major Harris was on fire, adrenalin pumped through his body, he turned to his bed partner who was now wide awake and looking at him, 'Good news?' she asked.

'Good News! Good News!' He was almost shouting, 'It's the best bloody news I've had for years my dear. Marcus and his team have pulled off the impossible and destroyed the OS cell in Paris. So my beautiful insatiable Mary, in order to mark this momentous occasion, we will break open a bottle or two of my very, very, expensive Champagne, and drink a toast to Marcus and his brave team. And then my dear you can be as rude with me as you wish.' With that he jumped out of bed laughing and waving his arms as he hurried to the kitchen.

In the telephone booth, MJ looked at the dead handset he was holding, he was shocked at the matter-of-fact way the Major had terminated their conversation and especially at his feeble joke about receipts, when CD was fighting for his life. Dropping the handset onto its cradle, he left the booth and slowly headed for the Intensive Care Ward.

As he approached the outer doors of the ward, he suddenly remembered something CD had said to him back in the woods of Fontainebleau just before they had parted company. He smiled to himself as he recalled Conrad telling him of his first day on duty at Post 7 and his brief conversation with General Norstad, the Supreme Commander. The words the General had uttered now seemed quite prophetic in view of the events of the past few days, "Such is the Price of Freedom, Corporal." With a wry smile on his face, he pushed open the doors of the unit and went inside.

THE END?